Hans Christian Andersen, Mary Botham Howitt

Hans Andersen's Story Book

Hans Christian Andersen, Mary Botham Howitt

Hans Andersen's Story Book

ISBN/EAN: 9783337392437

Printed in Europe, USA, Canada, Australia, Japan

Cover: Foto ©Andreas Hilbeck / pixelio.de

More available books at **www.hansebooks.com**

HANS ANDERSEN'S

STORY BOOK.

WITH

A MEMOIR BY MARY HOWITT,

AND

ILLUSTRATIONS.

New York and Boston:

C. S. FRANCIS AND COMPANY.

M.DCCC.LX.

CONTENTS.

Part I.

Part II.

Part III.

Part I.

MEMOIR OF HANS C. ANDERSEN:

BY MARY HOWITT:

A PICTURE-BOOK WITHOUT PICTURES,

AND OTHER STORIES.

c

MEMOIR.

WHETHER regarded as the human being asserting in his own person the true nobility of mind and moral worth, or the man of genius, whose works alone have raised him from the lowest poverty and obscurity, to be an honored guest with kings and queens, Hans Christian Andersen is one of the most remarkable men of his day.

Like most men of great original talent, he is emphatically one of the people; and writing as he has done, principally of popular life, he describes what he himself has suffered and seen. Poverty or hardship, however, never soured his mind; on the contrary, whatever he has written is singularly genial, and abounds with the most kindly and universal sympathy. Human life, with all its

9

trials, privations, and its tears, is to him a holy
thing; he lays bare the heart, not to bring
forth hidden and revolting passions or crimes,
but to show how lovely it is in its simplicity
and truth: how touching in its weaknesses
and its short-comings; how much it is to be
loved and pitied, and borne and striven with.
In short, this great writer, with all the ardor
of a strong poetical nature, and with great
power in delineating passion, is eminently
Christian in spirit.

It is a great pleasure to me that I have
been the means of making the principal
works of Hans Christian Andersen known,
through my translations, to English readers;
they have been well received by them, and I
now give a slight memoir of their author,
drawn from the True Story of his own Life,
sent by him to me for translation, and which
has lately been published.

The father of Hans Christian Andersen
was a shoemaker of Odense. When scarcely
twenty, he married a young girl about as
poor as himself. The poverty of this couple
may be imagined from the circumstance that
the house afforded no better bedstead than a

wooden frame, made to support the coffin of some count in the neighborhood, whose body lay in state before his interment. This frame, covered with black cloth, and which the young shoemaker purchased at a very low price, served as the family bedstead many years. Upon this humble bed was born, on the second of April, 1805, Hans Christian Andersen.

The father of Andersen was not without education; his mother was the kindest of human beings; they lived on the best terms with each other, but still the husband was not happy. He read comedies and the Arabian Tales, and made a puppet theatre for his little son, and often on Sundays took him out with him into the woods round Odense, where the solitude was congenial to his mind.

Andersen's grandmother had also great influence over him, and to her he was greatly attached. She was employed in taking care of a garden belonging to a lunatic asylum, and here he spent most of the summer afternoons of his early childhood.

Among his earliest recollections is the residence of the Spaniards in Funen, in the years

1808 and 1809. A soldier of an Asturian regiment took him one day in his arms, danced with him amid tears of joy, which no doubt were called forth by the remembrance of a child he had left at home, and pressed the Madonna to his lips, which occasioned great trouble to his pious mother, who was a Lutheran.

In Odense at that time many old festivities were still in use, which made a deep impression on the boy, and were as so much material laid up in his richly poetical mind for after use, as all who are familiar with his works must be well aware. His father, among other works, industriously read in his Bible. One day he closed it with these words: "Christ became a man like unto us, but a very uncommon man!" at which his wife burst into tears, greatly distressed and shocked at what she called "blasphemy." This made a deep impression on the boy, and he prayed in secret for the soul of his father. Another day his father said, "There is no other devil but what a man bears in his own breast!" After which, finding his arm scratched one morning when he awoke, his wife said it was a punishment of the devil, to teach him his real existence.

The unhappy temper of the father increased from day to day; he longed to go forth into the world. At that time war was raging in Germany. Napoleon was his hero, and as Denmark had now allied itself to France, he enlisted as a private soldier in a recruiting regiment, hoping that some time or other he might return as a lieutenant. The neighbors, however, thought it was all a folly to let himself be shot for no purpose at all. The corps in which he served went no farther than Holstein; the peace succeeded, and the poor shoemaker returned to his trade, only chagrined to have seen no service, nor even been in foreign lands. But though he had seen no service, his health had suffered; he awoke one morning delirious, and talked about campaigns and Napoleon. Young Andersen, then nine years old, was sent to the next village to ask counsel from a wise woman.

"Will my poor father die?" inquired he, anxiously.

"If thy father will die," replied she, "thou wilt meet his ghost on thy way home."

Terrified almost out of his senses lest he should meet the ghost, he set out on his homeward way, and reached his own door without any such apparition presenting itself, but for all that, his father died on the third day.

From this time young Andersen was left to himself. The whole instruction that he ever received was in a charity-school, and consisted of reading, writing, and arithmetic, but of the two last he knew scarcely anything.

About this time he was engaged by the widow of a clergyman in Odense, to read aloud to herself and her sister-in-law. She was the widow of a clergyman who had written poems. In this house Andersen first heard the appellation of *poet ;* and saw with what love the poetical talent of the deceased pastor was regarded. This sunk deeply into his mind ; he read tragedies, and resolved to become a poet, as this good man had been before him.

He wrote a tragedy, therefore, which the two ladies praised highly ; it was handed about in manuscript, and people laughed at it, and ridiculed him as the "play-writer." This wounded him so deeply, that he passed one whole night weeping, and was only pacified, or rather, silenced, by his mother threatening to give him a good beating for his folly. Spite, however, of his ill success, he wrote again and again, studying, among other devices, German and French words, to give dignity to his dialogue.   Again the whole town read his productions, and the boys shouted after him as he went, "Look! look: there goes the play-writer."

One day he took to his schoolmaster, as a birthday present, a garland, with which he had twisted up a little poem.   The schoolmaster was angry with him; he saw nothing but folly and false quantities in the verses, and thus the poor lad had nothing but trouble and tears.

The worldly affairs of the mother grew worse and worse, and as boys of his age earned money in a manufactory near, it was resolved that there also Hans Christian should be sent.   His old grandmother took him to the manufactory, and shed bitter tears because the lot of the boy was so early toil and sorrow. The workmen in the factory were principally German, and discovering that Andersen had a fine voice, and knew many popular songs, they made him sing to them while the other boys did his work. He knew himself that he had a good voice, because the neighbors always listened when he sang at home, and once a whole party of rich people had stopped to hear him, and had praised his beautiful voice. Everybody in the manufactory heard him with equal delight.

"I can act comedy as well!" said the poor boy one day, encouraged by their applause, and began to recite whole scenes from the comedies which his father had been in the habit of reading. The workmen were delighted, and the other boys were made to do his tasks while he amused them all. This smooth life of comedy acting and singing lasted but for a short time, and he returned home.

"The boy must go and act at the theatre!" many of the neighbors said to his mother; but as she knew of no other theatre than that of the strolling players, she shook her head, and resolved rather to put her son apprentice to a tailor.

He was now twelve, and had nothing to do; he devoured, therefore, the contents of every book which came in his way. His favorite reading was an old prose translation of Shakspere. From this, with little figures which he made of pasteboard, he performed the whole of King Lear, and the Merchant of Venice.

Andersen's passion for reading, and his beautiful voice, had in the meantime drawn upon him the attention of several of the higher families of the city, who introduced him to their houses. His simple, child-like behavior, his wonderful memory, and his sweet voice, gave to him a peculiar charm; people talked of him, and he soon had many friends; among others, a Colonel Guldborg, brother to the well-known poet of that name, and who afterwards introduced him to Prince Christian of Denmark.

About this time his mother married a second time, and as the step-father would not spend a penny, or do any thing for her son's education, he had still more leisure. He had

2   *b*

no playfellows, and often wandered by himself to the neighboring forest, or seated himself at home, in a corner of the house, and dressed up little dolls for his theatre, his mother in the meantime thinking that, as he was destined for a tailor, this was all good practice.

At length the time came when he was to be confirmed. On this occasion he had his first pair of boots; he was very vain of them, and that all the world might see them, he pulled them up over his trousers. An old sempstress was employed to make him a confirmation-suit out of his deceased father's great coat. Never before had he been possessed of such excellent clothes; the very thoughts of them disturbed his devotions on the day of consecration.

It had been determined that Andersen was to be apprenticed to a tailor after his confirmation, but he earnestly besought his mother to give up this idea, and consent to his going to Copenhagen, that he might get employment at the theatre there. He read to her the lives of celebrated men who had been quite as poor as himself, and assured her that he also would one day be a celebrated man.

For several years he had been hoarding up his money; he had now about thirty shillings, English, which seemed to him an inexhaustible sum. As soon as his mother heard of this fund, her heart inclined towards his wishes, and she promised to consent on condition that they should consult a wise woman, and that his going or staying should be decided by her augury. The sibyl was fetched to the house, and after she had read the cards, and studied the coffee-grounds, she pronounced these words.

"Your son will become a great man. The city of Odense will one day be illuminated in his honor."

A prophecy like this removed all doubts.

"Go, in God's name!" said his mother, and he lost no time in preparing for his great journey.

Some one had mentioned to him a certain female dancer at the Royal Theatre as a person of great influence; he obtained, therefore, from a gentleman universally esteemed in Odense, a letter of introduction to this lady; and with this, and his thirteen rix-dollars, he commenced the journey on which depended his whole fate. His mother accompanied him to the city gate, and there his good old grandmother met him; she kissed him with many tears, blessed him, and he never saw her more.   . .

It was not until he had crossed the Great Belt that he felt how forlorn he was in the world; he stepped aside from the road, fell on his knees, and besought God to be his friend. He rose up comforted, and walked on through towns and villages, until, on Monday morning, the 5th of September, 1819, he saw the towers of Copenhagen; and with his little bundle under his arm he entered that great city.

On the day after his arrival, dressed in his confirmation-suit, he betook himself, with his letter of introduction in his hand, to the house of the all-potential dancer. The lady allowed him to wait a long time on the steps of her house, and when at length he entered, his awkward, simple behavior and appearance displeased her; she fancied him insane, more particularly as the gentleman from whom he brought the letter was unknown to her.

He next went to the director of the theatre, requesting some appointment.

"You are too thin for the theatre," was the answer he obtained.

"Oh," replied poor Andersen, "only ensure me one hundred rix-dollars, and I will soon get fat!"

But the director would make no agreement of this kind, and then informed him that they engaged none at the theatre but people of education. This settled the question; he had nothing to say on his own behalf, and, dejected in spirit, went out into the street. He knew no human creature; he thought of death, and this thought turned his mind to God.

"When everything goes adversely," said he, "then God will help me; it is written so in every book that I ever read, and in God I will put my trust!"

Days and weeks went on, bringing with them nothing but disappointment and despair; his money was all gone, and for some time he worked with a joiner. At length, as, with a heavy heart, he was walking one day along the crowded streets of the city, it

occurred to him that as yet nobody had
heard his fine voice. Full of this thought,
he hastened at once to the house of Professor
Siboni, where a large party happened to be
at dinner, and among the guests Baggesen,
the poet, and the celebrated composer, Professor Weyse. He knocked at the door,
which was opened by a female servant, and
to her he related, quite open-heartedly, how
forlorn and friendless he was, and how great
a desire he had to be engaged at the theatre;
the young woman went in and related this
to the company. All were interested in the
little adventurer; he was ordered in, and de-
sired to sing, and to give some scenes from
Holberg. One of these scenes bore a resemblance to his own melancholy circumstances,
and he burst into tears. The company applauded him.

"I prophecy," said Baggesen, "that thou
wilt turn out something remarkable; only
don't become vain when the public admires
thee."

Professor Siboni promised immediately that
he would cultivate Andersen's voice, and that
he should make his debut at the Theatre

Royal. He had a good friend too in Professor Weyse, and a year and a half were spent in elementary instruction. But a new misfortune now befell him ; he lost his beautiful voice, and Siboni counselled him to put himself to some handicraft trade. He once more seemed abandoned to a hopeless fate. Casting about in his mind who might possibly befriend him, he bethought himself of the poet Guldborg, whose brother the colonel had been so kind to him in Odense. To him he went, and in him he happily found a friend; although poverty still pursued him, and his sufferings, which no one knew, almost overcame him.

He wrote a rhymed tragedy, which obtained some little praise from Oehlenschlager and Ingemann—but no *debut* was permitted him on the theatre. He wrote a second and third, but the theatre would not accept them. These youthful efforts fell, however, into the hand of a powerful and good man, Conference Counsellor Collin, who, perceiving the genius that slumbered in the young poet, went immediately to the king, and obtained permission from him that he should be sent, at Government charges, to one of the learned schools in the provinces, in which, however, he suffered immensely, till his heart was almost broken by unkindness. From this school he went to college, and became very soon favorably known to the public by true poetical works. Ingemann, Oehlenschlager, and others then obtained for him a royal stipend, to enable him to travel; and he visited Germany, France, Switzerland, and Italy. Italy, and the poetical character of life in that beautiful country, inspired him; and he wrote the "Improvisatore," one of the most exquisite works, whether for truthful delineation of character, or pure and noble sentiment, that ever was penned. This work most harmoniously combines the warm coloring and intensity of Italian life with the freshest and strong simplicity of the north. His romance of "O. T." followed; this is a true picture of the secluded, sober life of the north, and is a great favorite there. His third work, "Only a Fiddler," is remarkable for its strongly drawn personal and national characteristics, founded upon his own experience in early life. Perhaps there never was a more affecting picture of the hopeless attempts of a genius of second rate order to combat against and rise above poverty and adverse circumstances, than is given in the life of poor Christian, who dies at last "only a fiddler."

In all these works Andersen has drawn from his own experience, and in this lies their extraordinary power. There is a child-like tenderness and simplicity in his writings ; a sympathy with the poor and the struggling, and an elevation and purity of tone, which have something absolutely holy about them ; it is the inspiration of true genius, combined with great experience of life, and a spirit baptized with the tenderness of Christianity. This is it which is the secret of the extreme charm his celebrated stories have for children. They are as simple and as touching as the old Bible narratives of Joseph and his brethren, and the little lad who died in the corn field. We wonder not at their being the most popular books of their kind in Europe.

It has been my happiness, as I said before, to translate his three principal works, his Picture Book without Pictures, and several of his stories for children. They have been likewise translated into German, and some of them into Dutch, and even Russian. He speaks nobly of this circumstance in his life. "My works," says he, "seem to come forth under a lucky star, they fly over all lands. There is something elevating, but at the same time something terrific in seeing one's thoughts spread so far, and among so many people; it is indeed almost a fearful thing to belong to so many. The noble and good in us becomes a blessing, but the bad, one's errors, shoot forth also; and involuntarily the prayer forces itself from us—'God! let me never write down a word of which I shall not be able to give an account to thee!' a peculiar feeling, a mixture of joy and anxiety, fills my heart every time my good genius conveys my fictions to a foreign people."

Of Andersen's present life we need only say that he spends a great deal of his time in traveling; he goes from land to land, and from court to court, everywhere an honored guest, and enjoying the glorious reward of a manly struggle against adversity, and the triumph of a lofty and pure genius in seeing its claims generously acknowledged.

Let us now see the son of the poor shoemaker of Odense—the friendless, ill-clad, almost heart-broken boy of Copenhagen—on one of those occasions, which would make an era in the life of any other literary man, but which are of every day occurrence in his. I will quote from his own words.

"I received a letter from the ministry, Count Rantzau Breitenburg, containing an invitation from their majesties of Denmark to join them at the watering-place of Föhr; this island lies in the North Sea, on the coast of Sleswick. It was just now five and-twenty years since I, a poor lad, traveled alone and helpless to Copenhagen. Exactly the five-and twentieth anniversary would be celebrated by my being with my king and queen. Everything which surrounded me, man and nature, reflected themselves imperishably in my soul; I felt myself, as it were, conducted to a point from which I could look forth more distinctly over the past, with all the good fortune and happiness which it had evolved for me.

" Wyck, the largest town of Föhr, in which

are the baths, is built like a Dutch town with houses one story high, sloping roofs, and gables turned to the street. The number of strangers there, and the presence of the Court, gave a peculiar animation to it. The Danish flag was seen waving, and music was heard on all hands. I was soon established in my quarters, and was invited every day to dine with their majesties as well as to pass the evening in their circle. On several evenings I read aloud my little stories to them, and nothing could be more gracious and kind than they were. It is so well when a noble human nature will reveal itself, where otherwise only the king's crown and the purple mantle might be discovered.

"I sailed in the train of their majesties, to the largest of the Halligs, those grassy runes in the ocean, which bear testimony to a sunken country. The violence of the sea has changed the mainland into islands, has again riven these, and buried men and villages. Year after year are new portions rent away and in half a century's time there will be nothing left but sea. The Halligs are now low islets, covered with a dark turf, on which a few flocks graze. When the sea rises, these are driven to the garrets for refuge, and the waves roll over this little region, which lies miles distant from any shore. Oland, which we visited, contains a little town; the houses stand closely side by side, as if in their sore need they had huddled together; they are all erected on a platform, and have little windows like the cabin of a ship. There, solitary through half the year, sit the wives and daughters spinning. Yet I found books in all the houses; the people read and work, and the sea rises round the houses, which lie like a wreck on the ocean. The church-yard is half washed away; coffins and corpses are frequently exposed to view. It is an appalling sight, and yet the inhabitants of the Halligs are attached to their little home, and frequently die of home-sickness when removed from it.

"We found only one man upon the island, and he had only lately arisen from a sick-bed; the others were out on long voyages. We were received by women and girls; they had erected before the church a triumphal arch with flowers, which they had

fetched from Föhr, but it was so small and
low, that one was obliged to go round it; it
nevertheless showed their good will. The
Queen was deeply affected by their having
cut down their only shrub, a rose-bush, to lay
over a marshy place which she had to cross.

"On our return, dinner was served on board
the royal steamer, and afterwards as we sailed in a glorious sunset through this archipe-
lago, the deck of the vessel was changed to a
dancing hall : servants flew hither and thither with refreshments ; sailors stood upon the
paddle-boxes and took soundings, and their
deep tones might be heard giving the depth
of the water. The moon rose round and
large, and the promontory of Amrom assumed
the appearance of a snow-covered chain of
Alps."

The next day he visited the wild regions
about the promontory, but our space will not
admit of our giving any portions of wild and
grand sea-landscape which he here describes.
In the evening he returned to the royal din-
ner-table. It was on the above mentioned
five-and-twentieth anniversary, on the 5th of
September; he says,

"The whole of my former life passed in
review before my mind. I was obliged to
summon all my strength to prevent myself
bursting into tears. There are moments of
gratitude, in which we feel, as it were, a desire to press God to our hearts ! How deeply
I felt at this time my own nothingness, and
how all, all had come from him ! After dinner the king, to whom Rantzau had told how
interesting the day was to me, wished me
happiness, and that most kindly. He wished
me happiness in that which I had endured
and won. He asked me about my early,
struggling life, and I related to him some
traits of it.

"In the course of conversation he asked
me of my annual income. I told him.

" 'That is not much,' said he.

" 'But I do not need much,' I replied;
'my writings furnish something.'

" 'If I can in any way be serviceable to
you, come to me,' said the king in conclusion.

"In the evening, during the concert, some
of my friends reproached me for not making
use of my opportunity.

" ''The king,' said they 'put the words
into your mouth.'

" 'I could not have done more,' said I , 'if the king thought I required an additicn to my income, he would give it of his own free will.'

" And I was right ; in the following year the king increased my annual stipend, so that with this and my writings I can live honorably and free from care.

" The 5th of September was to me a festival day. Even the German visitors at the baths honored me by drinking my health in the pump-room.

" So many flattering circumstances, some people argue, may spoil a man and make him vain. But no, they do not spoil him, they make him, on the contrary, better; they purify his mind, and he thereby feels an impulse, a wish to deserve all that he enjoys."

Such are truly the feelings of a pure and noble nature. Andersen has stood the test through every trial, of poverty and adversity ; the harder trial that of a sun-bright prosperity, is now proving him, and so far, thank God, the sterling nature of the man has remained unspoiled.

A PICTURE-BOOK WITHOUT PICTURES.

33

Iт is wonderful! When my heart feels the most warmly, and my emotions are the noblest, it is as if my hands and my tongue were tied; I cannot describe, I cannot express my own inward state; and yet I am a painter; my eye tells me so; and every one who has seen my sketches and my tablets acknowledges it.

I am a poor youth; I live over there in one of the narrowest streets, but I have no want of light, because I live up aloft, with a view over all the house-tops. The first day I came into the city it seemed to me so confined and lonesome; instead of the woods and the green breezy heights, I had only the grey chimneys as far as I could see. I did not possess one friend here; not a single face which I knew saluted me.

One evening, very much depressed in mind, I stood at my window; I opened it and look-ed out. Nay, how glad it made me; I saw a face which I knew; a round, friendly face, that of my dearest` friend in heaven; it was the Moon—the dear old Moon, the very same, precisely the same, as when she peeped at me between the willow trees on the marshes. I kissed my hand to her; she shone right down into my chamber, and promised me, that every night when she was out she would take a peep at me. And she has honestly kept her word—pity only that she can re-main for so short a time!

Every night she comes she tells me one thing or another which she has seen either that night or the night before. "Make a sketch," said she, on her first visit, "of what

I tell thee, and thus thou shalt make a really beautiful picture-book!"

This I have done; and in this way I might give a new *Thousand and One Nights* in pictures: but that would be too much; those which I have given have not been selected, but are just as I heard them. A great, genial-hearted painter, a poet, or a musician, may make more of them if he will; that which I present is only a slight outline on paper, and mixed up with my own thoughts, because it was not every night that the moon came; there was now and then a cloud between us.

FIRST EVENING.

Last night,—these are the Moon's own words,—I glided through the clear air of India; I mirrored myself in the Ganges. My beams sought to penetrate the thick fence which the old plantains had woven, and which formed itself into an arch as firm as the shell of the tortoise. A Hindoo girl, light as the gazelle, beautiful as Eve, came forth from the thicket. There is scarcely anything so airy and yet so affluent in the luxuriance of beauty, as the daughter of India. I could see her thoughts through her delicate skin The thorny lianas tore her sandals from her feet, but she stepped rapidly forward; the wild beast which came from the river, where it had quenched its thirst, sprang past her,

for the girl held in her hand a burning lamp.
I could see the fresh blood in her fingers as
she curved them into a shade for the flame.
She approached the river; placed the lamp
on the stream; and the lamp sailed away.
The flame flickered as if it would go out;
but still it burned, and the girl's dark, flashing eyes followed it with her whole soul
beaming from under her long silken eyelashes;
she knew that if the lamp burned as long
as she could see it, then her beloved was alive;
but if it went out, then that he was dead.
The lamp burned and fluttered, and her heart
burned and fluttered also; she sank on her
knee and breathed a prayer: close beside
her, in the grass, lay a water-snake, but she
thought only of Brama and her beloved. " He
lives!" exclaimed she, rejoicingly, and the
mountains repeated her words, " he lives!"

SECOND EVENING.

It was last evening,—said the Moon,—
that I peeped down into a yard inclosed
by houses. A hen was there with eleven
chickens; a little girl was playing around
them; the hen set up a cackling cry, she
was frightened, and spread out her wings
over her eleven young ones. With that, out
came the father of the child and scolded her.
This evening (it is only a few minutes since,)
the moon looked down again into that yard.
Everything was quite still; presently, however, out came the little girl, and stole very
softly to the hen-house, lifted the latch, and
crept in to the hen and the chickens. The hen
and chickens set up a loud cry, and flew here
and there, and the little girl ran after them,

Again the father came out, and now he was very angry indeed, and scolded her, and pulled her out of the hen-house by her arm; she hung back her head, and there were large tears in her blue eyes.

" What wast thou doing here ?" asked the father. She wept; " I only wanted," said she, " to kiss the hen, and ask her to forgive me for yesterday: but I did not dare to tell thee."

The father kissed the sweet innocent on her forehead; the moonlight fell lovingly upon her eyes and mouth.

d

THIRD EVENING.

In a narrow street, just by,—said the Moon,—which is so very confined that only just for one minute can my beams fall upon the walls of the houses—and yet at this moment I can look abroad and see the world as it moves—into this narrow street I looked and saw a woman. Sixteen years ago and she was a child; she lived away in the country, and played in the old pastor's garden. The hedges of roses had grown out of bounds for many years; they threw their wild untrimmed branches across the path, and sent up long, green shoots into the apple-trees; there was only a rose here and there, and they were not beautiful as the queen of flowers may be, although the color and the odor were there. The pastor's little daughter, however, was a much more beautiful rose : she sate upon her little wooden stool under the wild untrimmed hedge, and kissed her doll with the broken face.

Ten years later I saw her again ; I saw her in the splendid dancing-hall; she was the lovely bride of a rich tradesman, and I rejoiced in her good fortune. I visited her in the still evening. Alas ! my rose had put forth also wild shoots like the roses in the pastor's garden !

Every-day life has its tragedy—this evening I saw the last act. Sick to death, she lay in that narrow street, upon her bed. The wicked landlord, her only protector, a man rude and cold-hearted, drew back the curtain. "Get up !" said he, "thy cheeks are pale and hollow; paint thyself ! Get money, or I will turn thee out into the streets ! Get up quickly !"

"Death is at my heart !" said she, "oh ! let me rest !"

He compelled her to rise; painted her cheeks, twined roses in her hair, placed her at the window, with a burning light beside

her, and went his way. I glanced at her;
she sate immoveable ; her hands fell upon her
lap.   The window blew open, so that one of
the panes of glass was broken ; but she
moved not ; the curtains of the window were
blown around her like a flame. She was
dead.   From that open window the dead
preached powerfully ; my rose of the pastor's
garden !

FOURTH EVENING.

I was last evening at a German play,—said the Moon;—it was in a little city. The theatre was a stable; that is to say, the stalls were made use of and decorated for boxes, the old wood-work was covered over with figured paper. There hung from the low roof a little iron chandelier, and in order that it might rise the moment the prompter's bell rang (as is the custom in large theatres), it was now covered by a tub turned upside down. The bell rang, and the little iron chandelier made a leap of half an ell, and by that token people knew that the comedy had begun. A young prince and his wife, who were traveling through the town, were to be present at the performance, and therefore it was a very full house, excepting that under the chandelier it was like a little crater. Not a single soul sate there; the chandelier kept dropping its oil—drop! drop! It was so hot in the little theatre that they were obliged to open all the holes in the walls to let in fresh air, and through all these peeped in lads and lasses from the outside, although the police sate by and drove them off with sticks.

Close by the orchestra, people saw the young princely couple sitting in two old arm-chairs, which otherwise would have been occupied by the burgomaster and his lady; as it was, however, they sate upon wooden benches, like other townsfolk. "One may see that there are falcons above falcons!" was Madame's silent observation; and after this all became more festal; the chandelier made a leap upwards, the people began counting on their fingers, and I—yes, the Moon—was present during the whole comedy.

FIFTH EVENING.

Yesterday,—said the Moon,—I looked down upon busy Paris. I gazed into the chambers of the Louvre. An old grandmother, wretchedly clad, and who belonged to the lower class, entered the large, empty throne-room, accompanied by one of the under servants of the palace. It had cost her many small sacrifices, and very much eloquence had she used before she could be admitted here. She folded her thin hands, and looked as reverentially around her as if she had been in a church.

"It was here!" she said, "here!" and she approached the throne which was covered with a cloth of rich velvet, trimmed with gold. "There!" said she, "there!" and she bowed her knee and kissed the crimson velvet—I think she wept.

"It was not *that* velvet," said the attendant, while a smile played round his mouth.

"But still it was here!" said the woman, "and it looked in this room just so!"

"Just so," replied he; "and yet it was not just so either: the windows were beaten out; the doors were torn off their hinges, and there was blood upon the floor! You can say, however, for all that, that your son died upon the throne of France!"

"Died!" repeated the old woman.

No more was said; they left the hall; the shades of evening fell deeper, and the moonlight streamed in with twofold brightness on the rich velvet of the throne of France.

I will tell thee a story. It was in the revolution of July, towards evening, on the most brilliant day of victory, when every house was a fortress, every window a redoubt, the people stormed the Tuilleries. Even women and children fought among the combatants; they thronged in through the chambers and halls of the palace. A poor, half-grown lad, in ragged clothing, fought desperately among the elder warriors; mortally wounded at length by the thrusts of many bayonets, he sank to the ground; this took place in the throne-room. They wrapped the velvet about his wounds; the blood streamed over the royal purple. It was a picture! The magnificent hall; the combating groups; a rent banner on the floor; the tri-colored flag floating above the bayonets; and upon the throne the poor lad, with his pale, glorified countenance, his eyes turned towards heaven; his limbs stiffening in death; his uncovered breast; his miserable garments, and around these the rich folds of the velvet, embroidered with silver lilies!

As that boy lay in the cradle, it had been foretold that he should die on the throne of France! His mother's heart had dreamed of a new Napoleon. The moonbeams have kissed the garland of everlasting upon his grave; her beams this night kissed the old grandmother's forehead as she dreamed of this picture—The poor lad upon the throne of France!

SIXTH EVENING.

I have been in Upsala,—said the Moon. She looked down upon the great castle, with the miserable grass of its trampled fields. She mirrored herself in the river Fyris, whilst the steam-boat drove the terrified fish among the reeds. Clouds careered along the moonlit sky, and cast long shadows over the graves, as they are called, of Odin, Thor, and Freya. Names are carved in the scanty turf upon the heights. Here there is no building-stone in which the visitors can hew their names; no walled fences on which they can paint them; they cut away, therefore, the turf, and the naked earth stares forth in the large letters of their names, which look like a huge net spread over the hill. An immortality which a fresh growth of turf destroys.

A man stood on the hill-top; he was a poet. He emptied a silver-rimmed mead-horn, and whispered a name, which he bade the wind not to reveal; a count's coronet shone above it, and therefore he breathed it low—the moonbeams smiled upon him, for a poet's crown shone above his! The noble name of Eleonora d'Este is united to Tasso's. I know where the rose of beauty grows. A cloud passed before the moon. May no cloud pass between the poet and his rose!

SEVENTH EVENING.

Down by the seaside there extends a wood of oaks and beeches, fresh and fragrant, and every branch is visited by hundreds of nightingales. Close beside is the sea, the eternally-moving sea, and between the sea and the wood runs the broad high-road. One carriage after another rolled past. I followed them not; my eye rested mostly on one spot where was a barrow, or old warrior's grave. Brambles and white thorns grew up from among the stones. There is the poetry of nature. Dost thou believe that this is felt by every one? Listen to what occurred there only last night.

First of all, two rich countrymen drove past. " 'There are some splendid trees there," said one. "There are ten loads of fire-wood in each," replied the other. "If the winter be severe, one should get forty rix dollars in spring for the measure!" and they were gone.

"The road is abominable here," said another traveller. "It is those cursed trees," replied his neighbor; "there is no circulation of air here, excepting from the sea:" and they advanced onward.

At that moment the diligence came by. All were asleep at the most beautiful point: the driver blew his horn, but he only thought, "I blow it capitally, and here it sounds well; what will they think of it?" And with that the diligence was gone.

Next came by two young country-fellows on horseback. The champagne of youth circulated through their blood; a smile was on their lips as they looked towards the moss-grown height, and the dark bushes. "I went there with Christine Miller," said one to the other; and they were gone.

The flowers sent forth their fragrance; every breeze slept; the sea looked like a portion of heaven spread out over a deep valley; a carriage drove along; there were six persons in it, four of whom were asleep; the fifth was thinking of his new summer-coat which was so becoming to him; the sixth leaned forward to the driver, and asked whether there was anything remarkable about that heap of stones : " No," said the fellow, " it's only a heap of stones, but the trees are remarkable !" "Tell me about them," said the other. " Yes, they are *very* remarkable ; you see, in winter, when the snow covers the ground, and everything, as it were, goes out in a twinkling, then those trees serve me as a landmark by which I can guide myself, and not drive into the sea; they are, therefore, you see, very remarkable,"—and by this time the carriage had passed the trees.

A painter now came up; his eyes flashed ; he said not a word, he whistled, and the nightingales sang, one louder than another ; " hold your tongues !" exclaimed he, and noted down with accuracy the colors and tints of the trees; "blue, black, dark-brown." It would be a beautiful painting ! He made a sketch, as hints for his intended picture, and all the time he whistled a march of Rossini's.

The last who came by was a poor girl;

she sate down to rest herself upon the old warrior's grave, and put her bundle beside her. Her lovely, pale face inclined itself towards the wood as she sate listening; her eyes flashed as she looked heaven-ward across the sea; her hands folded themselves, and she murmured the Lord's Prayer. She did not understand the emotions which penetrated her soul; but, nevertheless, in future years, this moment, in which she was surrounded by nature, will return to her much more beautifully, nay, will be fixed more faithfully in her memory, than on the tablets of the painter, though he noted down every shade of color. She went forward, and the moon-beams lighted her path, until daylight kissed her forehead !

EIGHTH EVENING.

There were thick clouds over the sky; the Moon was not visible; I stood in twofold solitude in my little room, and looked out into the night, which should have been illuminated by her beams. My thoughts fled far away, up to the great friend who told me stories so beautifully every evening, and showed me pictures. Yes, what has not she seen! She looked down upon the waters of the deluge, and smiled on the ark as she now smiles upon me, and brought consolation to a new world which should again bloom forth. When the children of Israel stood weeping by the rivers of Babylon, she looked mournfully down upon the willows where their harps hung. When Romeo ascended to the balcony, and the kiss of love went like a cherub's thought from earth, the round Moon stood in the transparent atmosphere, half concealed amid the dark cypresses. She saw the hero on St. Helena, when from his solitary rock he looked out over the ocean of the world, whilst deep thoughts were at work in his breast. Yes, what could not the Moon relate ! The life of the world is a history for her. This evening I see thee not, old friend! I can paint no picture in remembrance of thy visit !—and as I dreamingly looked up into the clouds, light shone forth ; it was a moon-beam, but it is gone again ; dark clouds float past ; but that ray was a salutation, a friend-ly evening salutation from the Moon.

NINTH EVENING.

Again the air is clear; I had again material for a sketch; listen to that which I
learned from the Moon.

The birds of the polar region flew onward, and the whale swam towards the
eastern coast of Greenland. Rocks covered
with ice and clouds shut in a valley in which
the bramble and whortleberry were in full
bloom. The fragrant lichen diffused its odor;
the Moon shone faintly; its crescent was pale
as the leaf of the water-lily, which, torn from
its stalk, has floated for weeks upon the water.
The northern-lights burned brightly; their
circle was broad, and rays went upwards
from them like whirling pillars of fire, ascending through the whole sphere of the

heavens, in colors of green and crimson.
The inhabitants of the valley assembled for
dance and mirth, but they looked not with
admiring eyes at the magnificent spectacle
which was familiar to them. " Let the dead
play at ball with the heads of the walrus!"
thought they, according to their belief, and
occupied themselves only with the dance and
the song. In the middle of the circle, wrapped in fur, stood a Greenlander with his
hand-drum, and accompanied himself as he
sung of seal-hunting, and the people answered in chorus with an " Eia! eia! a!" and
skipped round and round in their white furs
like so many bears dancing. With this, trial
and judgment began. They who were ad-
versaries came forward; the plaintiff impro-
vised in a bold and sarcastic manner the
crime of his opponent, and all the while
the dance went on to the sound of the drum;
the defendant replied in the same manner;
but the assembly laughed and passed sen-
tence upon him in the meantime. A loud
noise was now heard from the mountains:
the icy cliffs were cleft asunder, and the huge
tumbling masses were dashed to atoms in

their fall. That was a beautiful Greenland summer-night.

At the distance of a hundred paces, there lay a sick man within an open tent of skins; there was life still in his veins, but for all that he must die, because he himself believed it, and the people all around him believed it too. His wife, therefore, had sewn his cloak of skin tightly around him, that she might not be obliged to touch the dead; and she asked him—"Wilt thou be buried upon the mountains in the eternal snow? I will decorate the place with thy boat and thy arrows. The spirits of the mist shall dance away over it! Or wouldst thou rather be sunk in the sea?" "In the sea!" whispered he, and nodded with a melancholy smile. "There thou wilt have a beautiful summer-tent," said the wife; "there will gambol about thee thousands of seals; there will the walrus sleep at thy feet, and the hunting will be certain and merry!" The children, amid loud howlings, tore down the outstretched skin from the window, that the dying man might be borne out to the sea—the swelling sea, which gave him food during his lifetime, and now rest in death.

His funeral monument is the floating mountain of ice, which increases night and day. The seals slumber upon the icy blocks, and the birds of the tempest whirl about it. ·

TENTH EVENING.

I knew an old maid, — said the Moon, she wore every winter yellow satin trim-med with fur; it was always new; it was always her unvarying fashion; she wore every summer the same straw bonnet, and, I fancy, the very same blue-grey gown. She never went anywhere but to one old female friend of hers who lived on the other side the street;—during the last year, however, she did not even go there—because her old friend was dead. All solitarily sate my old maid working at her window, in which, through the whole summer, there stood ·beautiful flowers, and in the winter lovely cresses, grown on a little hillock of felt. During the last month, however, she no longer sate at her window; but I knew that she was still alive, because I had not seen her set out on that long journey of which she and her friend had so often talked. "Yes," she had said, "when I shall die, I shall have to take a longer journey than I ever took through my whole life; the family burial-place lies above twenty miles from here; thither must I be borne, and there shall I sleep with the rest of my kin."

Last night a carriage drew up at her door; they carried out a coffin, and by that I knew that she was dead; they laid straw around the coffin and drove away. There slept the quiet old maid, who for the last year had never been out of her house; and the carriage rattled along the streets and out of the city, as if it had been on a journey of pleasure. Upon the high road it went on yet faster; the fellow who drove looked over his shoulder several times; I fancy that he was afraid of seeing her sitting in her yellow satin upon the coffin behind him; he therefore urged on the horses thoughtlessly, holding them in so tightly that they foamed at the mouth: they were young and full of mettle:

a hare ran across the road, and off they set
at full speed. The quiet old maid, who
from one year's end to another had moved
only slowly in a narrow circle, now that she
was dead, drove over stock and stone along
the open high-road. The coffin, which was
wrapped in matting, was shook off, and now
lay upon the road, whilst horses, driver, and
carriage, sped onward in a wild career.

The lark which flew upward singing
from the meadow, warbled its morning song
above the coffin; it then descended and
alighted upon it, pecked at the matting with
its beak, as if it were rending to pieces some
strange insect.

The lark rose upward again, singing in
the clear ether, and I withdrew behind the
rosy clouds of morning.

ELEVENTH EVENING.

I will give thee a picture of Pompeii,—
said the Moon. I have been in the
suburbs, the Street of Tombs, as it is called,
where once the rejoicing youths, with roses
around their brows, danced with the lovely
sisters of Lais. Now the silence of death
reigns here; German soldiers in the pay of
Naples keep guard here, and play at cards
and dice. A crowd of foreigners, from the
other side of the mountains, wandered into
the city, accompanied by the guard. They
wished to see this city, arisen from the grave,
by the full clear light of the Moon; and I
showed to them the tracks of the chariot-
wheels in the streets paved with broad slabs
of lava; I showed to them the names upon

f   5

the doors and the signs which still remain
suspended from the shop-fronts; they looked
into the basin of the fountains ornamented
with shells and conches; but no stream of
water leaped upwards; no song resounded
from the richly painted chambers, where
dogs of bronze guarded the doors. It was
the city of the dead; Vesuvius alone still
thundered his eternal hymn.

We went to the temple of Venus, which
is built of dazzling white marble, with broad
steps ascending to its high altar, and a ver-
dant weeping-willow growing between its
columns. The air was exquisitely transparent and blue; and in the back-ground
towered Vesuvius, black as night: fires
ascended from the crater of the mountain
like the stem of a pine-tree; the illumined
cloud of smoke hung suspended in the stillness of night, like the pine-tree's crown, but
red as blood. Among the strangers there,
was a singer, a true and noble being, to whom
I had seen homage paid in the greatest cities
of Europe. When the party arrived at the
amphitheatre, they all seated themselves upon
the marble steps, and again, as in former

centuries, human beings occupied a portion of that space. The scene was now the same as in those former times; the walls of the theatre, and the two arches in the background, through which might be seen the same decoration as then—Nature itself—the mountains between Sorento and Amalfi. The singer, for fun, threw herself back into those ancient times, and sung; the scene inspired her; she reminded the listener of the wild horse of Arabia, when it snorts and careers away, with its mane lifted by the wind; there was the same ease, the same security; she brought to mind the agonized mother at the cross of Golgotha; there was the same heartfelt, deep sorrow. Once more resounded around her, as had resounded thousands of years before, the plaudits and acclamations of delight. "Happy! heavenly gifted one!" exclaimed they all. Three minutes after and the scene was changed; every one had departed; no tone was heard any longer; the whole party was gone; but the ruins still stood unchanged, as they will stand for centuries, and no one knows of the applause of the moment—of the beautiful singer—of her tones and her smile. All is past and forgotten; even to me is this hour a perished memory.

TWELFTH EVENING.

I peeped in at a critic's window,—said the Moon,—in a city of Germany. The room was filled with excellent furniture, books, and a chaos of papers; several young men were sitting there; the critic himself stood at his desk; two small books, both by young authors, were about to be reviewed. "One of these," said he, "has been sent to me; I have not read it though—but it is beautifully got up; what say you of its contents?"

"O," said one of the young men, who was himself a poet, "there is a deal that is good in it; very little to expunge; but, he is a young man, and the verses might be better! There is a healthy tone in the thoughts—but they are, after all, such thoughts as everybody has!—but as to that, where does one find anything new? You may very well praise him, but I never believe that he will turn out anything of a poet. He has read a deal, however; is an extraordinary orientalist, and has sound judgment. He it was who wrote that beautiful critique of my *Fancies of Domestic Life.* One ought to be gentle towards a young man."

"But he is a thorough ass !' said another gentleman in the room; "nothing worse in poetry than mediocrity, and he does not get above that !"

"Poor fellow," said a third, "and his aunt makes herself so happy about him. She it was, Mr. Critic, who obtained so many subscribers' names to your last translation."

"The good woman! yes, I have given a short notice of the book. Unmistakeable talent! a welcome gift! a flower out of the garden of poesy; beautifully got out, and so on. But the other book—he shall catch it! I had to buy it.—I hear it is praised; he has genius, don't you think?"

"That is the general opinion," said the poet, "but there is something wild about it."

"It will do him good to find fault and cut him up a little, else he will be getting too good an opinion of himself!"

"But that is unreasonable," interrupted a fourth; "don't let us dwell too much on trifling faults, but rejoice in the good—and ther is much here—though he thrusts in good and bad altogether."

"Unmistakeable talent!" wrote down the critic; "the usual examples of carelessness. That he also can write unlucky verse, may be seen at page five-and-twenty, where two hiatuses occur: the study of the ancients to be recommended, and so on."

I went away, said the Moon,—and peeped through the window into the aunt's house where sate our honored poet, the tame one, the worshipped of all the guests, and was happy.

"I sought out the other poet, the wild one, who also was in a great party of one of his patrons, where they talked about the other poet's book. "I shall also read yours!" said Mecænas, "but, honestly speaking, you know I never say to you what I do not mean; I do not expect great things from it. You are too wild for me! too fantastic—but I acknow-

ledge that as a man you are highly respectable!"

A young girl who sat in a corner read in
a book :—

> To the dust goes the poet's glory,
> And common-place to fame!--
> That is the trite old story,
> And 'twill ever be the same!

THIRTEENTH EVENING.

The Moon told me as follows:—There lie two peasants' cottages by the road through the wood. The doors are low, and the windows are irregular, but all around them grow buckthorn and barberries; the roof is mossy and grown over with yellow-flowered stone-crop and houseleek; nothing but cabbages and potatoes grow in the little garden, but there grows in the hedge an elder-tree, and under this sate a little girl; and there she sate with her brown eyes riveted upon an old oak tree between the houses. This tree has a tall and decayed hole, the top of it is sawn off, and there the stork has built his nest; there he stood and clattered with his beak.

g

A little boy came out of the cottage and placed himself by the little girl's side; they were brother and sister.

"What are you looking at?" cried he.

"I am looking at the stork," she replied; "the neighbor told me that this evening the stork will bring us either a little brother or sister; and so now I will stand and watch when they come."

"The storks do not bring anything," said the boy. "The neighbor's wife told me the same thing; but she laughed while she said it, and so I asked her if she durst say as sure as heaven, to it, but she dared not, and therefore I know that the story about the stork is only what they tell us children."

"Oh, really!" said the little girl.

"And I'll tell thee what," said the boy; "It is our Lord himself that brings little babies; he has them under his coat; but nobody can see our Lord now, and therefore we do not see him when he comes."

At that same moment the twigs of the elder-tree were moved; the children folded their hands and looked one at the other, for they thought that it was our Lord passing along with the little ones. They stood side by side, and took hold of each other's hand.

The house-door opened, and out came the neighbor.

"Come in now," said she, "and see what the stork has brought; he has brought a little brother!"

The children nodded their heads; they knew very well that the little brother was come.

FOURTEENTH EVENING.

I passed over Luneburg Heath,—said the Moon,—a solitary house stood by the roadside; some leafless trees grew beside it, and among these sung a nightingale which had lost its way. In the severity of the night it must perish; that was its song of death which I heard. With the early twilight there came along the road a company of emigrant peasants, who were on their way to Bremen or Hamburgh, to take ship for America, where happiness—the so much dreamed-of happiness—they expected should spring up for them. The women carried their youngest children upon their backs. the older ones sprang along by their side; a poor miserable horse dragged a car, on which were a few articles of household furniture. The cold wind blew ; the little girl clung closer to her mother, who looked up to my round waning face and thought upon her bitter want.

Her thoughts were those of the whole company, and therefore the red glimmering of daylight was like the evangile of the sun of prosperity which should again rise. They heard the song of the dying nightingale ; it was to them no false prophet, but a foreteller of happiness. The wind whistled, but they understood not the song ; "Sail securely across the sea ! thou hast paid for the long voyage with all that thou art possessed of ; poor and helpless shalt thou set foot on thy land of Canaan. Thou mayst sell thyself, thy wife, and thy child, yet you shall none of you suffer long. Behind the broad fragrant leaf sits the goddess of death ; her kiss of welcome breathes consuming fever into thy blood, far away, far away, over the swelling waters !"

The emigrant company listened joyfully to the song of the nightingale, which they thought announced to them happiness. Day beamed from behind light clouds, and the peasant people went over the heath to the church; the darkly-apparelled women, with their milk-white linen around their heads, looked like figures which had stepped forth from the old church paintings; all around them was nothing but the vast and death like landscape, the withered brown heath— dark, leafless plains, in the midst of white sand-banks. The women carried their hymn-books in their hands, and advanced towards the church. Oh, pray! pray for them who wander onward to their graves on the other side of the heaving water!

FIFTEENTH EVENING.

I know a theatrical Clown,—said the Moon,—the public applauds when it sees him; every one of his movements is comic, and throws the house into convulsions of laughter, and yet he is not moved thereby : that is his peculiarity. When he was yet a child, and played with other boys, he was already a punchinello. Nature had made him one ; had given him one lump upon his back, and another upon his breast. The inner man, however—the spiritual—that was really well-formed. No human being had deeper feeling, or greater elasticity of mind than he. The theatre was his ideal-world. Had he been slender and well proportioned, then he might have become a first-rate tragic actor, for the great, the heroic, filled his soul; but he was obliged to be the Clown. His sufferings, even, and his melancholy increased the comic expression of his strongly-marked countenance, and excited the laughter of the crowded public who applauded their favorite. The pretty little Columbine was friendly and kind to him, and yet she preferred marrying Harlequin. It would have been too comic in reality to have married the Clown; like the union of "Beauty and the Beast." When the Clown was most out of humor, she was the only one who could make him smile—nay, even burst into peals of laughter. First of all she would be melancholy with him, then rather cheerful, and at last full of fun.

"I know what it is thou art in want of!" said she—"yes, it is this love!" and so he was obliged to laugh.

"Me and love!" exclaimed he. "That would be a merry thing! How the public would applaud."

"It is love!" continued she; and added, with comic pathos—"It is me that you love!"

"Yes! and yet there are people who say there is no such thing as love!" The poor

Clown sprung up into the air, he was so diverted: his melancholy was now gone. And yet she had spoken the truth: he did love her—loved her like the sublime and great in art.

On her wedding-day he was more amusing than ever. At night he wept: had the public seen his distressed countenance then, they would have applauded him!

A few days ago Columbine died. On the day of her funeral Harlequin's appearance was excused on the stage, for he really was a mourning husband. The manager, however, was obliged to give something more merry than common, in order that the public should not miss too much the lovely Columbine and the light-bodied Harlequin, and for this reason it behoved the Clown to be doubly entertaining. He danced and sprung aloft with despair at his heart, and the public clapped their hands and shouted—"Bravo, bravissimo!" The clown was called for when the performance was over. Oh, he was invaluable!

This evening, after the play, the poor little man walked out from the city to the solitary churchyard. The garland of flowers

6

was withered on Columbine's grave; he sate down. It was something worth painting. His hands under his chin, his eyes fixed upon the moon; it was like a monumental figure. A clown upon a grave! very peculiar and very comic! Had the public seen their favorite then, how they would have shouted—" Bravo, Clown! bravo, bravissimo!"

SIXTEENTH EVENING

Listen to what the Moon said.—I have seen the cadet, become an officer, dress himself for the first time in his splendid uniform ; I have seen the young girl in her beautiful ball-dress; the young princely bride happy in her festival attire ; but the felicity of none of these could equal that which this evening I saw in a child, a little girl of four years. They had just put her on a new blue frock and a new pink bonnet. The beautiful things were scarcely on when they called for candles, because the moon-light through the window was too faint; they must have other light. There stood the little girl as stiff as a doll, her arms stretched out from her frock, her fingers spread out wide from each other—and oh! how her eyes, her whole being, beamed with delight!

"To-morrow you shall go out into the street," said the mother; and the little one looked up towards her bonnet and down towards her frock, and smiled joyfully.

"Mother," said she, "what will the dogs think, when they see me so beautifully dressed!"

SEVENTEENTH EVENING.

I have,—said the Moon,—told thee about Pompeii, that corpse of a city amongst living cities. I know another, one still more strange; not the corpse, but the ghost of a city. On all sides where the fountain splashes into a marble basin, I seem to hear stories of the floating city. Yes, the fountain-streams can tell them! The billows on the shore sing of them. Over the surface of the sea there often floats a mist, that is the widow's weeds. The sea's bridegroom is dead; his palace and city are now a mausoleum. Dost thou know this city? The rolling of the chariot-wheels, or the sound of the horse's hoof, were never heard in its streets. The fish swims, and like a spectre glides the black gondola over the green water.

I will,—continued the Moon,—show thee
the forum of the city, the city's great square,
and then thou wilt think it to be a city for
adventures. Grass grows between the broad
flag-stones, and thousands of tame pigeons
fly circling in the twilight around the lofty
tower. On three sides thou art surrounded
by colonnades. The Turk, with his long
pipe, sits silently beneath them; the handsome Greek-lad leans against a pillar, and
looks up to the elevated trophies, the tall
masts, the memorial of the ancient power.
The flag hangs drooping like mourning
crape; a girl stands there to rest herself, she
has set down the heavy buckets of water,
whilst the yoke on which she sustained them
rests upon her shoulders, and she supports
herself on the column of victory. That is
not a fairy palace but a church which thou
seest before thee! the gilded dome, the gilded
balls around it, shine in my beams; the
magnificent bronze horses upon it have
traveled about like bronze horses in a fairy
tale; they have traveled thither, away from
their place, and then again back! Seest
thou the beautiful painting on walls and win-

dow panes ? It is as if some genius had done
the will of a child and thus decorated this extraordinary temple. Dost thou see the winged
lion upon the pillar? Gold yet shines upon
it, but the wings are bound, the lion is dead
because the king of the sea is dead ; the vast
halls are empty, and where once hung costly
pictures the naked walls are now seen.
Lazzaroni sleep under the arches, where at
one time only the high noble dared to tread.
Either from the deep well or from the chamber
of the leaden roof, near to the Bridge of
Sighs, sounds forth a groan, whilst tamborines
are heard from the painted gondola as the
bridal-ring is cast from the glittering Bucen-
taur to Adria, the queen of the sea. Adria,
wrap thyself in mist ! let the widow's veil
cover the breast, and cast it over thy bridegroom's mausoleum ;—the marble-builder, the
spectre-like, Venice."

EIGHTEENTH EVENING.

I looked down upon a great theatre,—said the Moon,—the whole house was full of spectators, because a new actor made his debut; my beams fell upon a little window in the wall; a painted face pressed its forehead against the glass; it was the hero of the night. The chivalric beard curled upon his chin; but there were tears in the man's eyes, because he had been hissed—hissed with reason. Poor fellow! but the realm of art will not endure the feeble. He deeply felt and passionately loved art, but she did not love him.

The prompter's bell rung;—according to the piece, the hero stepped forth with a bold and determined air—thus had he to appear before a public which burst into peals of laughter.—The piece was ended; I saw a man wrapped in a cloak steal away down the steps; it was he, the spirit-crushed cavalier; the servants of the theatre whispered to each other as he passed. I followed the poor wretch home to his chamber. Hanging is such an ignominious death, and people have not always poison at hand. I know that he thought of both. He looked at his pale face in the glass; half closed his eyes to see whether he would look handsome as a corpse. It is possible for people to be unfortunate in the highest degree, and yet in the highest degree vain at the same time. He thought upon death, upon self-murder; I believe he wept in pity of himself—he wept bitterly, and when people have had a good fit of crying they do not kill themselves.

A year has passed since then. A comedy was acted, but this time in a little theatre, by a poor vagrant company. I saw again the well-known face, the painted cheeks, the curled beard. He again looked up to me and smiled—and yet for all that he had been hissed—hissed scarcely a minute before in

h

that miserable theatre, hissed by that miserable audience !

This very evening a poor hearse has driven out of the gate of the town ; not a single being accompanied it. There lay upon it a suicide, our painted and derided hero. The driver was the only attendant ; no one followed, no one except the Moon. In an angle of the churchyard wall is the self-murdered laid ; nettles will soon spring up thereon ; there will grave-diggers cast thorns and weeds from other graves.

NINETEENTH EVENING.

I come from Rome,—said the Moon,— there, in the middle of the city, upon one of the seven hills, lie the ruins of the palace of the Cæsars ; a wild fig-tree grows in a chink of the wall, and covers its nakedness with its broad, gray-green leaves ; the ass wanders over the heaps of rubbish among the laurel hedges, and feasts on the golden thistle. From this spot, whence the Roman eagle once flew forth, went, and saw, and conquered, the entrance is now through a small, miserable house, smeared with clay, between two broken pillars ; tendrils of the vine hang down, like a mourning garland, over the narrow window. An old woman, with her little grand-daughter lived there ; they ruled now

in the palace of the Cæsars, and showed to
strangers the buried treasures. There remains
of the rich throne-room nothing but a naked
wall; the shadow of the black cypress points
to the place where the throne stood. The
earth lies to the depth of some feet above the
broken floor; the little girl, now the daughter of the palace of the Cæsars, often sits
there upon her little stool, when the evening
bell rings. The keyhole in the door, close
beside her, she calls her balcony, and through
it she sees over half of Rome, as far as the
mighty dome of St. Peter's.

It was silent as ever, this evening, and
the little girl came homeward in my full,
bright light. She carried upon her head an
antiquely-formed earthen jug filled with water; her feet were bare; the black petticoat
and the little chemise sleeves were in tatters;
I kissed the child's beautiful round shoulder,
her black eyes, and her dark shining hair.
She mounted up the steps of the house, which
were steep, and were formed of broken pieces
of wall and a shattered capital. The bright-
colored lizard glided timidly past her feet,
but she was not frightened; she raised her

hand to ring at the door; there hung a hare's foot in the packthread, which is now the bell-pull at the palace of the Cæsars. She stood stock-still for a moment; what was she thinking about? Perhaps of the beautiful Jesus-child clothed in gold and silver, in the chapel below, where the silver lamp was burning, and where her little-girl friends were singing in chorus as she knew; I cannot tell if it was of this she thought! but again she made a movement, and stumbled; the earthen jug fell from her head and was shivered in pieces upon the broken marble pavement. She burst into tears; the beautiful daughter of the palace of the Cæsars wept over the poor, broken, earthen jug; she stood with her bare feet and wept, and dared not to pull at the pack-thread string, the bell-pull at the palace of the Cæsars.

•

TWENTIETH EVENING.

For upwards of fourteen days the Moon had not shone; now I saw it again, round and bright, standing above the slowly ascending clouds; listen to what the Moon related to me. I followed a caravan from one of the cities of Fez; it made a halt upon one of the salt plains, which glittered like an ice-field, and where one little stretch only was covered with moveable sand. The eldest of the caravan, with his water-flask hanging at his belt, and a bag of unleavened bread around his neck, marked out a square in the sand with his staff, and wrote therein some words of the koran; within this consecrated spot the whole caravan drew up. A young merchant, a child of the sun, as I could see by his eye and by his beautiful form, rode thoughtfully upon his white and spirited charger. Perhaps he was thinking of his young and lovely wife. It was only two days since the camel, adorned with skins and costly shawls, bore her, a beautiful bride, around the walls of the city; drums and bagpipes resounded, women sang, and shouts of joy were sent forth from those who surrounded the camel, the bridegroom shouted the gayest and the loudest of them all, and now —now he rode with the caravan across the desert. I accompanied them for many nights; saw them rest beside the wells, among the crested palm trees; they stabbed with a knife the fallen camel and cooked the flesh with fire. My beams cooled the burning sand; my beams showed them the black masses of rock, islands of death in the immense ocean of sand. No hostile power had they met with upon their trackless path; no storm was abroad; no pillars of sand carried death over the caravan.

The lovely wife prayed to heaven for her husband and father. "Are they dead?" inquired she from my gilded horn. "Are they dead?" inquired she from my beaming crescent. The desert now lies behind them; on this very evening they rest under the tall palm trees, around which circle the storks with their long wings; the pelican rushes down upon them from the branches of the mimosa. The luxuriant vegetation is trampled down by the many feet of the elephants; a troop of negro people come onward from a distant fair; women with copper buttons in their black hair, and in indigo-colored petticoats drive on the laden oxen on which the naked black children lie asleep. One negro leads in a thong a lion's cub, which he had purchased; they approach the caravan; the young merchant sits immoveable, silent; he thinks upon his lovely wife, dreams in this negro land of his white fragrant flower on the other side the desert; he lifts his head—A cloud passed over the Moon, and again a cloud. I heard no more that night.

TWENTY-FIRST EVENING.

I saw a little girl weeping,—said the Moon,
—she wept because of the wickedness of the
world. She had had a present made her of
the most beautiful doll—Oh, it was a doll, so
lovely and delicate, not at all fitted to struggle with misfortune! But the little girl's
brother, a tall lad, had taken the doll and set
it up in a high tree in the garden, and then
had run away. The little girl could not
reach the doll, could not help it down, and
therefore she cried. The doll cried too, and
stretched out her arms from among the green
branches, and looked so distressed. Yes, this
was one of the misfortunes of life of which her
mamma had so often spoken. Oh, the poor
doll! It already began to get dusk, and then

i   7

dismal night would come! And was she to sit up there in the tree, and by herself all night? No, the little girl would not endure the thought of that.

"I will stay with you!" said she, although she was not at all courageous. She began already to see quite plainly the little elves, in their tall pointed hats, peeping from between the bushes, and down the dusky alleys danced tall spectres, which came nearer and nearer. She stretched her hands up towards the tree in which the doll sate, and they laughed and pointed their fingers at her. Ah, how terrified was the little girl! "But if one has not done anything wrong," thought she, "nothing can do one any harm! Have I done anything wrong?"

She thought. "Ah, yes!" said she, "I laughed at the poor duck with the red rag tied round its leg; it hobbled so comically, and that made me laugh; but it is wrong to laugh at poor animals."

"Have you laughed at poor animals?" inquired she, looking up to the doll, and it seemed to her as if the doll shook her head.

TWENTY-SECOND EVENING.

I looked into the Tyrol,—said the Moon,—
I caused the dark fir-trees to cast strong sha
dows upon the rocks. I saw the holy Chris
topher, with the child Jesus upon his shoulder, as he stood there against the wall of the
houses, colossal in size from the foundation
to the gable. The holy Florian carries water
to the burning house, and Christ hangs bleeding upon the great cross by the wayside.
These are old pictures for the new generation :
I have, nevertheless, seen them depart one
after another.

Aloft, in the projection of the mountains, a
solitary nunnery hangs like a swallow's nest
Two sisters stood up in the tower, and rung
the bell. They were both young, and there

fore they looked out beyond the mountains into the world. A traveling carriage drove below along the high road, the postillion's horn resounded, and the poor nuns riveted with kindred thoughts their eyes upon it: there were tears in the eyes of the younger of the two. The horn sounded fainter and fainter: the bell of the nunnery overpowered its dying tones.

TWENTY-THIRD EVENING.

Listen to what the Moon said.—Many years ago, in Copenhagen, I peeped in at the window of a poor chamber. The father and mother slept, but the little son slept not. I saw the flowered cotton bed-hangings move, and the child peeped out. 1 fancied at first that he was looking at the Bornholm time-piece, it was so beautifully painted with red and green, and a cuckoo sate on the top of it; there were heavy leaden weights, and the pendulum with its shining brass surface, went to and fro, "dik, dik !" but it was not that which he was looking at—no, it was his mother's spinning-wheel, which stood under the clock. That was the most precious piece of furniture in the whole house to the boy, but he did not dare to touch it, for if he did, he got a rap on the fingers. All the time his mother was spinning he would sit beside her, and watch the humming spole and the turning wheel, and he had the while his own peculiar thoughts about them. Ah! if he could only dare thus to spin on the wheel! Father and mother were asleep; he looked at them, he looked at the wheel, and presently afterwards one little naked foot was pushed out of bed, and then another naked foot, then two little legs—thump! stood he upon the floor. He turned himself once round, however, to see whether father and mother slept. Yes, that they did! and so he went softly, very softly—in nothing but his short little shirt—to the wheel, and began to spin. The cord flew off, and the wheel ran round faster than ever. I kissed his yellow hair and his light blue eyes; it was a lovely picture. At that moment the mother awoke—the curtains moved—she looked out and thought about elves, or some other kind of little sprite.

"In the name of Jesus!" said she; and full of alarm, awoke her husband. He opened his eyes, rubbed them with his hands, and looked at the busy little creature.

" It is actually Bertel !" said he.

I withdrew my gaze from that poor chamber—I can see so far around me ! I looked at that very moment into the hall of the Vatican where the marble gods stand. I illumined the group of the Laocoon ; the stone seemed to sigh. I pressed my quiet kiss upon the muses' breast; I fancy it heaved. But my beams tarried longest upon the group of the Nile, upon the colossal god. He lay full of thought, supporting himself upon sphinxes: dreaming there as if he were thinking of the fleeting year ; little loves played around him with crocodiles. In the horn of plenty sate, with folded arms, and gazing upon the great river-god, a very little love, a true picture of the little boy with the wheel ; it was the same expression. Living and charming, here stood the little marble child ; and yet more than a thousand times had the wheel of the year gone round since it stood forth in stone. Just so many times as the boy in the poor chamber turned the wheel has the great wheel of time hummed round, and still shall hum, before the age creates another marble-god like this.

See, it is now many years since then. Last
evening,—continued the Moon,—I looked
down upon a creek in the east coast of Zea
land.   Beautiful woods were there, lofty
mounds, an old mansion-house with red walls,
swans in the moat, and a little trading town,
with its church among the apple-orchards. A
fleet of boats, each bearing a torch, glided
over the unruffled water; it was not to catch
fish that the torches were burning—no! everything was festal!   Music sounded, a song
was sung; and in the middle of one of the
boats stood he whom they honored, a tall,
strong man in a large cloak; he had blue
eyes, and long white hair.   I knew him, and
thought upon the Vatican, and the Nile-group,
and all the marble gods; I thought upon the
poor little chamber where little Bertel sate in
his short shirt and spun.

The wheel of time has gone round; new
gods have ascended from the marble.   "Hurrah!" resounded from the boats—"Hurrah for
Bertel Thorwaldsen!"

TWENTY-FOURTH EVENING.

I will give thee a picture from Frankfort, —said the Moon :—I took notice of one building in particular. It was not the birth-place of Goethe, nor was it the old town-house, where, through the grated windows, are still exhibited the horned fronts of the oxen which were roasted and given to the people at the emperor's coronation, but it was the house of a citizen painted green and unpretending, at the corner of the narrow Jews' street. It was the house of the Rothschilds. I looked in at the open door; the flight of steps was strongly lighted; servants stood there with burning lights in massive silver candlesticks, and bowed themselves lowly before the old woman who was carried forth down the steps in a sedan chair. The master of the house

stood with bare head, and impressed reverentially a kiss upon the old woman's hand. It
was his mother. She nodded kindly to him,
and to the servants; and they carried her out
into the narrow, dark street, into a little
house, where she lived, and where her child
was born, from whom all her good fortune
had proceeded. If she were now to leave the
despised street and the little house, then, perhaps, good fortune would leave him!—that
was her belief.

The Moon told nothing more. Her visit
to me was too short this evening; but I
thought of the old woman in the narrow, despised street. Only one word about her—
and she had her splendid house near the
Thames; only one word about her—and her
villa was situated on the Gulf of Naples.

"Were I to leave the mean little house
where my son's good fortune began, then,
perhaps, good fortune would leave him!"

This is a superstition, but of that kind
which only requires, when the history is
known and the picture seen, two words as
a superscription to make it intelligible—A
MOTHER.

TWENTY-FIFTH EVENING.

It was yesterday, in the morning twilight, —these were the Moon's own words,—not a chimney was yet smoking in the whole city, and it was precisely the chimneys that I was looking at. From one of these chimneys at that very moment came forth a little head, and then a half body, the arms of which rested on the coping stone of the chimney. "Hurrah!" It was a little chimney-sweeper lad, who, for the first time in his life, had mounted a chimney, and had thus put forth his head. "Hurrah!" Yes, there was some difference between this and creeping upwards in the narrow chimney! The air blew so fresh; he could look out over the whole city to the green wood. The sun had just risen round and large, it looked brightly into his face, which beamed with happiness, although it was famously smeared with soot.

" Now the whole city can see me, and the moon can see me, and the sun also !" and with that he flourished about his brush.

TWENTY-SIXTH EVENING.

Last night I looked down upon a city in China,—said the Moon. My beams illumined the long naked walls which form the streets ; here and there, to be sure, is a door, but it is closed, because the Chinese troubled not themselves about the world outside. Impenetrable Venetian shutters covered the windows of the houses behind the walls ; from the temple alone light shone faintly through the window-glass. I looked in— looked in upon the brilliant splendor ; from floor to ceiling was covered with pictures in strong colors and rich gilding, which represented the works of the gods on earth. Their statues themselves stood in every niche, but mostly concealed by brilliant dra-

peries and suspended fans; and before every
divinity—they were all of tin—stood a little
altar with holy water, flowers, and burning
wax-lights. Supreme in the temple, however,
stood Fu, the supreme divinity, dressed in a
garment of silken stuff of the holy yellow
color. At the foot of the altar sate a living
figure, a young priest. He appeared to be
praying, but in the midst of his prayer he
sunk into deep thought; and it certainly was
sinful, because his cheeks burned, and his
head bowed very low.   Poor Souihoung!
Perhaps he was dreaming about working in
one of the little flower-gardens which lie before every house behind the long wall of the
street, and which was a far pleasanter occu-
pation to him than trimming the wax-lights
in the temple ; or was he longing to be seated
at the well-covered board, and between every
course to be wiping his lips with silver paper?
or was i. a sin so great that if he had dared
to utter it, the heavenly powers must have
punished him with death ? Were his thoughts
bold enough to take flight with the ship of
the barbarians to their home, the remote
England ? No, his thoughts did not fly so

far ; and yet they were as sinful as the warm blood of youth could make them—sinful here, in the temple before the statues of Fu and the holy deities. I knew where his thoughts were. In the most distant corner of the city, upon the flat, flagged roof, the parapet of which seemed to be made of porcelain, and where stood the beautiful vases in which grew large white campanulas, sate the youthful Pe, with her small roguish eyes, her pouting lips, and her least of all little feet. Her shoes pinched, but there was a more severe pinching at her heart ; she raised her delicate, blooming arms, and the satin rustled. Before her stood a glass bowl, in which were four gold fish : she stirred the water very softly with a beautifully painted and japaned stick. Oh, so slowly she stirred it because she was deep in thought ! Perhaps she was thinking how rich and golden was the apparel of the fish, how safely they lived in the glass bowl, and how luxuriously they were fed ; and yet, for all that, how much more happy they might be in freedom : yes, the idea distressed the beautiful Pe. Her thoughts passed away from her home ; her thoughts went into the church, but it was not for the sake of the gods that they went there. Poor Pe! poor Soui-houng! Their earthly thoughts met, but my cold beam lay like a cherub's sword between them.

TWENTY-SEVENTH EVENING.

There was a calm,—said the Moon—the water was as transparent as the pure air through which I floated. I could see, far below the surface of the sea, the strange plants which, like giant trees in groves, heaved themselves up towards me with stems a fathom long, whilst the fish swam over their tops. High up in the air flew a flock of wild swans, one of which sank with wearied wings lower and lower: its eyes followed the airy caravan, which every moment became more distant; its pinions were expanded widely, and it sank, like a soap-bubble in the still air; it touched the surface of the water, bowed back its head between its wings, and lay still, like a white lotus

k

upon the calm Indian Sea. The breeze blew and lifted up the bright surface of the water, which was brilliant as the air; there rolled on a large, broad billow—the swan lifted its head, and the shining water was poured, like blue fire, over its breast and back.

The dawn of day illumined the red clouds, and the swan rose up refreshed, and flew towards the ascending sun, towards the blue coast, whither had betaken themselves the airy caravan; but it flew alone—with longing in its breast, flew alone over the blue, the foaming water!

TWENTY-EIGHTH EVENING.

I will now give thee a picture from Sweden, said the Moon.—In the midst of black pine woods, not far from the melancholy shore of Roxe, lies the old convent-church of Wreta. My beams passed through the grating in the walls into the spacious vault where kings sleep in great stone coffins. On the wall above them, is placed, as an image of earthly magnificence, a king's crown, made of wood, painted and gilded, and held firm by a wooden pin, which is driven into the wall. The worm has eaten through the gilded wood, the spider has spun its web from the crown to the coffin; it is a mourning banner, perishable, as mourning for the dead! How still they sleep! I remember them so well! I see now the bold smile on the lips which expressed joy or sorrow so strongly, so decisively. When the steam-vessel, like an enchanted ship, sails hither from the mountains, many a stranger comes to the church, visits this vault, and inquires the names of the kings, and these names sound forgotten and dead; he looks upon the worm-eaten crown, smiles, and if he be of a pious turn of mind, there is melancholy in his smile.

Slumber ye dead! the Moon remembers you. The Moon sends in the night her cold beams to your quiet kingdom, over which hangs the wooden crown!

TWENTY-NINTH EVENING.

Close beside the high road,—said the Moon, —lies a little public house, and just opposite to it is a great coach house. As the roof was under repair, I looked down between the beams and saw through the open trap-door into the great desolate space; the turkey slept upon the beam, and the saddle was laid to rest in the empty manger. In the middle of the place stood a travelling-carriage, within which the gentlefolks were sound asleep, whilst the horses were feeding, and the driver stretched his limbs, although I know very well that he slept soundly more than half the way. The door of the fellow's chamber stood open, and the bed looked as if he had tumbled neck and heels into it; the candle stood on the floor, and burned low in the socket. The wind blew cold through the barn; and the time was nearer to daybreak than midnight. Upon the floor within the stall, slept a family of wandering musicians; father and mother were dreaming about the burning drop in the bottle; the pale little girl, she dreamed about the burning tears in her eyes. The harp lay at their head, and the dog at their feet.

THIRTIETH EVENING.

It was in a little trading town—said the Moon—I saw it last year; but that is nothing, for I saw it so plainly. This evening I read about it in the newspaper, but it was not nearly as plain there.

Down in the parlor of the public-house sate the master of the bear, and ate his supper. Bams, the bear, stood outside, tied to the faggot-stake. The poor bear! he would not have done the least harm to any soul, for all his grim looks. Up in the garret there lay, in the bright light of the Moon, three little children: the eldest was six years old, the youngest not more than two. "Clap, clap!" came something up the stairs! What could it be? The door sprang open—it was Bams, the great rough bear! He had grown tired of standing out there in the yard, and he now found his way up the steps. I saw the whole thing,—said the Moon. The children were very much frightened at the great grim-looking beast, and crept each one of them into his corner; but he found them all out, rubbed them with his snout, but did them no harm at all! "It is certainly a big dog!" thought they; and with that they patted him. He laid himself down on the floor, and the least boy tumbled upon him, and played at hiding his yellow curly head among his thick black hair. The eldest boy now took his drum and made a tremendous noise, and the bear rose up on his hind legs and began to dance. It was charming! Each boy took his weapons; the bear must have a gun, too, and he held it like a regular soldier. What a glorious comrade they had found! and so they marched—" One, two! one, two!"

Presently the door opened; it was the children's mother. You should have seen her — seen her speechless horror; her face as white as a wall, her half-opened mouth, her

staring eyes ; the least of the children, however, nodded so joyfully, and shouted with all
his might—" We are playing at soldiers !"
And with that, up came the bear's master !

l

STORIES.

123

MY BOOTS.

THERE is a street in Rome which is called *Via della Purificazione;* yet nobody can say of it that it is purified. It goes up-hill and down-hill; cabbage stalks and old broken pots lie scattered about it; the smoke comes curling out of the door of the public-house, and the lady who lives opposite to me —yes, I cannot help it, but it is true—the lady on the opposite side, she shakes her sheets every morning out of the window. In this street there generally live many foreigners; this year, however, fear of the fever and malignant sickness keeps most of them in Naples and Florence. I lived quite alone in a great big house; neither the host nor hostess ever slept there at night.

It was a great, big, cold house, with a little wet garden, in which there grew only one row of peas, and a half-extinguished gilly-flower; and yet, in the very next garden, which lay higher, there were hedges of monthly roses, and trees full of yellow lemons. These last, spite of the incessant rain, looked vigorous; the roses, on the contrary, looked as if they had lain for eight days in the sea.

The evenings were so lonesome in the cold large rooms; the black chimney yawning between the windows, and without were rain and mist. All the doors were fastened with locks and iron bolts; but what good could that do? The wind whistled in a tone sharp enough to cut one in two through the cracks in the doors; the thin faggots kindled in the chimney, but did not send out their warmth very far; the cold stone floor, the damp walls and the lofty ceiling seemed only suited to the summer season.

If I would make myself right comfortable, I was obliged to put on my traveling fur-boots, my great coat, my cloak, and my fur-cap,—yes, and then I could do tolerably well.

To be sure, the side next the fire was half roasted; but then, in this world, people must learn to turn and twist themselves about, and I turned myself like a sunflower.

The evenings were somewhat long; but then the teeth took it into their heads to get up a nervous concert, and it was extraordinary with what alacrity the proposal was accepted. A downright Danish toothache cannot compare itself to an Italian one. Here the pain played upon the very fangs of the teeth, as if there sate a Liszt or a Thalberg at them; now it thundered in the foreground, now in the background. There was an accordance and strength in the whole thing which at last drove me beside myself.

Besides the evening concerts, there were also nocturnal concerts; and during such a one, while the windows rattled in the storm, and rain poured down in torrents, I threw a half-melancholy glance upon my night-lamp. My writing implements stood just by, and I saw, quite plainly, that the pen was dancing along over the paper as if it were guided by an invisible hand; but it was not so; it was guided by its own hand; it wrote from dictation ; and who dictated ? Yes, it may sound incredible, but is the truth for all that. And when I say so, people will believe me. It was my boots,—my old Copenhagen boots— which, being soaked through and through with rain-water, now had their place in the chimney, near to the red glowing fire. Whilst I was suffering from toothache, they were suffering from dropsy ; they dictated their own autobiography, which, as it seems to me, may throw some light upon the Italian winter of 1840-41.

The Boots said,—

" We are two brothers, Right and Left Boot. Our earliest recollection is of being strongly rubbed over with wax, and after that highly polished. I could see myself reflected in my brother ; my brother could see himself reflected in me ; and we saw that we were only one body,—a sort of Castor and Pollux ; a pair of together-grown Siamese, which fate has ordained to live and die, to exist, and not to exist, together. We were, both of us, native Copenhageners.

The shoemaker's apprentice carried us out into the world in his own hands, and this

gave rise to sweet, but alas! false hopes of
our destination. The person to whom we
were thus brought, pulled us on by the ears,
until we fitted to his legs, and then he went
down stairs in us. We creaked for joy!
When we got out of doors it rained—we kept
creaking on, however; but only for the first
day.

"Ah! there is a great deal of bad weather
to go through in this world! We were not
made for water boots, and therefore did not
feel happy. No brushing ever gave us again
the polish of our youth; the polish which
we possessed when the shoemaker's apprentice carried us through the streets in his hand.
Who can describe our joy, therefore, when
we heard it said one morning, that we were
going into foreign parts! yes, were even going to Italy, to that mild, warm country,
where we should only tread upon marble and
classic ground; drink in the sunshine, and,
of a certainty, recover the brightness of our
youth.

"We set out. Through the longest part
of our journey we slept in the trunk, and
dreamed about the warm countries. In the

cities or the country, we made good use of
our eyes; it was, however, bad weather, and
wet there also as in Denmark. Our soles
were taken ill of palsy, and in Munich were
obliged tc be taken off, and we had a new
pair; but these were so well done, that they
looked like native soles.

" 'Oh, that we were but across the Alps!'
sighed we; there the weather is mild and
good.'

" We came to the other side of the Alps,
but we found neither mild nor good weather.
It rained and blew; and when we trod upon
marble, it was so icy-cold, that it forced the
cold perspiration out of our soles; wherever
we trod we left behind a wet impression.
In the evenings, however, it was very amusing when the shoe-boys at the hotels collected
and numbered the boots and shoes; and we
were set among all these foreign companions
and heard them tell about all the cities where
they had been. There was once a pair of
beautiful red morocco boots, with black feet,
I think it was in Bologna, that told us all
about their ascending Vesuvius, where their
feet were burned off with the subterranean

heat. Ah! we could not help longing to die such a death.

" 'If we were but across the Appenines! If we were but in Rome!' sighed we. And we came thither; but for one week after another have been tramping about in nothing but wet and mud. People must see everything; and wonderful sights and rainy weather, never come to an end. Not a single warm sunbeam has refreshed us; the cold wind is always whistling round us. Oh Rome! Rome! For the first time this night do we inhale warmth in this blessed chimney corner, and we will inhale it till we burst! The upper leathers are gone already,—nothing remains but the hind quarters, and they will soon give way. Before, however, we die this blessed death, we wish to leave our history behind us; and we wish also that our corpses should be taken to Berlin, to repose near to that man who had the heart and the courage to describe 'Italy as it is,'—even by the truth-loving Nicolai."

And with these words the boots crumbled to pieces.

All was still: my night-lamp had gone

out.   I myself slumbered a little; and when
towards morning I awoke, I found it was all
a dream; but when I glanced towards the
chimney-corner, I saw the boots all shrivelled
up, standing like mummies beside the cold
ashes !   I looked at the paper which lay near
to my lamp—it was grey paper, full of ink
spots —the pen unquestionably had been over
it, but the words had all run one into another;
however the pen had written the Memoirs of
the Boots on grey paper.   That, however,
which was legible I copied out; and the peo
ple will be so good as to recollect that it is
not I, but my boots, which make this com·
plaint of La bella Italia.

SCENES ON THE DANUBE.

TO-DAY IS SUNDAY.

IT is Sunday in the calendar; it is Sunday in God's beautiful nature! Let us go out into the hills toward Mehadia, the most delightfully situated of all the watering-places in Hungary. What a mass of flowers are in bloom in the tall green grass! What gushes of sunshine upon the wood-covered sides of the hills! The air is blue and transparent. To-day it is Sunday, and therefore all the people whom we meet are in holiday attire. The smooth, black, plaited hair of the girls is adorned with real flowers; with a spray of laburnum, or a dark red carnation; the white chemise sleeves are embroidered with green and red; the petticoat resembles a deep fringe of red, blue, and yellow: even the old

133

grandmother is dressed in fringe, and wears a flower in her white linen head-band. Young men and boys have roses in their hats; the very least is arrayed in his best, and looks splendid; his short shirt hangs outside his dark-colored breeches; a spray of laburnum is wreathed round his large hat, which soon half buries his eyes. Yes, it is Sunday to-day!

What a solitude there is in these hills! Life and health gush in water out of these springs; music resounds from the stately, large pump-room; the nightingale sings in the clear sunshine, among the fragrant trees, where the wild vines climb from branch to branch.

Thou wonderful nature! to me the best, the holiest of churches! In the midst of thee my heart tells me that "this day is Sunday!"

We are again in Orsova. The brass ball upon the church-tower shines in the sun: the door is open. How solitary it is within. The priest stands in his robes and lifts up his voice; it is Father Adam; little Antonius kneels before him, and swings to and fro the censer; the elder boy, Hieronymus, has his

place in the middle of the church, and repre-
sents the whole Armenian congregation.

In front of the church, in the market-place,
where the lime-trees are in blossom, there is
a great dance of young and old. In the
middle of the circle stand the musicians; one
blows the bag-pipe, the other scrapes the
fiddle. The circle twists itself first to the
right, then to the left. Everybody is in their
utmost grandeur, with fringe, flowers, and
bare feet. To-day it is Sunday!

Several little lads run about in nothing but
a shirt; upon their heads, however, they wear
a large man's hat, and in the hat a flower.
Official people, gentlemen and ladies all
dressed in the fashion of Vienna, walk about
to look at the people, the dancing people.
The red evening sun illumines the white
church tower, the amber-colored Danube, and
the wood-crowned mountains of Servia: may
it shine also in my song when I sing of it!
How beautiful and animated! How fresh
and peculiar! Everything indicates a holiday.
Everything shows that to-day is Sunday!

At Drencova.

About sunset I walked alone in the wood near the little town, where I fell in with some gipseys who had encamped round a fire for the night. When I returned back through the wood, I saw a handsome peasant-lad standing among the bushes, who bade me good evening in German. I asked him if this were his native tongue; he replied in the negative, and told me that he commonly spoke in the Wallacian language, but that he had learned German in the school. To judge by his dress he appeared very poor · but everything that he wore was so clean his hair so smoothly combed ; his eyes beamed with such an expression of happiness; there was something so thoughtful and so good in his countenance, as I rarely have seen in a child before. I asked him if he were intended for a soldier, and he replied, " Yes, we are all of us soldiers here, but I wish to be an officer, and therefore I learn everything that I can." There was a something in his whole manner so innocent, so noble, that actually, if I had been rich, I would have adopted that boy. I told him that he certainly must be an officer; and that no doubt he would be one if he only zealously strove after it, and put his trust in God.

In reply to my question, whether he knew where Denmark was, he thought with himself for some time, and then said, "I fancy it is a long way from here—near Hamburgh."

I could not give an alms to this boy; he seemed too noble to receive charity; I asked him, therefore, to gather me a few flowers; he ran away readily, and soon gathered me a beautiful nosegay. I took and said I shall buy these flowers. In that way he received payment; he blushed deeply, and thanked me sweetly. He told me that his name was Adam Marco. I took one of my cards out of my pocket, and gave it to him, saying, "Some day when you are an officer, and perhaps may come to Denmark, then inquire for me, and your happiness will give me great pleasure. Be industrious, and put your trust in God! There is no knowing what may happen."

Never did any unknown child make such a strong impression on me at the first meet
m

ing, as did this. His noble deportment, his
thoughtful innocent countenance, were his
best patent of nobility. He *must* become an
officer; and I will do my little towards it;
committing it, it is true, to the hand of
chance. And here I make my bow to every
noble, rich, Hungarian lady, who, by any
chance, may read this book, and who, perhaps, for the "Improvisatore" and "The
Fiddler," may have a kindly thought; the
poet beseeches of her—or if he have, unknown
to himself, a wealthy friend in Hungary, or
in Wallacia, he beseeches also of him, to
think of Adam Marco in Drencova, and to
help your little countryman forward, if he
deserve it!

The Swineherds.

Before a cottage, plastered of mud and
straw, sat an old swineherd, a real Hungarian,
and consequently a nobleman.* Very often

* The number of indigent nobles in Hungary is very
great and they live like peasants, in the most miserable
huts.

had he laid his hand upon his heart, and said this to himself. The sun burnt hotly, and therefore he had turned the woolly side of his sheepskin outwards; his silver white hair hung around his characteristic brown countenance. He had got a new piece of linen, a shirt, and he was now preparing it for wear, according to his own fashion, which was this: he rubbed the fat of a piece of bacon into it; by this means it would keep clean so much the longer, and he could turn it first on one side and then on the other.

His grandson, a healthy-looking lad, whose long black hair was smoothed with the same kind of pomatum which the old man used to his shirt, stood just by, leaning on a staff. A long leathern bag hung on his shoulder. He also was a swineherd, and this very evening was going on board a vessel, which, towed by the steamboat Eros, was taking a freight of pigs to the imperial city of Vienna.

"You will be there in five days," said the old man. "When I was a young fellow, like you, it used to take six weeks for the journey. Step by step we went on through marshy roads, through forests, and over rocks. The pigs, which at the beginning of the journey, were so fat that many of them died by the way, became thin and wretched before we came to our destination. Now, the world strides onward : everything gets easier !"

"We can smoke our pipes," said the youth ; "lie in the sun in our warm skin-cloaks. Meadows and cities glide swiftly past us; the pigs fly along with us, and get fat on the journey. That is the life !"

"Everybody has his own notions," replied the old man; "I had mine. There is a pleasure even in difficulty. When in the forest I saw the gypsies roasting and boiling, I had to look sharply about me, to mind that my best pigs did not get into their clutches. Many a bit of fun have I had. I had to use my wits. I was put to my shifts; and sometimes had to use my fists as well. On the plain between the rocks, where, you know, the winds are shut in, I drove my herd : I drove it across the field where the invisible castle of the winds is built. There was neither house nor roof to be seen: the castle of the winds can only be felt. I drove the herd through the invisible chambers and halls.

I could see it very well; the wall was storm
the door whirlwind! Such a thing as that
is worth all the trouble; it gives a man
something to talk about. What do you come
to know, you who lie idling in the sunshine,
in the great floating pig-sty?"

And all the time the old man was talking,
he kept rubbing the bacon-fat into his new
shirt.

"Go with me to the Danube," returned
the youth; "there you will see a dance of
pigs, all so fat, till they are ready to burst.
They do not like to go into the vessel; we
drive them with sticks; they push one
against another; set themselves across;
stretch themselves out on the earth, run
hither and thither, however fat and heavy
they may be. That is a dance! You would
shake your sides with laughing! What a
squealing there is! All the musicians in
Hungary could not make such a squealing
as that out of all their bagpipes, let them
blow as hard as they would! How beautifully bright you have made your shirt look ;
you can't improve it. Go with me—now do
—to the Danube! I'll give you something

to drink, grandfather! In four days I snall be in the capital: what pomp and splendor I shall see there! I will buy you a pair of red trowsers and plaited spurs!"

The old swineherd proudly lifted his head, regarded the youthful Magyar with flashing eyes; hung his shirt on the hook in the wall of the low mud cottage, in which there was nothing but a table, a bench, and a wooden chest; he nodded with his head, and muttered to himself. "Nemes-ember van, nemes-ember én és vagyok." (He is a nobleman: I am also a nobleman!)

THE REAL PRINCESS.

THERE was once a Prince who wished to marry a Princess; but then she must be a real Princess. He travelled all over the world in hopes of finding such a lady; but there was always something wrong. Princesses he found in plenty; but whether they were real Princesses it was impossible for him to decide, for now one thing, now another, seemed to him not quite right about the ladies. At last he returned to his palace quite cast down, because he wished so much to have a real Princess for his wife.

One evening a fearful tempest arose, it thundered and lightened, and the rain poured down from the sky in torrents: besides, it was as dark as pitch. All at once there was heard a violent knocking at the door, and the old King, the Prince's father, went out himself to open it.

It was a Princess who was standing outside the door. What with the rain and the wind, she was in a sad condition; the water trickled down from her hair, and her clothes clung to her body. She said she was a real Princess.

"Ah! we shall soon see that!" thought the old Queen-mother; however, she said not a word of what she was going to do; but went quietly into the bed-room, took all the bed-clothes off the bed, and put three little peas on the bedstead. She then laid twenty mattrasses one upon another over the three peas, and put twenty feather beds over the mattrasses.

Upon this bed the Princess was to pass the night.

The next morning she was asked how she had slept. "Oh, very badly indeed!" she replied. "I have scarcely closed my eyes the whole night through. I do not know what was in my bed, but I had something hard under me, and am all over black and blue. It has hurt me so much!"

Now it was plain that the lady must be a

real Princess, since she had been able to feel the three little peas through the twenty mattrasses and twenty feather beds. None but a real Princess could have had such a delicate sense of feeling.

The Prince accordingly made her his wife; being now convinced that he had found a real Princess. The three peas were however put into the cabinet of curiosities, where they are still to be seen, provided they are not lost.

Was not this lady a real delicacy.

THERE was once a poor Prince, who had a kingdom; his kingdom was very small, but still quite large enough to marry upon; and he wished to marry.

It was certainly rather cool of him to say to the Emperor's daughter, Will you have me? But so he did; for his name was renowned far and wide; and there were a hundred princesses who would have answered, "Yes!" and "Thank you kindly." We shall see what this princess said.

Listen!

It happened that where the Prince's father lay buried, there grew a rose tree—a most beautiful rose tree, which blossomed only once in every five years, and even then bore only one flower, but that *was* a rose! It smelt so

sweet tnat all cares and sorrows were forgotten
by him who inhaled its fragrance.

And furthermore, the Prince had a nightingale, who could sing in such a manner that
it seemed as though all sweet melodies dwelt
in her little throat. So the Princess was to
have the rose, and the nightingale ; and they
were accordingly put into large silver caskets, and sent to her.

The Emperor had them brought into a
large hall, where the Princess was playing at
" Visiting," with the ladies of the court ; and
when she saw the caskets with the presents,
she clapped her hands for joy.

" Ah, if it were but a little pussy-cat !" said
she ; but the rose tree, with its beautiful rose
came to view.

" Oh, how prettily it is made !" said all the
court ladies.

" It is more than pretty," said the Emperor,
" it is charming !"

But the Princess touched it, and was almost ready to cry.

" Fie, papa !" said she, " it is not made at
all, it is natural !"

" Let us see what is in the other casket,

before we get into a bad humor," said the
Emperor.   So the nightingale came forth
and sang so delightfully that at first no one
could say anything ill-humored of her.

"*Superbe! charmant!*" exclaimed the
ladies ; for they all used to chatter French,
each one worse than her neighbor.

"How much the bird reminds me of the
musical box that belonged to our blessed
Empress," said an old knight.   "Oh yes!
these are the same tones, the same execu-
tion."

"Yes! yes!" said the Emperor, and he
wept like a child at the remembrance.

"I will still hope that it is not a real bird,"
said the Princess.

"Yes, it is a real bird," said those who had
brought it.   "Well then let the bird fly," said
the Princess ; and she positively refused to
see the Prince.

However, he was not to be discouraged ;
he daubed his face over brown and black ;
pulled his cap over his ears, and knocked at
the door.

"Good day to my lord, the Emperor !" said
he.   "Can I have employment at the palace ?"

"Why, yes," said the Emperor, "I want some one to take care of the pigs, for we have a great many of them."

So the Prince was appointed "Imperial Swineherd." He had a dirty little room close by the pig-sty; and there he sat the whole day, and worked. By the evening he had made a pretty little kitchen-pot. Little bells were hung all round it; and when the pot was boiling, these bells tinkled in the most charming manner, and played the old melody,

> "Ach! du lieber Augustin,
> Allest ist weg, weg, weg!"*

But what was still more curious, whoever held his finger in the smoke of the kitchen-pot, immediately smelt all the dishes that were cooking on every hearth in the city— this, you see, was something quite different from the rose.

Now the Princess happened to walk that way; and when she heard the tune, she stood quite still, and seemed pleased; for she could play "Lieber Augustine;" it was

> * "Ah! dear Augustine!
> All is gone, gone, gone!"

the only piece she knew; and she played it with one finger.

"Why there is my piece," said the Princess: "that swineherd must certainly have been well educated! go in and ask him the price of the instrument."

So one of the court ladies must run in; however, she drew on wooden slippers first.

"What will you take for the kitchen-pot?" said the lady.

"I will have ten kisses from the Princess," said the swineherd.

"Yes, indeed!" said the lady.

"I cannot sell it for less," rejoined the swineherd.

"He is an impudent fellow!" said the Princess, and she walked on; but when she had gone a little way, the bells tinkled so prettily

"Ach! du lieber Augustin,
Alles ist weg, weg, weg!"

"Stay," said the Princess. "Ask him if he will have ten kisses from the ladies of my court."

"No, thank you!" said the swineherd, "ten kisses from the Princess, or I keep the the kitchen-pot myself."

"That must not be, either!" said the Princess, "but do you all stand before me that no one may see us."

And the court-ladies placed themselves in front of her, and spread out their dresses—the swineherd got ten kisses, and the Princess—the kitchen-pot.

That was delightful! the pot was boiling the whole evening, and the whole of the following day. They knew perfectly well what was cooking at every fire throughout the city, from the chamberlain's to the cobbler's; the court-ladies danced and clapped their hands.

"We know who has soup, and who has pancakes for dinner to-day, who has cutlets, and who has eggs. How interesting!"

"Yes, but keep my secret, for I am an Emperor's daughter."

The swineherd—that is to say—the Prince, for no one knew that he was other than an ill-favored swineherd, let not a day pass without working at something; he at last constructed a rattle, which, when it was swung round, played all the waltzes and jig tunes which have ever been heard since the creation of the world.

"Ah, that is *superbe!*" said the Princess when she passed by, "I have never heard prettier compositions! Go in and ask him the price of the instrument; but mind, he shall have no more kisses!"

"He will have a hundred kisses from the Princess!" said the lady who had been to ask.

"I think he is not in his right senses!" said the Princess, and walked on, but when she had gone a little way, she stopped again. "One must encourage art," said she, "I am the Emperor's daughter. Tell him he shall, as on yesterday, have ten kisses from me, and may take the rest from the ladies of the court."

"Oh!—but we should not like that at all!" said they. "What are you muttering?" asked the Princess; "if I can kiss him, surely you can. Remember that you owe everything to me." So the ladies were obliged to go to him again.

"A hundred kisses from the Princess!" said he, "or else let every one keep his own."

"Stand round!" said she; and all the ladies stood round her whilst the kissing was going on.

" What can be the reason for such a crowd close by the pig-sty ?" said the Emperor, who happened just then to step out on the balcony ; he rubbed his eyes, and put on his spec tacles. "They are the ladies of the court ; I must go down and see what they are about !" So he pulled up his slippers at the heel, for he had trodden them down.

As soon as he had got into the court-yard, he moved very softly, and the ladies were so much engrossed with counting the kisses, that all might go on fairly, that they did not perceive the Emperor. He rose on his tiptoes.

" What is all this ?" said he, when he saw what was going on, and he boxed the Princess's ears with his slipper, just as the swineherd was taking the eighty-sixth kiss.

" March out !" said the Emperor, for he was very angry ; and both Princess and swineherd were thrust out of the city.

The Princess now stood and wept, the swineherd scolded, and the rain poured down.

" Alas ! unhappy creature that I am !" said the Princess "If I had but married the

handsome young Prince! ah! how unfortunate I am!"

And the swineherd went behind a tree,
washed the black and brown color from his
face, threw off his dirty clothes, and stepped
forth in his princely robes; he looked so noble that the Princess could not help bowing
before him.

"I am come to despise thee," said he.
"Thou would'st not have an honorable
Prince! thou could'st not prize the rose and
the nightingale, but thou wast ready to kiss
the swineherd for the sake of a trumpery
plaything.   Thou art rightly served."

He then went back to his own little kingdom, and shut the door of his palace in her
face.   Now she might well sing

> " Ach ! du lieber Augustine,
> Alles ist weg, weg, weg!"

Part II.

THE SHOES OF FORTUNE

THE SNOW-QUEEN,

ETC

Q

THE SHOES OF FORTUNE.

I.

A BEGINNING.

VERY author
has some peculiarity in his descriptions or in
his style of writing. Those who do not
like him, magnify it, shrug up their shoulders, and exclaim—There he is again !—I,
for my part, know very well how I can
bring about this movement and this excla-
mation. It would happen immediately if I

7

were to begin here, as I intended to do, with : " Rome has its Corso, Naples its Toledo "—" Ah ! that Andersen ; there he is again !" they would cry ; yet I must, to please my fancy, continue quite quietly, and add : " But Copenhagen has its East Street."

Here, then, we will stay for the present. In one of the houses not far from the new market a party was invited—a very large party, in order, as is often the case, to get a return invitation from the others. One half of the company was already seated at the card-table, the other half awaited the result of the stereotype preliminary observation of the lady of the house :

" Now let us see what we can do to amuse ourselves."

They had got just so far, and the conversation began to crystallise, as it could but do with the scanty stream which the commonplace world supplied. Amongst other things they spoke of the middle ages : some praised that period as far more interesting, far more poetical than our own too sober present; indeed Councillor Knap defended this opinion so warmly, that the hostess declared imme-

diately on his side, and both exerted themselves with unwearied eloquence. The
Councillor boldly declared the time cf King
Hans to be the noblest and the most happy
period.*

While the conversation turned on this
subject, and was only for a moment interrupted by the arrival of a journal that contained nothing worth reading, we will just
step out into the antechamber, where cloaks,
mackintoshes, sticks, umbrellas, and shoes,
were deposited. Here sat two female figures,
a young and an old one. One might have
thought at first they were servants come to
accompany their mistresses home ; but on
looking nearer, one soon saw they could
scarcely be mere servants ; their forms were
too noble for that, their skin too fine, the
cut of their dress too striking. Two fairies
were they ; the younger, it is true, was not
Dame Fortune herself, but one of the
waiting-maids of her handmaidens who
carry about the lesser good things that she
distributes ; the other looked extremely
gloomy—it was Care. She always attends

* A.D. 1482—1513.

to her own serious business herself, as then
she is sure of having it done properly.

They were telling each other, with a
confidential interchange of ideas, where they
had been during the day. The messenger
of Fortune had only executed a few unimportant commissions, such as saving a new
bonnet from a shower of rain, &c. &c.; but
what she had yet to perform was something
quite unusual.

"I must tell you," said she, "that to-day
is my birth-day; and in honor of it, a pair
of walking-shoes or galoshes has been en-
trusted to me, which I am to carry to mankind. These shoes possess the property of
instantly transporting him who has them on
to the place or the period in which he most
wishes to be; every wish, as regards time or
place, or state of being, will be immediately
fulfilled, and so at last man will be happy,
here below."

"Do you seriously believe it?" replied
Care, in a severe tone of reproach. "No;
he will be very unhappy, and will assuredly
bless the moment when he feels that he has
freed himself from the fatal shoes."

"Stupid nonsense!" said the other angri.
ly. "I will put them here by the door.
Some one will make a mistake for certain
and take the wrong ones—he will be a
happy man."

Such was their conversation.

WHAT BEFF? THE COUNCILLOR.

IT was late; Councillor Knap, deeply
occupied with the times of King Hans,
intended to go home, and malicious Fate
managed matters so that his feet, instead of
finding their way to his own galoshes,
slipped into those of Fortune. Thus ca-
parisoned the good man walked out of the
well-lighted rooms into East Street. By the
magic power of the shoes he was carried
back to the times of King Hans; on which
account his foot very naturally sank in the
mud and puddles of the street, there having

been in those days no pavement in Copen
hagen.

"Well! this is too bad! How dirty it is
here!" sighed the Councillor. "As to a
pavement, I can find no traces of one, and
all the lamps, it seems, have gone to sleep."

The moon was not yet very high; it was
besides rather foggy, so that in the darkness
all objects seemed mingled in chaotic confusion. At the next corner hung a votive
lamp before a Madonna, but the light it gave
was little better than none at all; indeed,
he did not observe it before he was exactly
under it, and his eyes fell upon the bright
colors of the pictures which represented the
well-known group of the Virgin and the in-
fant Jesus.

"That is probably a wax-work show,"
thought he; "and the people delay taking
down their sign in hopes of a late visitor or
two."

A few persons in the costume of the time
of King Hans passed quickly by him.

"How strange they look! The good
folks come probably from a masquerade!"

Suddenly was heard the sound of drums

and fifes; the bright blaze of a fire shot up from time to time, and its ruddy gleams seemed to contend with the bluish light of the torches. The Councillor stood still, and watched a most strange procession pass by. First came a dozen drummers, who understood pretty well how to handle their instruments; then came halberdiers, and some armed with cross-bows. The principal person in the procession was a priest. Astonished at what he saw, the Councillor asked what was the meaning of all this mummery, and who that man was.

"That's the Bishop of Zealand," was the answer.

"Good Heavens! what has taken possession of the Bishop?" sighed the Councillor, shaking his head. It certainly could not be the Bishop; even though he was considered the most absent man in the whole kingdom, and people told the drollest anecdotes about him. Reflecting on the matter, and without looking right or left, the Councillor went through East Street and across the Häbro Platz. The bridge leading to Palace Square was not to be found; scarcely trusting his senses, the nocturnal wanderer discovered a shallow piece of water, and here fell in with two men who very comfortably were rocking to and fro in a boat.

"Does your honor want to cross the ferry to the Holme?" asked they.

"Across to the Holme!" said the Councillor, who knew nothing of the age in which he at that moment was; "no, I am going to Christianshafen, to Little Market Street."

Both men stared at him in astonishment.

"Only just tell me where the bridge is," said he. "It is really unpardonable that there are no lamps here; and it is as dirty as if one had to wade through a morass."

The longer he spoke with the boatmen, the more unintelligible did their language become to him.

"I don't understand your Bornholmish dialect," said he at last, angrily, and turning his back upon them. He was unable to find the bridge: there was no railway either. "It is really disgraceful what a state this place is in," muttered he to himself. Never had his age, with which, however, he was

always grumbling, seemed so miserable as
on this evening. "I'll take a hackney-
coach!" thought he. But where were the
hackney-coaches? Not one was to be seen.

"I must go back to the New Market;
there, it is to be hoped, I shall find some
coaches; for if I don't, I shall never get
safe to Christianshafen."

So off he went in the direction of East
Street, and had nearly got to the end of it
when the moon shone forth.

"God bless me! What wooden scaffold-
ing is that which they have set up there?"
cried he involuntarily, as he looked at East
Gate, which, in those days, was at the end
of East Street.

He found, however, a little side-door open,
and through this he went, and stepped into
our New Market of the present time. It
was a huge desolate plain; some wild
bushes stood up here and there, while across
the field flowed a broad canal or river. Some
wretched hovels for the Dutch sailors, resembling great boxes, and after which the
place was named, lay about in confused dis-
order on the opposite bank.

"I either behold a *fata morgana,* or I am regularly tipsy," whimpered out the Councillor. But what's this?"

He turned round anew, firmly convinced that he was seriously ill. He gazed at the street formerly so well known to him, and now so strange in appearance, and looked at the houses more attentively: most of them were of wood, slightly put together; and many had a thatched roof.

"No—I am far from well," sighed he; "and yet I drank only one glass of punch; but I cannot suppose it:——it was, too, really very wrong to give us punch and hot salmon for supper. I shall speak about it at the first opportunity. I have half a mind to go back again, and say what I suffer. But no, that would be too silly; and Heaven only knows if they are up still."

He looked for the house. but it had vanished.

"It is really dreadful," groaned he with increasing anxiety; I cannòt recognise East Street again; there is not a single decent shop from one end to the other! Nothing but wretched huts can I see any where·

just as if I were at Ringstead. Oh! I am ill! I can scarcely bear myself any longer. Where the deuce can the house be? It must be here on this very spot; yet there is not the slightest idea of resemblance, to such a degree has every thing changed this night!—At all events here are some people up and stirring. Oh! oh! I am certainly very ill."

He now hit upon a half-open door, through a chink of which a faint light shone. It was a sort of hostelry of those times; a kind of public-house. The room had some resemblance to the clay-floored halls in Holstein; a pretty numerous company, consisting of seamen, Copenhagen burghers, and a few scholars, sat here in deep converse over their pewter cans, and gave little heed to the person who entered.

"By your leave!" said the Councillor to the Hostess, who came bustling towards him; "I've felt so queer all of a sudden; would you have the goodness to send for a hackney-coach to take me to Christianshafen?"

The woman examined him with eyes of

z

astonishment, and shook her head; she then addressed him in German. The Councillor thought she did not understand Danish, and therefore repeated his wish in German. This, in connection with his costume, strengthened the good woman in the belief that he was a foreigner. That he was ill, she comprehended directly; so she brought him a pitcher of water, which tasted certainly pretty strong of the sea, although it had been fetched from the well.

The Councillor supported his head on his hand, drew a long breath, and thought over all the wondrous things he saw around him.

"Is this the *Daily News* of this evening?" he asked mechanically, as he saw the Hostess push aside a large sheet of paper.

The meaning of this councillorship query remained, of course, a riddle to her, yet she handed him the paper without replying. It was a coarse wood-cut, representing a splendid meteor "as seen in the town of Cologne," which was to be read below in bright letters.

"That is very old!" said the Councillor, whom this piece of antiquity began to make considerably more cheerful. " Pray how did you come into possession of this rare print? It is extremely interesting, although the whole is a mere fable. Such meteorous appearances are to be explained in this way· —that they are the reflections of the Aurora Borealis, and it is highly probable they are caused principally by electricity."

Those persons who were sitting nearest him and heard his speech, stared at him in wonderment; and one of them rose, took off his hat respectfully, and said with a serious countenance, "You are no doubt a very learned man, Monsieur."

"Oh no," answered the Councillor, "I can only join in conversation on this topic and on that, as indeed one must do according to the demands of the world at present."

"*Modestia* is a fine virtue," continued the gentleman; "however, as to your speech, I must say *mihi secus videtur :* yet I am willing to suspend my *judicium.*"

"May I ask with whom I have the pleasure of speaking?" asked the Councillor.

"I am a Bachelor in *Theologia,*" answered the gentleman with a stiff reverence.

This reply fully satisfied the Councillor;

the title suited the dress. "He is certainly," thought he, "some village schoolmaster,— some queer old fellow, such as one still often meets with in Jutland."

"This is no *locus docendi*, it is true," began the clerical gentleman ; "yet I beg you earnestly to let us profit by your learning. Your reading in the ancients is, *sine dubio*, of vast extent ?"

"Oh yes, I've read a something, to be sure," replied the Councillor. "I like reading all useful works ; but I do not on that account despise the modern ones ; 'tis only the unfortunate 'Tales of Ever-day Life' that I cannot bear—we have enough and more than enough such in reality."

"Tales of Every-day Life?" said our Bachelor inquiringly.

"I mean those new fangled novels, twisting and writhing themselves in the dust of commonplace, which also expect to find a reading public."

"Oh," exclaimed the clerical gentleman smiling, "there is much wit in them ; besides they are read at court. The King likes the history of Sir Iffven and Sir Gaudian particularly, which treats of King Arthur, and his Knights of the Round Table; he has more than once joked about it with his high vassals."

"I have not read that novel," said the Councillor; "it must be quite a new one, that Heiberg has published lately."

"No," answered the theologian of the time of King Hans: "that book is not written by a Heiberg, but was imprinted by Godfrey von Gehmen."

"Oh, is that the author's name?" said the Councillor. "It is a very old name: and, as well as I recollect, he was the first printer that appeared in Denmark."

"Yes, he is our first printer," replied the clerical gentleman hastily.

So far all went on well. Some one of the worthy burghers now spoke of the dreadful pestilence that had raged in the country a few years back, meaning that of 1484. The Councillor imagined it was the cholera that was meant, which people made so much fuss about; and the discourse passed off satisfactorily enough. The war of the buccanneers of 1490 was so recent that it could not fail

r

being alluded to; the English pirates had, they said, most shamefully taken their ships while in the roadstead; and the Councillor, before whose eyes the Herostratic* event of 1801 still floated vividly, agreed entirely with the others in abusing the rascally English. With other topics he was not so fortunate; every moment brought about some new confusion, and threatened to become a perfect Babel; for the worthy bachelor was really too ignorant, and the simplest observations of the Councillor sounded to him too daring and phantastical. They looked at one another from the crown of the head to the soles of the feet; and when matters grew to too high a pitch, then the Bachelor talked Latin, in the hope of being better understood—but it was of no use after all.

"What's the matter?" asked the Hostess, plucking the Councillor by the sleeve; and now his recollection returned, for in the course of the conversation he had entirely forgotten all that had preceded it.

---

* Herostratus, or Eratostratus,—an Ephesian, who wantonly set fire to the famous temple of Diana, in order to commemorate his name by so uncommon an action.

"Merciful God, where am I!" exclaimed
he in agony; and while he so thought, all
his ideas and feelings of overpowering dizziness, against which he struggled with the
utmost power of desperation, encompassed
him with renewed force. "Let us drink
claret and mead, and Bremen beer," shouted
one of the guests—"and you shall drink
with us !"

Two maidens approached. One wore a
cap of two staring colors, denoting the class
of persons to which she belonged. They
poured out the liquor, and made the most
friendly gesticulations; while a cold perspiration trickled down the back of the poor
Councillor.

"What's to be the end of this! What's
to become of me !" groaned he; but he was
forced, in spite of his opposition, to drink
with the rest. They took hold of the worthy
man; who, hearing on every side that he
was intoxicated, did not in the least doubt
the truth of this certainly not very polite
assertion; but on the contrary, implored the
ladies and gentlemen present to procure him

a hackney-coach: they, however, imagined he was talking Russian.

Never before, he thought, had he been in such a coarse and ignorant company; one might almost fancy the people had turned heathens again. "It is the most dreadful moment of my life: the whole world is leagued against me!" But suddenly it occurred to him that he might stoop down under the table, and then creep unobserved out of the door. He did so; but just as he was going, the others remarked what he was about; they laid hold of him by the legs; and now, happily for him, off fell his fatal shoes—and with them the charm was at an end.

The Councillor saw quite distinctly before him a lantern burning, and behind this a large handsome house. All seemed to him in proper order as usual; it was East Street, splendid and elegant as we now see it. He lay with his feet towards a doorway, and exactly opposite sat the watchman asleep.

"Gracious Heaven!" said he, "have I lain here in the street and dreamed? Yes; 'tis East Street! how splendid and light it is!

But really it is terrible what an effect that one glass of punch must have had on me!"

Two minutes later, he was sitting in a hackney-coach and driving to Frederick-shafen. He thought of the distress and agony he had endured, and praised from the very bottom of his heart the happy reality—our own time—which, with all its deficiencies, is yet much better than that in which, so much against his inclination, he had lately been.

———

III.

THE WATCHMAN'S ADVENTURE.

"WHY, there is a pair of galoshes, as sure as I'm alive!" said the watchman, awaking from a gentle slumber. "They belong no doubt to the lieutenant who lives over the way. They lie close to the door."

The worthy man was inclined to ring and deliver them at the house, for there was still a light in the window; but he did not like disturbing the other people in their beds, and so very considerately he left the matter alone.

"Such a pair of shoes must be very warm and comfortable," said he; "the leather is so soft and supple." They fitted his feet as though they had been made for him. "'Tis a curious world we live in," continued he, soliloquising. "There is the lieutenant, now, who might go quietly to bed if he chose, where no doubt he could stretch himself at his ease; but does he do it? No; he saunters up and down his room, because, probably, he has enjoyed too many of the good things of this world at his dinner. That's a happy fellow! he has neither an infirm mother, nor a whole troop of everlastingly hungry children to torment him. Every evening he goes to a party, where his nice supper costs him nothing: would to Heaven I could but change with him! how happy should I be!"

While expressing his wish, the charm of the shoes, which he had put on, began to work; the watchman entered into the being

and nature of the lieutenant. He stood in
the handsomely furnished apartment, and
held between his fingers a small sheet of
rose-colored paper, on which some verses
were written,—written indeed by the officer
himself; for who has not, at least once in his
life, had a lyrical moment? and if one then
marks down one's thoughts, poetry is produced. But here was written:

OH, WERE I RICH!

"Oh, were I rich!" Such was my wish, yea such
    When hardly three feet high, I longed for much.
        Oh, were I rich! an officer were I,
        With sword, and uniform, and plume so high.
        And the time came, and officer was I!
    But yet I grew not rich. Alas, poor me!
    Have pity, Thou, who all man's wants dost see.

    I sat one evening sunk in dreams of bliss,
    A maid of seven years old gave me a kiss,
        I at that time was rich in poesy
        And tales of old, though poor as poor could be;
        But all she asked for was this poesy.
    Then was I rich, but not in gold, poor me!
As Thou dost know, who all men's hearts canst see.

    Oh, were I rich! Oft asked I for this boon.
    The child grew up to womanhood full soon.

She is so pretty, clever, and so kind;
Oh, did she know what's hidden in my mind :—
  A tale of old. Would she to me were kind!
But I'm condemned to silence ! oh, poor me !
As Thou dost know, who all men's hearts canst see

Oh, were I rich in calm and peace of mind,
My grief you then would not here written find!
  O thou, to whom I do my heart devote,
  Oh read this page of glad days now remote,
  A dark, dark tale, which I to night devote!
Dark is the future now. Alas, poor me !
Have pity Thou, who all men's pains dost see.

Such verses as these people write when
they are in love ! but no man in his senses
ever thinks of printing them. Here one of
the sorrows of life, in which there is real poetry, gave itself vent ; not that barren grief
which the poet may only hint at, but never
depict in its detail—misery and want: that
animal necessity, in short, to snatch at least
at a fallen leaf of the bread-fruit tree, if not
at the fruit itself. The higher the position
in which one finds oneself transplanted, the
greater is the suffering. Every-day necessity
is the stagnant pool of life—no lovely picture
reflects itself therein. Lieutenant, love, and
lack of money—that is a symbolic triangle,

or much the same as the half of the shattered die of Fortune. This the lieutenant felt most poignantly, and this was the reason he leant his head against the window, and sigh--ed so deeply.

"The poor watchman out there in the street is far happier than I. He knows not what I term privation. He has a home, a wife, and children, who weep with him over his sorrows, who rejoice with him when he is glad. Oh, far happier were I, could I exchange with him my being—with his desires and with his hopes perform the weary pilgrimage of life! oh, he is a hundred times happier than I!"

In the same moment the watchman was again watchman. It was the shoes that caused the metamorphosis by means of which, unknown to himself, he took upon him the thoughts and feelings of the officer; but, as we have just seen, he felt himself in his new situation much less contented, and now preferred the very thing which but some minutes before he had rejected. _So then the watchman was again watchman.

"That was an unpleasant dream," said

ne . "but 'twas droll enough altogether. I fancied that I was the lieutenant over there : and yet the thing was not very much to my taste after all.   I missed my good old mother and the dear little ones; who almost tear me to pieces for sheer love."

He seated himself once more and nodded : the dream continued to haunt him, for he still had the shoes on his feet. A falling star shone in the dark firmament.

" There falls another star," said he : " but what does it matter; there are always enough left. I should not much mind examining the little glimmering things somewhat nearer, especially the moon ; for that would not slip so easily through a man's fingers. When we die—so at least says the student, for whom my wife does the washing —we shall fly about as light as a feather from one such a star to the other. That's, of course, not true : but 'twould be pretty enough if it were so. If I could but once take a leap up there, my body might stay here on the steps for what I care."

Behold !—there are certain things in the world to which one ought never to give utter-

ance except with the greatest caution; but
doubly careful must one be when we have
the Shoes of Fortune on our feet.   Now just
listen to what happened to the watchman.

As to ourselves, we all know the speed
produced by the employment of steam; we
have experienced it either on railroads, or in
boats when crossing the sea; but such a
flight is like the travelling of a sloth in comparison with the velocity with which light
moves.   It flies nineteen million times faster
than the best race-horse; and yet electricity
is quicker still.   Death is an electric shock
which our heart receives; the freed soul
soars upwards on the wings of electricity.
The sun's light wants eight minutes and some
seconds to perform a journey of more than
twenty million of our Danish* miles; borne
by electricity, the soul wants even some minutes less to accomplish the same flight.   To
it the space between the heavenly bodies is
not greater than the distance between the
homes of our friends in town is for us, even
if they live a short way from each other;
such an electric shock in the heart, however,

* A Danish mile is nearly 4¾ English.

costs us the use of the body here below ; unless, like the watchman of East Street, we
happen to have on the Shoes of Fortune.

In a few seconds the watchman had done
the fifty-two thousand of our miles up to the
moon, which, as every one knows, was formed out of matter much lighter than our
earth ; and is, so we should say, as soft as
newly-fallen snow. He found himself on
one of the many circumjacent mountain-
ridges with which we are acquainted by
means of Dr. Mädler's "Map of the Moon."
Within, down it sunk perpendicularly into a
caldron, about a Danish mile in depth ;
while below lay a town, whose appearance
we can, in some measure, realize to ourselves
by beating the white of an egg in a glass of
water. The matter of which it was built was
just as soft, and formed similar towers, and
domes, and pillars, transparent and rocking
in the thin air ; while above his head our
earth was rolling like a large fiery ball.

He perceived immediately a quantity of
beings who were certainly what we call
"men ;" yet they looked different to us. A
far more correct imagination than that of

the pseudo-Herschel* had created them; and if they had been placed in rank and file, and copied by some skilful painter's hand, one would, without doubt, have exclaimed involuntarily, "What a beautiful arabesque!" They had a language too; but surely nobody can expect that the soul of the watchman should understand it. Be that as it may, it did comprehend it; for in our souls there germinate far greater powers than we poor mortals, despite all our cleverness, have any notion of. Does she not show us—she the queen in the land of enchantment—her astounding dramatic talent in all our dreams? There every acquaintance appears and speaks upon the stage, so entirely in character, and with the same tone of voice, that none of us, when awake, were able to imitate it. How well can she recall persons to our mind, of

* This relates to a book published some years ago in Germany, and said to be by Herschel, which contained a description of the moon and its inhabitants, written with such a semblance of truth that many were deceived by the imposture.—C. B.

Probably a translation of the celebrated Moon hoax, written by Richard A. Locke, and originally published in New York.

C

whom we have not thought for years; when suddenly they step forth "every inch a man," resembling the real personages, even to the finest features, and become the heroes or heroines of our world of dreams. In reality, such remembrances are rather unpleasant: every sin, every evil thought, may, like a clock with alarm or chimes, be repeated at pleasure; then the question is if we can trust ourselves to give an account of every unbecoming word in our heart and on our lips.

The watchman's spirit understood the language of the inhabitants of the moon pretty well. The Selenites* disputed variously about our earth, and expressed their doubts if it could be inhabited: the air, they said, must certainly be too dense to allow any rational dweller in the moon the necessary free respiration. They considered the moon alone to be inhabited: they imagined it was the real heart of the universe or planetary system, on which the genuine Cosmopolites, or citizens of the world. dwelt. What strange things men—no, what strange things Selenites sometimes take into their heads!

* Dwellers in the moon.

About politics they had a good deal to say. But little Denmark must take care what it is about, and not run counter to the moon; that great realm, that might in an ill-humor bestir itself, and dash down a hail-storm in our faces, or force the Baltic to overflow the sides of its gigantic basin.

We will, therefore, not listen to what was spoken, and on no condition run the possibility of telling tales out of school; but we will rather proceed, like good quiet citizens, to East Street, and observe what happened meanwhile to the body of the watchman.

He sat lifeless on the steps: the morning-star,* that is to say, the heavy wooden staff, headed with iron spikes, and which had nothing else in common with its sparkling brother in the sky, had glided from his hand; while his eyes were fixed with glassy stare on the moon, looking for the good old fellow of a spirit which still haunted it.

"What's the hour, watchman?" asked a passer-by. But when the watchman gave

---

* The watchmen in Germany, had formerly, and in some places they still carry with them, on their rounds at night, a sort of mace or club, known in ancient times by the above denomination.—C. B.

no reply, the merry roysterer, who was now returning home from a noisy drinking bout, took it into his head to try what a tweak of the nose would do, on which the supposed sleeper lost his balance, the body lay motionless, stretched out on the pavement : the man was dead. When the patrol came up, all his comrades, who comprehended nothing of the whole affair, were seized with a dreadful fright, for dead he was, and he remained so. The proper authorities were informed of the circumstance, people talked a good deal about it, and in the morning the body was carried to the hospital.

Now that would be a very pretty joke, if the spirit when it came back and looked for the body in East Street, were not to find one. No doubt it would, in its anxiety, run off to the police, and then to the "*Hue and Cry*" office, to announce that "the finder will be handsomely rewarded," and at last away to the hospital; yet we may boldly assert that the soul is shrewdest when it shakes off every fetter, and every sort of leading-string,—the body only makes it stupid.

The seemingly dead body of the watchman

wandered, as we have said, to the hospital,
where it was brought into the general view-
ing-room : and the first thing that was done
here was naturally to pull off the galoshes—
when the spirit, that was merely gone out on
adventures, must have returned with the
quickness of lightning to its earthly tene-
ment.   It took its direction towards the body
in a straight line ; and a few seconds after,
life began to show itself in the man.   He
asserted that the preceding night had been
the worst that ever the malice of fate had al-
lotted him ; he would not for two silver
marks again go through what he had endured while moon-stricken ; but now, however, it was over.

The same day he was discharged from the
hospital as perfectly cured ; but the Shoes
meanwhile remained behind.

s

IV.

A MOMENT OF HEAD IMPORTANCE—AN EVENING'S " DRAMATIC READINGS"—A MOST STRANGE JOURNEY.

EVERY inhabitant of Copenhagen knows, from personal inspection, how the entrance to Frederick's Hospital looks; but as it is possible that others, who are not Copenhagen people, may also read this little work, we will beforehand give a short description of it.

The extensive building is separated from the street by a pretty high railing, the thick iron bars of which are so far apart, that in all seriousness, it is said, some very thin fellow had of a night occasionally squeezed himself through to go and pay his little visits in the town. The part of the body most difficult to manage on such occasions was, no doubt, the head; here, as is so often the case in the world, long-headed people get through best. So much, then, for the introduction.

One of the young men, whose head, in a

physical sense only, might be said to be of the thickest, had the watch that evening. The rain poured down in torrents; yet despite these two obstacles, the young man was obliged to go out, if it were but for a quarter of an hour; and as to telling the door-keeper about it, that, he thought, was quite unnecessary, if, with a whole skin, he were able to slip through the railings. There, on the floor lay the galoshes, which the watchman had forgotten; he never dreamed for a moment that they were those of Fortune; and they promised to do him good service in the wet; so he put them on. The question now was, if he could squeeze himself through the grating, for he had never tried before. Well, there he stood.

"Would to Heaven I had got my head through!" said he, involuntarily; and instantly through it slipped, easily and without pain, notwithstanding it was pretty large and thick. But new the rest of the body was to be got through!

"Ah! I am much too stout," groaned he aloud, while fixed as in a vice; "I had thought the head was the most difficult part of the matter—oh! oh! I really cannot squeeze myself through!"

He now wanted to pull his over-hasty head back again, but he could not. For his neck there was room enough, but for nothing more. His first feeling was of anger; his next that his temper fell to zero. The Shoes of Fortune had placed him in the most dreadful situation; and, unfortunately, it never occurred to him to wish himself free. The pitch-black clouds poured down their contents in still heavier torrents; not a creature was to be seen in the streets. To reach up to the bell was what he did not like; to cry aloud for help would have availed him little; besides, how ashamed would he have been to be found caught in a trap, like an outwitted fox! How was he to twist himself through! He saw clearly that it was his irrevocable destiny to remain a prisoner till dawn, or, perhaps, even late in the morning; then the smith must be fetched to file away the bars; but all that would not be done so quickly as he could think about it. The whole Charity School, just opposite, would be in motion; all the new booths, with their not very courtier-like swarm of seamen, would join them out of curiosity, and would greet him with a wild "hurrah!" while he was stand-ing in his pillory : there would be a mob, a hissing, and rejoicing, and jeering, ten times worse than in the rows about the Jews some years ago—"Oh, my blood is mounting to my brain ; 'tis enough to drive one mad ! I shall go wild ! I know not what to do. Oh ! were I but loose; my dizziness would then cease ; oh, were my head but loose !"

You see he ought to have said that sooner ; for the moment he expressed the wish his head was free ; and cured of all his parox-ysms of love, he hastened off to his room, where the pains consequent on the fright the Shoes had prepared for him, did not so soon take their leave.

But you must not think that the affair is over now ; it grows much worse.

The night passed, the next day also; but nobody came to fetch the Shoes.

In the evening "Dramatic Readings" were to be given at the little theatre in King Street. The house was filled to suffocation, and among other pieces to be recited was a new poem by H. C. Andersen, called, *My Aunt's Spectacles;* the contents of which were pretty nearly as follows: "A certain person had an aunt, who boasted of particular skill in fortune-telling with cards, and who was constantly being stormed by persons that wanted to have a peep into futurity. But she was full of mystery about her art, in which a certain pair of magic spectacles did her essential service. Her nephew, a merry boy, who was his aunt's darling, begged so long for these spectacles, that, at last, she lent him the treasure, after having informed him, with many exhortations, that in order to execute the interesting trick, he need only repair to some place where a great many persons were assembled; and then, from a higher position, whence he could overlook the crowd, pass the company in review before him through his spectacles. Immediately 'the inner man' of each individual would be displayed before him, like a game of cards, in which he unerringly might read what the future of every person presented was to be. Well pleased the little magician hastened away to prove the powers of the spectacles in the theatre; no place seeming to him more fitted for such a trial. He begged permission of the worthy audience, and set his spectacles on his nose. A motley phantasmagori presents itself before him, which he describes in a few satirical touches, yet without expressing his opinion openly : he tells the people enough to set them all thinking and guessing; but in order to hurt nobody, he wraps his witty oracular judgments in a transparent veil, or rather in a lurid thundercloud, shooting forth bright sparks of wit, that they may fall in the powder-magazine of the expectant audience."

The humorous poem was admirably recited, and the speaker much applauded. Among the audience was the young man of the hospital, who seemed to have forgotten his adventure of the preceding night. He had on the Shoes; for as yet no lawful owner had appeared to claim them ; and besides it was so very dirty out of doors, they were just the thing for him, he thought.

The beginning of the poem he praised with great generosity : he even found the idea original and effective. But that the end of it, like the Rhine, was very insignificant, proved, in his opinion, the author's want of invention ; he was without genius, &c. &c. &c. This was an excellent opportunity to have said something clever.

Meanwhile he was haunted by the idea,— he should like to possess such a pair of spectacles himself; then, perhaps, by using them circumspectly, one would be able to look into people's hearts, which, he thought, would be far more interesting than merely to see what was to happen next year ; for that we should all know in proper time, but the other never.

"I can now," said he to himself, " fancy the whole row of ladies and gentlemen sitting there in the front row ; if one could but see into their hearts ;—yes, that would be a revelation—a sort of bazar. In that lady yonder, so strangely dressed, I should find for certain a large milliner's shop ; in that one the shop is empty, but it wants cleaning plain enough. But there would also be some good stately shops among them. Alas !" sighed he, " I know one in which all is stately ; but there sits already a spruce young shopman, which is the only thing that's amiss in the whole shop. All would be splendidly decked out, and we should hear, 'Walk in, gentlemen, pray walk in ; here you will find all you please to want.' Ah ! I wish to Heaven I could walk in and take a trip right through the hearts of those present !"

And behold ! to the Shoes of Fortune this was the cue ; the whole man shrunk together and a most uncommon journey through the hearts of the front row of spectators, now began. The first heart through which he came, was that of a middle-aged lady, but he instantly fancied himself in the room of the "Institution for the cure of the crooked and deformed," where casts of mis-shapen limbs are displayed in naked reality on the wall. Yet there was this difference, in the institution the casts were taken at the entry of the patient ; but here they were retained and guarded in the heart while the sound persons went away. They were, namely, casts of female friends, whose bodily or mental deformities were here most faithfully preserved.

t

With the snake-like writhings of an idea he glided into another female heart ; but this seemed to him like a large holy fane. The white dove of innocence fluttered over the altar. How gladly would he have sunk upon his knees ; but he must away to the next heart ; yet he still heard the pealing tones of the organ, and he himself seemed to have become a newer and a better man ; he felt unworthy to tread the neighboring sanctuary which a poor garret, with a sick bed-rid mother, revealed. But God's warm sun streamed through the open window ; lovely roses nodded from the wooden flower-boxes on the roof, and two sky-blue birds sang rejoicingly, while the sick mother implored God's richest blessings on her pious daughter.

He now crept on hands and feet through a butcher's shop ; at least on every side, and above and below, there was nought but flesh. It was the heart of a most respectable rich man, whose name is certain to be found in the Directory.

He was now in the heart of the wife of this worthy gentleman. It was an old, dilapidated, mouldering dovecot. The husɔand's portrait was used as a weather-cock, which was connected in some way or other with the doors, and so they opened and shut of their own accord, whenever the stern old husband turned round.

Hereupon he wandered into a boudoir formed entirely of mirrors, like the one in Castle Rosenburg; but here the glasses magnified to an astonishing degree. On the floor, in the middle of the room, sat, like a Dalai-Lama, the insignificant "Self" of the person, quite confounded at his own greatness. He then imagined he had got into a needle-case full of pointed needles of every size.

"This is certainly the heart of an old maid," thought he. But he was mistaken. It was the heart of a young military man; a man, as people said, of talent and feeling.

In the greatest perplexity, he now came out of the last heart in the row; he was unable to put his thoughts in order, and fancied that his too lively imagination had run away with him.

"Good Heavens!" sighed he; "I have surely a disposition to madness—'tis dreadfully hot here; my blood boils in my veins and my head is burning like a coal." And he now remembered the important event of the even ing before, how his head had got jammed in between the iron railings of the hospital. "That's what it is, no doubt," said he. "I must do something in time : under such cir- cumstances a Russian bath might do me good. I only wish I were already on the up- per bank."*

And so there he lay on the uppermost bank in the vapor-bath; but with all his clothes on, in his boots and galoshes, while the hot drops fell scalding from the ceiling on his face.

"Holloa!" cried he, leaping down. The bathing attendant, on his side, uttered a loud cry of astonishment when he beheld in the bath, a man completely dressed.

The other, however, retained sufficient presence of mind to whisper to him, "'T is a bet, and I have won it !" But the first thing

---

* In these Russian (vapor) baths the person extends himself on a bank or form, and as he gets accustomed to the heat, moves to another higher up towards the ceil ing, where, of course, the vapor is warmest. In this manner he ascends gradually to the highest.

he did as soon as he got home, was to have a large blister put on his chest and back to draw out his madness.

The next morning he had a sore chest and a bleeding back; and, excepting the fright, that was all that he had gained by the Shoes of Fortune.

V.

METAMORPHOSIS OF THE COPYING-CLERK.

THE watchman, whom we have certainly not forgotten, thought meanwhile of the galoshes he had found and taken with him to the hospital; he now went to fetch them; and as neither the lieutenant, nor any body else in the street, claimed them as his property, they were delivered over to the police-office.*

---

* As on the continent, in all law and pol'ce practices nothing is verbal, but any circumstance, however trifling, is reduced to writing, the labor, as well as the

"Why, I declare the Shoes look just like my own," said one of the clerks, eyeing the newly-found treasure, whose hidden powers, even he, sharp as he was, was not able to discover. "One must have more than the eye of a shoemaker to know one pair from the other," said he, soliloquizing; and putting, at the same time, the galoshes in search of an owner, beside his own in the corner.

"Here, sir!" said one of the men, who panting brought him a tremendous pile of papers.

The copying-clerk turned round and spoke awhile with the man about the reports and legal documents in question; but when he had finished, and his eye fell again on the Shoes, he was unable to say whether those to the left or those to the right belonged to him. "At all events it must be those which are wet," thought he; but this time, in spite of his cleverness, he guessed quite wrong, for it was just those of Fortune which played as

number of papers that thus accumulate, is enormous. In a police-office, consequently, we find copying-clerks among many other scribes of various denominations, o ᵕ·ᵕ᎓h. it seemₑ ᵕ᎑r hero was one.

it were into his hands, or rather on his feet
And why, I should like to know, are the po
lice never to be wrong? So he put them on
quickly, stuck his papers in his pocket, and
took besides a few under his arm, intending
to look them through at home to make the
necessary notes. It was noon; and the
weather, that had threatened rain, began to
clear up, while gaily dressed holiday folks
filled the streets. "A little trip to Fredericksburg would do me no great harm," thought
he; "for I, poor beast of burden that I am,
have so much to annoy me, that I don't
know what a good appetite is. 'T is a bitter
crust, alas! at which I am condemned to
gnaw!"

Nobody could be more steady or quiet than
this young man; we therefore wish him joy
of the excursion with all our heart; and it
will certainly be beneficial for a person who
leads so sedentary a life. In the park he
met a friend, one of our young poets, who
told him that the following day he should set
out on his long-intended tour.

"So you are going away again!" said the
clerk. "You are a very free and happy be-

ing ; we others are chained by the leg and held fast to our desk."

" Yes ; but it is a chain, friend, which en-sures you the blessed bread of existence," answered the poet. " You need feel no care for the coming morrow : when you are old, you receive a pension."

" True," said the clerk, shrugging his shoulders ; " and yet you are the better off. To sit at one's ease and poetise—that is a pleasure ; every body has something agreea-ble to say to you, and you are always your own master. No, friend, you should but try what it is to sit from one year's end to the other occupied with and judging the most trivial matters."

The poet shook his head, the copying-clerk did the same. Each one kept to his own opinion, and so they separated.

" It's a strange race, those poets !" said the clerk, who was very fond of soliloquizing. " I should like some day, just for a trial, to take such nature upon me, and be a poet myself ; I am very sure I should make no such miserable verses as the others. To-day, methinks, is a most delicious day for a poet :

Nature seems anew to celebrate her awakening into life. The air is so unusually clear, the clouds sail on so buoyantly, and from the green herbage a fragrance is exhaled that fills me with delight. For many a year have I not felt as at this moment."

We see already, by the foregoing effusion, that he is become a poet; to give further proof of it, however, would in most cases be insipid, for it is a most foolish notion to fancy a poet different from other men. Among the latter there may be far more poetical natures than many an acknowledged poet, when examined more closely, could boast of; the difference only is, that the poet possesses a better mental memory, on which account he is able to retain the feeling and the thought till they can be embodied by means of words; a faculty which the others do not possess. But the transition from a commonplace nature to one that is richly endowed, demands always a more or less breakneck leap over a certain abyss which yawns threateningly below; and thus must the sudden change with the clerk strike the reader.

"The sweet air!" continued he of the po

lice office, in his dreamy imaginings ; " how it reminds me of the violets in the garden of my aunt Magdalena ! Yes, then I was a little wild boy, who did not go to school very regularly. O heavens ! 'tis a long time since I have thought on those times. The good old soul ! She lived behind the Exchange. She always had a few twigs or green shoots in water—let the winter rage without as it might. The violets exhaled their sweet breath, whilst I pressed against the window-panes covered with fantastic frost-work the copper coin I had heated on the stove, and so made peep-holes. What splendid vistas were then opened to my view ! What change—what magnificence ! Yonder in the canal lay the ships frozen up, and deserted by their whole crews, with a screaming crow for the sole occupant. But when the spring, with a gentle stirring motion, announced her arrival, a new and busy life arose ; with songs and hurrahs the ice was sawn asunder, the ships were fresh tarred and rigged, that they might sail away to distant lands. But I have remained here— must always remain here, sitting at my desk in the office, and patiently see other people fetch their passports to go abroad. Such is my fate! Alas!"—sighed he, and was again silent. "Great Heaven! what is come to me! never have I thought or felt like this before! It must be the summer air that affects me with feelings almost as disquieting as they are refreshing." He felt in his pocket for the papers. "These police-reports will soon stem the torrent of my ideas, and effectually hinder any rebellious overflowing of the time-worn banks of official duties;" he said to himself consolingly, while his eye ran over the first page. "DAME TIGBRITH, tragedy in five acts." "What is that? And yet it is undeniably my own handwriting. Have I written the tragedy? Wonderful, very wonderful! —And this—what have I here? 'INTRIGUE ON THE RAMPARTS; or THE DAY OF REPENTANCE: vaudeville with new songs to the most favorite airs.' The deuce! where did I get all this rubbish? Some one must have slipped it slyly into my pocket for a joke. There is too a letter to me; a crumpled letter and the seal broken."

Yes, it was not a very polite epistle from

the manager of a theatre, in which both pieces were flatly refused.

"Hem! hem!" said the clerk breathlessly, and quite exhausted he seated himself on a bank. His thoughts were so elastic, his heart so tender; and involuntarily he picked one of the nearest flowers. It is a simple daisy, just bursting out of the bud. What the botanist tells us after a number of imperfect lectures, the flower proclaimed in a minute. It related the mythus of its birth, told of the power of the sun-light that spread out its delicate leaves, and forced them to impregnate the air with their incense :—and then he thought of the manifold struggles of life, which in like manner awaken the budding flowers of feeling in our bosom. Light and air contend with chivalric emulation for the love of the fair flower that bestowed her chief favors on the latter; full of longing she turned towards the light, and as soon as it vanished, rolled her tender leaves together and slept in the embraces of the air. "It is the light which adorns me," said the flower. "But 'tis the air which enables thee to breathe," said the poet's voice.

Close by stood a boy who dashed his stick into a wet ditch. The drops of water splashed up to the green leafy roof, and the clerk thought of the million of ephemera which in a single drop were thrown up to a height, that was as great doubtless for their size, as for us if we were to be hurled above the clouds. While he thought of this and of the whole metamorphosis he had undergone, he smiled and said, "I sleep and dream; but it is wonderful how one can dream so naturally, and know besides so exactly that it is but a dream. If only to-morrow on awaking, I could again call all to mind so vividly! I seem in unusually good spirits; my perception of things is clear, I feel as light and cheerful as though I were in heaven; but I know for a certainty, that if to-morrow a dim remembrance of it should swim before my mind, it will then seem nothing but stupid nonsense, as I have often experienced already—especially before I enlisted under the banner of the police, for that dispels like a whirlwind all the visions of an unfettered imagination. All we hear or say in a dream that is fair and beautiful is like the gold of the subterra nean spirits ; it is rich and splendid when it is given us, but viewed by daylight we find only withered leaves. " Alas !" he sighed quite sorrowful, and gazed at the chirping birds that hopped contentedly from branch to branch, " they are much better off than I ! To fly must be a heavenly art; and happy do I prize that creature in which it is innate. Yes ! could I exchange my nature with any other creature, I fain would be such a happy little lark !"

He had hardly uttered these hasty words when the skirts and sleeves of his coat folded themselves together into wings ; the clothes became feathers, and the galoshes claws. He observed it perfectly, and laughed in his heart. " Now then, there is no doubt that I am dreaming ; but I never before was aware of such mad freaks as these." And up he flew into the green roof and sang ; but in the song there was no poetry, for the spirit of the poet was gone. The Shoes, as is the case with anybody who does what he has to do properly, could only attend to one thing at a time. He wanted to be a poet, and he was one ; he now wished to be a merry chirping bird : but when he was metamorphosed into one, the former peculiarities ceased immediately. "It is really pleasant enough," said he: "the whole day long I sit in the office amid the driest law-papers, and at night I fly in my dream as a lark in the gardens of Fredericksburg; one might really write a very pretty comedy upon it." He now fluttered down into the grass, turned his head gracefully on every side, and with his bill pecked the pliant blades of grass, which, in comparison to his present size, seemed as majestic as the palm-branches of northern Africa.

Unfortunately the pleasure lasted but a moment. Presently black night overshadowed our enthusiast, who had so entirely missed his part of copying-clerk at a police-office ; some vast object seemed to be thrown over him. It was a large oil-skin cap, which a sailor-boy of the quay had thrown over the struggling bird ; a coarse hand sought its way carefully in under the broad rim, and seized the clerk over the back and wings. In the first moment of fear, he called, indeed, as loud as he could—"You impudent little

blackguard ! I am a copying-clerk at the police office ; and you know you cannot insult
any belonging to the constabulary force without a chastisement. Besides, you good-for-
nothing rascal, it is strictly forbidden to catch
birds in the royal gardens of Fredericksburg ;
but your blue uniform betrays where you
come from." This fine tirade sounded, however, to the ungodly sailor-boy like a mere
" Pip-pi-pi." He gave the noisy bird a knock
on his beak, and walked on.

He was soon met by two schoolboys of the
upper class,—that is to say as individuals,
for with regard to learning they were in the
lowest class in the school ; and they bought
the stupid bird. So the copying-clerk came
to Copenhagen as guest, or rather as prisoner
in a family living in Gother Street.

" 'T is well that I'm dreaming," said the
clerk, " or I really should get angry. First
I was a poet ; now sold for a few pence as a
lark ; no doubt it was that accursed poetical
nature which has metamorphosed me into
such a poor harmless little creature. It is
really pitiable, particularly when one gets
into the hands of a little blackguard, perfect

in all sorts of cruelty to animals : all I should like to know is, how the story will end."

The two school-boys, the proprietors now of the transformed clerk, carried him into an elegant room. A stout stately dame received them with a smile ; but she expressed much dissatisfaction that a common field bird, as she called the lark, should appear in such high society. For to-day, however, she would allow it; and they must shut him in the empty cage that was standing in the window. "Perhaps he will amuse my good Polly," added the lady, looking with a benignant smile at a large green parrot that swung himself backwards and forwards most comfortably in his ring, inside a magnificent brass-wired cage. "To-day is Polly's birthday," said she with stupid simplicity : "and the little brown field-bird must wish him joy."

Mr. Polly uttered not a syllable in reply, but swung to and fro with dignified condescension ; while a pretty canary, as yellow as gold, that had lately been brought from his sunny fragrant home, began to sing aloud.

"Noisy creature ! will you be quiet !"
u

screamed the lady of the house, covering the cage with an embroidered white pocket hand-kerchief.

"Chirp, chirp!" sighed he; "that was a dreadful snow-storm;" and he sighed again, and was silent.

The copying-clerk, or, as the lady said, the brown field-bird, was put into a small cage, close to the Canary, and not far from "my good Polly." The only human sounds that the Parrot could bawl out were, "Come, let us be men!" Everything else that he said was as unintelligible to everybody as the chirping of the Canary, except to the clerk, who was now a bird too: he understood his companion perfectly.

"I flew about beneath the green palms and the blossoming almond-trees," sang the Canary; "I flew around, with my brothers and sisters, over the beautiful flowers, and over the glassy lakes, where the bright water-plants nodded to me from below. There, too, I saw many splendidly-dressed paro-quets, that told the drollest stories, and the wildest fairy-tales without end."

"Oh! those were uncouth birds," answered the Parrot. "They had no education, and talked of whatever came into their head. If my mistress and all her friends can laugh at what I say, so may you too, I should think. It is a great fault to have no taste for what is witty or amusing—come, let us be men."

"Ah, you have no remembrance of love for the charming maidens that danced beneath the outspread tents beside the bright fragrant flowers? Do you no longer remember the sweet fruits, and the cooling juice in the wild plants of our never-to-be-forgotten home?" said the former inhabitant of the Canary Isles, continuing his dithyrambic.

"Oh, yes," said the Parrot; "but I am far better off here. I am well fed, and get friendly treatment. I know I am a clever fellow; and that is all I care about. Come, let us be men. You are of a poetical nature, as it is called,—I, on the contrary, possess profound knowledge and inexhaustible wit. You have genius; but clear-sighted, calm discretion does not take such lofty flights, and utter such high natural tones. For this they have covered you over,—they never do the like to me; for I cost more. Besides, they are afraid of my beak; and I have always a witty answer at hand. Come, let us be men!"

"O warm spicy land of my birth," sang the Canary bird; "I will sing of thy dark-green bowers, of the calm bays where the pendent boughs kiss the surface of the water; I will sing of the rejoicing of all my brothers and sisters where the cactus grows in wanton luxuriance."

"Spare us your elegiac tones," said the Parrot giggling. "Rather speak of something at which one may laugh heartily. Laughing is an infallible sign of the highest degree of mental development. Can a dog, or a horse laugh? No, but they can cry. The gift of laughing was given to man alone. Ha! ha! ha!" screamed Polly, and added his stereotype witticism, "come, let us be men!"

"Poor little Danish grey-bird," said the Canary; "you have been caught too. It is, no doubt, cold enough in your woods, but there at least is the breath of liberty; therefore fly away. In the hurry they have for-

gotten to shut your cage, and the upper window is open. Fly, my friend; fly away,
Farewell!"

Instinctively the Clerk obeyed; with a few
strokes of his wings he was out of the cage;
but at the same moment the door, which was
only ajar, and which led to the next room,
began to creak, and supple and creeping
came the large tom-cat into the room, and
began to pursue him. The frightened Canary fluttered about in his cage; the Parrot
flapped his wings, and cried, "Come, let us
be men!" The Clerk felt a mortal fright,
and flew through the window, far away over
the houses and streets. At last he was
forced to rest a little.

The neighboring house had a something
familiar about it; a window stood open; he
flew in; it was his own room. He perched
upon the table.

"Come, let us be men!" said he, involuntarily imitating the chatter of the Parrot,
and at the same moment he was again a
copying-clerk; but he was sitting in the
middle of the table.

"Heaven help me!" cried he. "How did

5

I get up here—and so buried in sleep, too? After all, that was a very unpleasant, disagreeable dream that haunted me! The whole story is nothing but silly, stupid nonsense!"

VI.

THE BEST THAT THE GALOSHES GAVE.

THE following day, early in the morning, while the Clerk was still in bed, some one knocked at his door. It was his neighbor, a young Divine, who lived on the same floor. He walked in.

"Lend me your Galoshes," said he; "it is so wet in the garden, though the sun is shining most invitingly. I should like to go out a little."

He got the Galoshes, and he was soon below in a little duodecimo garden, where between two immense walls a plum-tree and an apple-tree were standing. Even such a

little garden as this was considered in the
metropolis of Copenhagen as a great luxury.

The young man wandered up and down
the narrow paths, as well as the prescribed
limits would allow; the clock struck six;
without was heard the horn of a post-boy.

"To travel! to travel!" exclaimed he,
overcome by most painful and passionate remembrances; "that is the happiest thing in
the world! that is the highest aim of all my
wishes! Then at last would the agonizing
restlessness be allayed, which destroys my
existence! But it must be far, far away! I
would behold magnificent Switzerland; I
would travel to Italy, and ——"

It was a good thing that the power of the
Galoshes worked as instantaneously as lightning in a powder-magazine would do, otherwise the poor man with his overstrained
wishes would have travelled about the world
too much for himself as well as for us. In
short, he was travelling. He was in the
middle of Switzerland, but packed up with
eight other passengers in the inside of an
eternally-creaking diligence; his head ached
till it almost split, his weary neck could

hardly bear the heavy load, and his feet,
pinched by his torturing boots, were terribly
swollen. He was in an intermediate state
between sleeping and waking; at variance
with himself, with his company, with the
country, and with the government. In his
right pocket he had his letter of credit, in the
left, his passport, and in a small leathern
purse some double louis-d'or, carefully sewn
up in the bosom of his waistcoat. Every
dream proclaimed that one or the other of
these valuables was lost; wherefore he started up as in a fever; and the first movement
which his hand made, described a magic triangle from the right pocket to the left, and
then up towards the bosom, to feel if he had
them all safe or not. From the roof inside
the carriage, umbrellas, walking-sticks, hats,
and sundry other articles were depending,
and hindered the view, which was particularly imposing. He now endeavored as well
as he was able to dispel his gloom, which
was caused by outward chance circumstances merely, and on the bosom of nature im-
bibe the milk of purest human enjoyment.

Grand, solemn, and dark was the whole

landscape around. The gigantic pine-forests, on the pointed crags, seemed almost like little tufts of heather, colored by the surrounding clouds. It began to snow, a cold wind blew and roared as though it were seeking a bride.

"Augh!" sighed he, "were we only on the other side the Alps, then we should have summer, and I could get my letters of credit cashed. The anxiety I feel about them prevents me enjoying Switzerland. Were I but on the other side!"

And so saying he was on the other side in Italy, between Florence and Rome. Lake Thracymene, illumined by the evening sun, lay like flaming gold between the dark-blue mountain-ridges; here, where Hannibal defeated Flaminius, the rivers now held each other in their green embraces; lovely, half-naked children tended a herd of black swine, beneath a group of fragrant laurel-trees, hard by the road-side. Could we render this inimitable picture properly, then would everybody exclaim, "Beautiful, unparalleled Italy!" But neither the young Divine said so, nor any one of his grumbling companions in the coach of the vetturino.

w

The poisonous flies and gnats swarmed
around by thousands; in vain one waved
myrtle-branches about like mad; the auda-
cious insect population did not cease to sting;
nor was there a single person in the well-
crammed carriage whose face was not swollen and sore from their ravenous bites. The
poor horses, tortured almost to death, suffered most from this truly Egyptian plague;
the flies alighted upon them in large disgusting swarms; and if the coachman got down
and scraped them off, hardly a minute elaps-
ed before they were there again. The sun
now set: a freezing cold, though of short
duration pervaded the whole creation; it
was like a horrid gust coming from a burial-
vault on a warm summer's day,—but all
around the mountains retained that wonderful green tone which we see in some old
pictures, and which, should we not have seen
a similar play of color in the South, we declare at once to be unnatural. It was a
glorious prospect; but the stomach was empty, the body tired; all that the heart cared
and longed for was good night-quarters; yet
how would they be? For these one looked

much more anxiously than for the charms
of nature, which every where were so pro-
fusely displayed.

The road led through an olive-grove, and
here the solitary inn was situated. Ten or
twelve crippled-beggars had encamped outside. The healthiest of them resembled, to
use an expression of Marryat's, "Hunger's
eldest son when he had come of age;" the
others were either blind, had withered legs
and crept about on their hands, or withered
arms and fingerless hands. It was the most
wretched misery, dragged from among the
filthiest rags. "Excellenza, miserabili!" sighed they, thrusting forth their deformed limbs
to view. Even the hostess, with bare feet,
uncombed hair, and dressed in a garment of
doubtful color, received the guests grumbling-
ly. The doors were fastened with a loop of
string; the floor of the rooms presented a
stone paving half torn up; bats fluttered
wildly about the ceiling; and as to the smell
therein—no—that was beyond description.

"You had better lay the cloth below in
the stable," said one of the travellers; "there,

at all events, one knows what one is breath
ing."

The windows were quickly opened, to let
in a little fresh air. Quicker, however, than
the breeze, the withered, sallow arms of the
beggars were thrust in, accompanied by the
eternal whine of "Miserabili, miserabili, excellenza !" On the walls were displayed in-
numerable inscriptions, written in nearly
every language of Europe, some in verse,
some in prose, most of them not very lauda-
tory of "bella Italia."

The meal was served. It consisted of a
soup of salted water, seasoned with pepper
and rancid oil. The last ingredient played
a very prominent part in the salad; stale
eggs and roasted cocks'-combs furnished the
grand dish of the repast; the wine even was
not without a disgusting taste—it was like a
medicinal draught.

At night the boxes and other effects of
the passengers were placed against the rick-
etty doors. One of the travelers kept watch
while the others slept. The sentry was our
young Divine. How close it was in the

chamber! The heat oppressive to suffoca-
cation—the gnats hummed and stung unceasingly—the "miserabili" without whined
and moaned in their sleep.

"Travelling would be agreeable enough,"
said he groaning, " if one only had no body,
or could send it to rest while the spirit went
on its pilgrimage unhindered, whither the
voice within might call it. Wherever I go,
I am pursued by a longing that is insatiable,
—that I cannot explain to myself, and that
tears my very heart. I want something better than what is but momentary—than what
is fled in an instant. But what is it, and
where is it to be found? Yet, I know in
reality what it is I wish for. Oh! most
happy were I, could I but reach one aim,—
could but reach the happiest of all!"

And as he spoke the word he was again
in his home; the long white curtains hung
down from the windows, and in the middle
of the floor stood the black coffin; in it he
lay in the sleep of death. His wish was fulfilled—the body rested, while the spirit went
unhindered on its pilgrimage. "Let no one
deem himself happy before his end," were

the words of Solon; and here was a new
and brill.ant proof of the wisdom of the old
apothegm.

Every corpse is a sphynx of immortality;
here too on the black coffin the sphynx gave
us no answer to what he who lay within
had written two days before:

> " O mighty Death ! thy silence teaches nought,
>   Thou leadest only to the near grave's brink ;
> Is broken now the ladder of my thoughts ?
>   Do I instead of mounting only sink ?
>
> Our heaviest grief the world oft seeth not,
>   Our sorest pain we hide from stranger eyes :
> And for the sufferer there is nothing left
>   But the green mound that o'er the coffin lies."

Two figures were moving in the chamber.
We knew them both ; it was the fairy of
Care, and the emissary of Fortune. They
both bent over the corpse.

"Do you now see," said Care, "what happiness your Galoshes have brought to mankind ?"

"To him, at least, who slumbers here,
they have brought an imperishable blessing,"
answered the other.

"Ah no!" replied Care, "he took his departure himself; he was not called away. His mental powers here below were not strong enough to reach the treasures lying beyond this life, and which his destiny ordained he should obtain. I will now confer a benefit on him."

And she took the Galoshes from his feet; nis sleep of death was ended; and he who had been thus called back again to life arose from his dread couch in all the vigor of youth. Care vanished, and with her the Galoshes. She has no doubt taken them for herself, to keep them to all eternity.

UT in the woods stood a nice little Fir-tree. The place he had was a very good one: the sun shone on him: as to fresh air, there was enough of that, and round him grew many large-sized comrades, pines as well as firs. But the little Fir wanted so very much to be a grown up tree.

He did not think of the warm sun and of the fresh air; he did not care for the little cottage children that ran about and prattled when they were in the woods looking for wild-strawberries. The children often came

76

with a whole pitcher full of berries, or a long
row of them threaded on a straw, and sat
down near the young tree and said, "Oh,
how pretty he is! what a nice little fir!"
But this was what the tree could not bear to
hear.

At the end of a year he had shot up a
good deal, and after another year he was another long bit taller; for with fir-trees one can
always tell by the shoots how many years
old they are.

"Oh! were I but such a high tree as the
others are," sighed he. "Then I should be
able to spread out my branches, and with the
tops to look into the wide world! Then
would the birds build nests among my branches: and when there was a breeze, I could
bend with as much stateliness as the others!"

Neither the sunbeams, nor the birds, nor
the red clouds which morning and evening
sailed above him, gave the little tree any
pleasure.

In winter, when the snow lay glittering
on the ground, a hare would often come
leaping along, and jump right over the little
tree. Oh, that made him so angry! But

twc winte.s were past, and, in the third the
tree was so large that the hare was obliged
to go round it. "To grow and grow, to get
older and be tall," thought the Tree,—"that,
after all, is the most delightful thing in the
world !"

In autumn the wood-cutters always came
and felled some of the largest trees. This
happened every year ; and the young Fir-
tree, that had now grown to a very comely
size, trembled at the sight ; for the magnificent great trees fell to the earth with noise
and cracking, the branches were lopped off,
and the trees looked long and bare ; they were
hardly to be recognised ; and then they were
laid in carts, and the horses dragged them
out of the wood.

Where did they go to ?   What became of
them ?

In spring, when the swallows and the
storks came, the Tree asked them, "Don't
you know where they have been taken ?
Have you not met them any where ?"

The swallows did not know any thing
about it ; but the Stork looked musing, nodded his head, and said, "Yes ; I think 1

know; I met many ships as I was flying
hither from Egypt; on the ships were magnificent masts, and I venture to assert that it
was they that smelt so of fir. I may con-
gratulate you, for they lifted themselves on
high most majestically!"

"Oh, were I but old enough to fly across
the sea! But how does the sea look in reality? What is it like?"

"That would take a long time to explain,"
said the Stork, and with these words off he
went.

"Rejoice in thy growth!" said the Sunbeams, "rejoice in thy vigorous growth, and
in the fresh life that moveth within thee!"

And the Wind kissed the Tree, and the
Dew wept tears over him; but the Fir understood it not.

When Christmas came, quite young trees
were cut down: trees which often were not
even as large or of the same age as this Fir-
tree, who could never rest, but always wanted to be off. These young trees, and they
were always the finest looking, retained their
branches; they were laid on carts, and the
horses drew them out of the wood.

"Where are they going to?" asked the Fir "They are not taller than I; there was one indeed that was considerably shorter; and why do they retain all their branches? Whither are they taken?"

"We know! we know!" chirped the Sparrows. "We have peeped in at the windows in the town below! We know whither they are taken! The greatest splendor and the greatest magnificence one can imagine await them. We peeped through the windows, and saw them planted in the middle of the warm room and ornamented with the most splendid things, with gilded apples, with gingerbread, with toys, and many hundred lights!"

"And then?" asked the Fir-tree, trembling in every bough. "And then? What happens then?"

"We did not see any thing more: it was incomparably beautiful."

"I would fain know if I am destined for so glorious a career," cried the Tree, rejoic ing. "That is still better than to cross the sea! What a longing do I suffer! Were Christmas but come! I am now tall, and my branches spread like the others that were carried off last year! Oh! were I but already on the cart! Were I in the warm room with all the splendor and magnificence! Yes; then something better, something still grander, will surely follow, or wherefore should they thus ornament me? Something better, something still grander *must* follow— but what? Oh, how I long, how I suffer! I do not know myself what is the matter with me!"

"Rejoice in our presence!" said the Air and the Sunlight; "rejoice in thy own fresh youth!"

But the Tree did not rejoice at all; he grew and grew, and was green both winter and summer. People that saw him said, "What a fine tree!" and towards Christmas he was one of the first that was cut down. The axe struck deep into the very pith; the tree fell to the earth with a sigh; he felt a pang—it was like a swoon; he could not think of happiness, for he was sorrowful at being separated from his home, from the place where he had sprung up. He well knew that he should never see his dear old comrades, the little bushes and flowers around

G

him, any more; perhaps not even the birds! The departure was not at all agreeable.

The Tree only came to himself when he was unloaded in a court-yard with the other trees, and heard a man say, "That one is splendid! we don't want the others." Then two servants came in rich livery and carried the fir-tree into a large and splendid drawing-room. Portraits were hanging on the walls, and near the white porcelain stove stood two large Chinese vases with lions on the covers. There, too, were large easy-chairs, silken so-fas, large tables full of picture-books and full of toys, worth hundreds and hundreds of crowns—at least the children said so. And the Fir-tree was stuck upright in a cask that was filled with sand; but no one could see that it was a cask, for green cloth was hung all round it, and it stood on a large gaily-colored carpet. Oh! how the tree quivered! What was to happen? The servants, as well as the young ladies, decorated it. On one branch there hung little nets cut out of color-ed paper, and each net was filled with sugar-plums; and among the other boughs gilded apples and walnuts were suspended, looking as though they had grown there, and little blue and white tapers were placed among the leaves. Dolls that looked for all the world like men—the Tree had never beheld such before—were seen among the foliage, and at the very top a large star of gold tinsel was fixed. It was really splendid—beyond description splendid.

"This evening!" said they all, "how it will shine this evening!"

"Oh!" thought the Tree, "if the evening were but come! If the tapers were but lighted! And then I wonder what will happen! Perhaps the other trees from the forest will come to look at me! Perhaps the sparrows will beat against the window-panes! I wonder if I shall take root here, and winter and summer stand covered with ornaments!"

He knew very much about the matter!— but he was so impatient that for sheer longing he got a pain in his back, and this with trees is the same thing as a headache with us.

The candles were now lighted—What brightness! What splendor! The Tree trembled so in every bough that one of the tapers set fire to the foliage. It blazed up famously.

"Help! help!" cried the young ladies, and they quickly put out the fire.

Now the tree did not even dare tremble. What a state he was in! He was so uneasy lest he should lose something of his splendor, that he was quite bewildered amidst the glare and brightness; when suddenly. both folding-doors opened and a troop of children rushed in as if they would upset the Tree. The older persons followed quietly; the little ones stood quite still. But it was only for a moment; then they shouted that the whole place re-echoed with their. rejoicing; they danced round the Tree, and one present after the other was pulled off.

"What are they about?" thought the Tree. ("What is to happen now!") And the lights burned down to the very branches, and as they burned down they were put out one after the other, and then the children had permission to plunder the Tree. So they fell upon it with such violence that all its branches cracked; if it had not been fixed firmly in the ground, it would certainly have tumbled down.

The children danced about with their beautiful play-things; no one looked at the Tree except the old nurse, who peeped between the branches; but it was only to see if there was a fig or an apple left that had been forgotten.

"A story! a story!" cried the children, drawing a little fat man towards the Tree. He seated himself under it and said, " Now we are in the shade, and the Tree can listen too. But I shall tell only one story. Now which will you have; that about Ivedy-Avedy, or about Humpy-Dumpy, who tumbled down stairs, and yet after all came to the throne and married the princess?"

"Ivedy-Avedy," cried some; "Humpy-Dumpy," cried the others. There was such a bawling and screaming!—the Fir-tree alone was silent, and he thought to himself, "Am I not to bawl with the rest?—am I to do nothing whatever?" for he was one of the company, and had done what he had to do.

And the man told about Humpy-Dumpy that tumbled down, who notwithstanding

x

came to the throne, and at last married the princess. And the children clapped their hands, and cried. " Oh, go on ! Do go on !" They wanted to hear about Ivedy-Avedy too, but the little man only told them about Humpy-Dumpy. The Fir-tree stood quite still and absorbed in thought; the birds in the wood had never related the like of this. " Humpy-Dumpy fell down stairs, and yet he married the princess! Yes, yes! that's the way of the world !" thought the Fir-tree, and believed it all, because the man who told the story was so good-looking. " Well, well! who knows, perhaps I may fall down stairs, too, and get a princess as wife! And he looked forward with joy to the morrow, when he hoped to be decked out again with lights, playthings, fruits, and tinsel.

" I won't tremble to-morrow !" thought the Fir-tree. " I will enjoy to the full all my splendor! To morrow I shall hear again the story of Humpy-Dumpy, and perhaps that of Ivedy-Avedy too." And the whole night the Tree stood still and in deep thought.

In the morning the servant and the house-maid came in.

"Now then the splendor will begin again,"
thought the Fir. But they dragged him out
of the room, and up the stairs into the loft:
and here, in a dark corner, where no daylight
could enter, they left him. "What's the
meaning of this?" thought the Tree. "What
am I to do here? What shall I hear now, I
wonder?" And he leaned against the wall
lost in reverie. Time enough had he too for
his reflections; for days and nights passed
on, and nobody came up; and when at last
somebody did come, it was only to put some
great trunks in a corner, out of the way.
There stood the Tree quite hidden; it seemed as if he had been entirely forgotten.

"'T is now winter out of doors!" thought
the Tree. "The earth is hard and covered
with snow; men cannot plant me now, and
therefore I have been put up here under shelter
till the spring-time comes! How thoughtful that is! How kind man is, after all! If
it only were not so dark here, and so terribly
lonely! Not even a hare!—And out in the
woods it was so pleasant, when the snow was
on the ground, and the hare leaped by; yes
—even when he jumped over me; but I did

not like it then ! It is really terribly lonely here !"

"Squeak ! squeak !" said a little Mouse, at the same moment, peeping out of his hole. And then another little one came. They snuffed about the Fir-tree, and rustled among the branches.

"It is dreadfully cold," said the Mouse. "But for that, it would be delightful here, old Fir, wouldn't it ?"

"I am by no means old," said the Fir-tree. "There's many a one considerably older than I am."

"Where do you come from," asked the Mice ; "and what can you do ?" They were so extremely curious. "Tell us about the most beautiful spot on the earth. Have you never been there ? Were you never in the larder, where cheeses lie on the shelves, and hams hang from above ; where one dances about on tallow candles : that place where one enters lean, and comes out again fat and portly ?"

"I know no such place," said the Tree. "But I know the wood, where the sun shines and where the little birds sing." And then

he told all about his youth; and the little
Mice had never heard the like before; and
they listened and said,

"Well, to be sure! How much you have
seen! How happy you must have been!"

"I!" said the Fir-tree, thinking over what
he had himself related. "Yes, in reality
those were happy times." And then he told
about Christmas-eve, when he was decked
out with cakes and candles.

"Oh," said the little Mice, " how fortunate
you have been, old Fir-tree!"

"I am by no means old," said he. "I came
from the wood this winter; I am in my
prime, and am only rather short for my age."

"What delightful stories you know!" said
the Mice: and the next night they came with
four other little Mice, who were to hear what
the Tree recounted: and the more he related,
the more he remembered himself; and it appeared as if those times had really been happy times. "But they may still come—they
may still come! Humpy-Dumpy fell down
stairs, and yet he got a princess!" and he
thought at the moment of a nice little Birch

tree growing out in the woods: to the Fir, that would be a real charming princess.

"Who is Humpy-Dumpy?" asked the Mice. So then the Fir-tree told the whole fairy tale, for he could remember every single word of it; and the little Mice jumped for joy up to the very top of the Tree. Next night two more Mice came, and on Sunday two Rats even ; but they said the stories were not interesting, which vexed the little Mice; and they, too, now began to think them not so very amusing either.

"Do you know only one story ?" asked the Rats.

"Only that one," answered the Tree. "I heard it on my happiest evening; but I did not then know how happy I was."

"It is a very stupid story ! Don't you know one about bacon and tallow candles? Can't you tell any larder stories ?"

"No," said the Tree.

"Then good-bye," said the Rats ; and they went home.

"At last the little Mice stayed away also ; and the Tree sighed: "After all, it was very

pleasant when the sleek little Mice sat round
me, and listened to what I told them. Now
that too is over. But I will take good care
to enjoy myself when I am brought out
again."

But when was that to be? Why, one
morning there came a quantity of people and
set to work in the loft. The trunks were
moved, the tree was pulled out and thrown,
—rather hard, it is true,—down on the floor,
but a man drew him towards the stairs,
where the daylight shone.

"Now a merry life will begin again,"
thought the Tree. He felt the fresh air, the
first sunbeam,—and now he was out in the
court-yard. All passed so quickly, there was
so much going on around him, the Tree
quite forgot to look to himself. The court
adjoined a garden, and all was in flower;
the roses hung so fresh and odorous over the
balustrade, the lindens were in blossom, the
Swallows flew by, and said, "Quirre-vit! my
husband is come!" but it was not the Fir-
tree that they meant.

"Now, then, I shall really enjoy life," said
he exultingly, and spread out his branches;

but, alas! they were all withered and yellow.
It was in a corner that he lay, among weeds
and nettles. The golden star of tinsel was
still on the top of the Tree, and glittered in
the sunshine.

In the court-yard some of the merry children were playing who had danced at Christmas round the Fir-tree, and were so glad at
the sight of him. One of the youngest ran
and tore off the golden star.

"Only look what is still on the ugly old
Christmas tree!" said he, trampling on the
branches, so that they all cracked beneath
his feet.

And the Tree beheld all the beauty of the
flowers, and the freshness in the garden; he
beheld himself, and wished he had remained
in his dark corner in the loft; he thought of
his first youth in the wood, of the merry
Christmas-eve, and of the little Mice who had
listened with so much pleasure to the story
of Humpy-Dumpy.

"'T is over—'t is past!" said the poor Tree.
"Had I but rejoiced when I had reason to do
so! But now 't is past, 't is past!"

And the gardener's boy chopped the Tree

into small pieces; there was a whole heap lying there. The wood flamed up splendidly under the large brewing copper, and it sighed so deeply! Each sigh was like a shot.

The boys played about in the court, and the youngest wore the gold star on his breast which the Tree had had on the happiest evening of his life. However, that was over now, —the Tree gone, the story at an end. All all was over;—every tale must end at last.

y

THE SNOW QUEEN.

FIRST STORY,

WHICH TREATS OF A MIRROR AND OF THE SPLINTERS.

NOW then, let us begin. When we are at the end of the story, we shall know more than we know now : but to begin.

Once upon a time there was a wicked sprite, indeed he was the most mischievous of all sprites. One day he was in a very good humor, for he had made a mirror with the power of causing all that was good and beautiful when it was reflected therein, to look poor and mean; but that which was good for nothing and looked ugly was shown magnified and increased in ugliness. In this mirror the most beautiful landscapes looked like boiled spinach, and the best persons were turned into frights, or appeared to stand on their heads; their faces were so distorted that they were not to be recognised; and if any one had a mole, you might be sure that it would be magnified and spread over both nose and mouth. " That's glorious fun !" said the sprite. If a good thought passed through a man's mind, then a grin was seen in the mirror, and the sprite laughed heartily at his clever discovery. All the little sprites who went to his school—for he kept a sprite school—told each other that a miracle had happened; and that now only, as they thought, it would be possible to see how the world really looked. They ran about with the mirror; and at last there was not a land or a person who was not represented distorted in the mirror. So then they thought they would fly up to the sky, and have a joke there. The higher they flew with the mirror, the more terribly it grinned: they could hardly hold it fast. Higher and higher still they flew, nearer and nearer to the stars, when suddenly the mirror shook so terribly

with grinning, that it flew out of their hands
and fell to the earth, where it was dashed in
a hundred million and more pieces. And
now it worked much more evil than before;
for some of these pieces were hardly so large
as a grain of sand, and they flew about in
the wide world, and when they got into people's eyes, there they stayed; and then people saw everything perverted, or only had an
eye for that which was evil. This happened
because the very smallest bit had the same
power which the whole mirror had possessed.
Some persons even got a splinter in their
heart, and then it made one shudder, for
their heart became like a lump of ice. Some
of the broken pieces were so large that they
were used for window-panes, through which
one could not see one's friends. Other pieces
were put in spectacles; and that was a
sad affair when people put on their glasses to
see well and rightly. Then the wicked
sprite laughed till he almost choked, for all
this tickled his fancy. The fine splinters
still flew about in the air: and now we shall
hear what happened next.

SECOND STORY.

A LITTLE BOY AND A LITTLE GIRL.

IN a large town, where there are so many houses, and so many people, that there is no roof left for every body to have a little garden; and where, on this account, most persons are obliged to content themselves with flowers in pots; there lived two little children, who had a garden somewhat larger than a flower-pot. They were not brother and sister; but they cared for each other as much as if they were. Their parents lived exactly opposite. They inhabited two garrets; and where the roof of the one house joined that of the other, and the gutter ran along the extreme end of it, there was to each house a small window: one needed only to step over the gutter to get from one window to the other.

The children's parents had large wooden boxes there, in which vegetables for the kitchen were planted, and little rose-trees besides: there was a rose in each box, and they

7

grew splendidly. They now thought of placing the boxes across the gutter, so that they nearly reached from one window to the other, and looked just like two walls of flowers. The tendrils of the peas hung down over the boxes; and the rose-trees shot up long branches, twined round the windows, and then bent towards each other: it was almost like a triumphant arch of foliage and flowers. The boxes were very high, and the children knew that they must not creep over them; so they often obtained permission to get out of the windows to each other, and to sit on their little stools among the roses, where they could play delightfully. In winter there was an end of this pleasure. The windows were often frozen over; but then they heated copper farthings on the stove, and laid the hot farthing on the window-pane, and then they had a capital peep-hole, quite nicely rounded; and out of each peeped a gentle friendly eye—it was the little boy and the little girl who were looking out. His name was Kay, hers was Gerda. In summer, with one jump, they could get to each other; but in winter they were obliged

first to go down the long stairs, and then up
the long stairs again : and out of doors there
was quite a snow-storm.

"It is the white bees that are swarming,"
said Kay's old grandmother.

"Do the white bees choose a queen ?" asked the little boy ; for he knew that the ho-
ney-bees always have one.

"Yes," said the grandmother, "she flies
where the swarm hangs in the thickest clus-
ters. She is the largest of all ; and she can
never remain quietly on the earth, but goes
up again into the black clouds. Many a
winter's night she flies through the streets of
the town; and peeps in at the windows ; and
they then freeze in so wondrous a manner
that they look like flowers."

"Yes, I have seen it," said both the children ; and so they knew that it was true.

"Can the Snow Queen come in ?" said the
little girl.

"Only let her come in !" said the little boy,
"then I'd put her on the stove, and she'd
melt."

And then his grandmother patted his head
and told him other stories.

In the evening, when little Kay was at home, and half undressed, he climbed up on the chair by the window, and peeped out of the little hole. A few snow-flakes were falling, and one, the largest of all, remained lying on the edge of a flower-pot. The flake of snow grew larger and larger; and at last it was like a young lady, dressed in the finest white gauze, made of a million little flakes like stars. She was so beautiful and delicate, but she was of ice, of dazzling, sparkling ice; yet she lived; her eyes gazed fixedly, like two stars; but there was neither quiet or repose in them. She nodded towards the window, and beckoned with her hand. The little boy was frightened, and jumped down from the chair; it seemed to him as if, at the same moment, a large bird flew past the window.

The next day it was a sharp frost:—and then the spring came; the sun shone, the green leaves appeared, the swallows built their nests, the windows were opened, and the little children again sat in their pretty garden, high up on the leads at the top of the house.

That summer the roses flowered in unwonted beauty. The little girl had learned a hymn, in which there was something about roses; and then she thought of her own flowers; and she sang the verse to the little boy, who then sang it with her:

"The rose in the valley is blooming so sweet,
  And angels descend there the children to greet."

And the children held each other by the hand, kissed the roses, looked up at the clear sunshine, and spoke as though they really saw angels there. What lovely summer-days those were! How delightful to be out in the air, near the fresh rose-bushes, that seem as if they would never finish blossoming!

Kay and Gerda looked at the picture-book full of beasts and of birds; and it was then— the clock in the church-tower was just striking five,—that Kay said, "Oh! I feel such a sharp pain in my heart; and now something has got into my eye!"

The little girl put her arms around his neck. He winked his eyes; now there was nothing to be seen.

"I think it is out now," said he; but it

was not. It was just one of those pieces of glass from the magic mirror that had got into his eye ; and poor Kay had got another piece right in his heart. It will soon become like ice. It did not hurt any longer, but there it was.

"What are you crying for?" asked he. "You look so ugly! There's nothing the matter with me. Ah," said he at once, "that rose is cankered! and look, this one is quite crooked! after all, these roses are very ugly! they are just like the box they are planted in!" And then he gave the box a good kick with his foot, and pulled both the roses up.

"What are you doing?" cried the little girl ; and as he perceived her fright, he pulled up another rose, got in at the window, and hastened off from dear little Gerda.

Afterwards, when she brought her picture-book, he asked, "What horrid beasts she had there ?" And if his grandmother told them stories, he always interrupted her ; besides, if he could manage it, he would get behind her, put on her spectacles, and imitate her way of speaking ; he copied all her ways, and then every body laughed at him. He was soon able to imitate the gait and manner of every one in the street. Every thing that was peculiar and displeasing in them,—that Kay knew how to imitate: and at such times all the people said, "The boy is certainly very clever!" But it was the glass he had got in his eye; the glass that was sticking in his heart, which made him tease even little Gerda, whose whole soul was devoted to him.

His games now were quite different to what they had formerly been, they were so very knowing. One winter's day, when the flakes of snow were flying about, he spread the skirts of his blue coat, and caught the snow as it fell.

"Look through this glass, Gerda," said he. And every flake seemed larger, and appeared like a magnificent flower, or a beautiful star; it was splendid to look at!

"Look, how clever!" said Kay. "That's much more interesting than real flowers! They are as exact as possible; there is not a fault in them, if they did not melt!"

It was not long after this, that Kay came

one day with large gloves on, and his little sledge at his back, and bawled right into Gerda's ears, "I have permission to go out into the square, where the others are play-ing ;" and off he was in a moment.

There, in the market-place, some of the boldest of the boys used to tie their sledges to the carts as they passed by, and so they were pulled along, and got a good ride. It was so capital ! Just as they were in the very height of their amusement, a large sledge passed by : it was painted quite white, and there was some one in it wrapped up in a rough white mantle of fur, with a rough white fur cap on his head. The sledge drove round the square twice, and Kay tied on his as quickly as he could, and off he drove with it. On they went quicker and quicker into the next street ; and the person who drove turn-ed round to Kay, and nodded to him in a friendly manner, just as if they knew each other. Every time he was going to untie his sledge, the person nodded to him, and then Kay sat quiet ; and so on they went till they came outside the gates of the town. Then the snow began to fall so thickly that the little boy could not see an arm's length before him, but still on he went: when suddenly he let go the string he held in his hand in order to get loose from the sledge, but it was of no use ; still the little vehicle rushed on with the quickness of the wind. He then cried as loud as he could, but no one heard him ; the snow drifted and the sledge flew on, and sometimes it gave a jerk as though they were driving over hedges and ditches. He was quite frightened, and he tried to repeat the Lord's prayer ; but all he could do, he was only able to remember the multiplication table.

The snow-flakes grew larger and larger, till at last they looked just like great white fowls. Suddenly they flew on one side ; the large sledge stopped, and the person who drove rose up. It was a lady ; her cloak and cap were of snow. She was tall and of slender figure, and of a dazzling whiteness. It was the Snow-Queen.

"We have travelled fast," said she ; "but it is freezingly cold. Come under my bear-skin." And she put him in the sledge beside her, wrapped the fur round him, and he felt as though he were sinking in a snow wreath.

"Are you still cold?" asked she; and then she kissed his forehead. Ah! it was colder than ice; it penetrated to his very heart, which was already almost a frozen lump; it seemed to him as if he were about to die,— but a moment more and it was quite congenial to him, and he did not remark the cold that was around him.

"My sledge! Do not forget my sledge!" It was the first thing he thought of. It was there tied to one of the white chickens, who flew along with it on his back behind the large sledge. The Snow-Queen kissed Kay once more, and then he forgot little Gerda, grandmother, and all whom he had left at his home.

"Now you will have no more kisses," said she, "or else I should kiss you to death!"

Kay looked at her. She was very beautiful; a more clever, or a more lovely countenance he could not fancy to himself; and she no longer appeared of ice as before, when she sat outside the window, and beckoned to him; in his eyes she was perfect, he did not fear her at all, and told her that he could calculate in his head and with fractions, even; that he knew the number of square miles there were in the different countries, and how many inhabitants they contained; and she smiled while he spoke. It then seemed to him as if what he knew was not enough, and he looked upwards in the large huge empty space above him, and on she flew with him; flew high over the black clouds, while the storm moaned and whistled as though it were singing some old tune. On they flew over woods and lakes, over seas, and many lands; and beneath them the chilling storm rushed fast, the wolves howled, the snow crackled; above them flew large screaming crows, but higher up appeared the moon, quite large and bright; and it was on it that Kay gazed during the long long winter's night; while by day he slept at the feet of the Snow-Queen.

THIRD STORY.

OF THE FLOWER-GARDEN AT THE OLD WOMAN'S WHO UNDERSTOOD WITCHCRAFT.

BUT what became of little Gerda when Kay did not return? Where could he be? Nobody knew; nobody could give any intelligence. All the boys knew was, that they had seen him tie his sledge to another large and splendid one, which drove down the street and out of the town. Nobody knew where he was; many sad tears were shed, and little Gerda wept long and bitterly; at last she said he must be dead; that he had been drowned in the river which flowed close to the town. Oh! those were very long and dismal winter evenings!

At last spring came, with its warm sunshine.

"Kay is dead and gone!" said little Gerda.

"That I don't believe," said the Sunshine.

"Kay is dead and gone!" said she to the Swallows.

"That I don't believe," said they: and at

last little Gerda did not think so any longer either.

"I'll put on my red shoes," said she, one morning; "Kay has never seen them, and then I'll go down to the river and ask there."

It was quite early; she kissed her old grandmother, who was still asleep, put on her red shoes, and went alone to the river.

"Is it true that you have taken my little playfellow? I will make you a present of my red shoes, if you will give him back to me."

And, as it seemed to her, the blue waves nodded in a strange manner; then she took off her red shoes, the most precious thing she possessed, and threw them both into the river. But they fell close to the bank, and the little waves bore them immediately to land; it was as if the stream would not take what was dearest to her; for in reality it had not got little Kay; but Gerda thought that she had not thrown the shoes out far enough, so she clambered into a boat which lay among the rushes, went to the farthest end, and threw out the shoes. But the boat was not fastened, and the motion which she oc-

z

casioned, made it drift from the shore. She
observed this, and hastened to get back; but
before she could do so, the boat was more
than a yard from the land, and was gliding
quickly onward.

Little Gerda was very frightened, and be
gan to cry; but no one heard her except the
sparrows, and they could not carry her to
land; but they flew along the bank, and
sang as if to comfort her, "Here we are!
here we are!". The boat drifted with the
stream, little Gerda sat quite still without
shoes, for they were swimming behind the
boat, but could not reach it, because it went
much faster than they did.

The banks on both sides were beautiful;
lovely flowers, venerable trees, and slopes
with sheep and cows, but not a human being
was to be seen.

"Perhaps the river will carry me to little
Kay," said she; and then she grew less sad.
She rose, and looked for many hours at the
beautiful green banks. Presently she sailed
by a large cherry-orchard, where was a little
cottage with curious red and blue windows;
it was thatched, and before it two wooden

soldiers stood sentry, and presented arms when any one went past.

Gerda called to them, for she thought they were alive; but they, of course, did not answer. She came close to them, for the stream drifted the boat quite near the land.

Gerda called still louder, and an old woman then came out of the cottage, leaning upon a crooked stick. She had a large broad-brimmed hat on, painted with the most splendid flowers.

"Poor little child!" said the old woman; "how did you get upon the large rapid river, to be driven about so in the wide world!" And then the old woman went into the water, caught hold of the boat with her crooked stick, drew it to the bank, and lifted little Gerda out.

And Gerda was so glad to be on dry land again; but she was rather afraid of the strange old woman.

"But come and tell me who you are, and how you came here," said she.

And Gerda told her all; and the old woman shook her head and said, "A-hem! a-hem!" and when Gerda had told her anything, and asked her if she had not seen little Kay, the woman answered that he had not passed there, but he no doubt would come; and she told her not to be cast down, but taste her cherries, and look at her flowers, which were finer than any in a picture-book, each of which could tell a whole story. She then took Gerda by the hand, led her into the little cottage, and locked the door.

The windows were very high up; the glass was red, blue, and green, and the sunlight shone through quite wondrously in all sorts of colors. On the table stood the most exquisite cherries, and Gerda ate as many as she chose, for she had permission to do so. While she was eating, the old woman combed her hair with a golden comb, and her hair curled and shone with a lovely golden color around that sweet little face, which was so round and so like a rose.

" I have often longed for such a dear little girl," said the old woman. " Now you shall see how well we agree together;" and while she combed little Gerda's hair, the child forgot her foster-brother Kay more and more, for the old woman understood magic; but

. ..

she was no evil being, she only practised witchcraft a little for her own private amuse‐ ment, and now she wanted very much to keep little Gerda. She therefore went out in the garden, stretched out her crooked stick towards the rose-bushes, which, beautifully as they were blowing, all sank into the earth and no one could tell where they had stood. The old woman feared that if Gerda should see the roses, she would then think of her own, would remember little Kay, and run away from her.

She now led Gerda into the flower-garden. Oh, what odour and what loveliness was there! Every flower that one could think of, and of every season, stood there in fullest bloom; no picture-book could be gayer or more beautiful. Gerda jumped for joy, and played till the sun set behind the tall cherry- tree; she then had a pretty bed, with a red silken coverlet filled with blue violets. She fell asleep, and had as pleasant dreams as ever a queen on her wedding-day.

The next morning she went to play with the flowers in the warm sunshine, and thus passed away a day. Gerda knew every

8

flower ; and, numerous as they were, it still
seemed to Gerda that one was wanting,
though she did not know which. One day
while she was looking at the hat of the old
woman painted with flowers, the most beautiful of them all seemed to her to be a rose.
The old woman had forgotten to take it from
her hat when she made the others vanish in
the earth. But so it is when one's thoughts
are not collected. "What!" said Gerda,
" are there no roses here?" and she ran about
amongst the flower-beds, and looked, and
looked, but there was not one to be found.
She then sat down and wept ; but her hot
tears fell just where a rose-bush had sunk ;
and when her warm tears watered the
ground, the tree shot up suddenly as fresh
and blooming as when it had been swallowed
up. Gerda kissed the roses, thought of her
own dear roses at home, and with them of
little Kay.

"Oh, how long I have stayed!" said the
little girl. I intended to look for Kay!
Don't you know where he is?" asked she
of the roses. "Do you think he is dead and
gone?"

" Dead he certainly is not," said the Roses.
" We have been in the earth where all the
dead are, but Kay was not there."

" Many thanks !" said the little Gerda ; and
she went to the other flowers, looked into
their cups, and asked, " Don't you know
where little Kay is ?"

But every flower stood in the sunshine, and
dreamed its own fairy-tale or its own story:
and they all told her very many things, but
not one knew anything of Kay.

Well, what did the Tiger-Lily say ?

" Hearest thou not the drum ?   Bum !
bum ! those are the only two tones.   Always
bum ! bum !   Hark to the plaintive song of
the old woman ! to the call of the priests !
The Hindoo woman in her long robe stands
upon the funeral pile ; the flames rise around
her and her dead husband, but the Hindoo
woman thinks on the living one in the surrounding circle ; on him whose eyes burn hot-
ter than the flames—on him, the fire of whose
eyes pierces her heart more than the flames
which soon will burn her body to ashes.
Can the heart's flame die in the flame of the
funeral pile ?"

"I don't understand that at all," said little Gerda.

"That is my story," said the Lily.

What did the Convolvulus say?

"Projecting over a narrow mountain-path there hangs an old feudal castle. Thick evergreens grow on the dilapidated walls, and around the altar, where a lovely maiden is standing: she bends over the railing and looks out upon the rose. No fresher rose hangs on the branches than she; no apple-blossom carried away by the wind is more buoyant! How her silken robe is rustling!

"'Is he not yet come?'"

"Is it Kay that you mean?" asked little Gerda.

"I am speaking about my story—about my dream," answered the Convolvulus.

What did the Snow-drops say?

"Between the trees a long board is hang-ing—it is a swing. Two little girls are sit-ting in it, and swing themselves backwards and forwards; their frocks are as white as snow, and long green silk ribands flutter from their bonnets. Their brother, who is older than they are, stands up in the swing;

he twines his arms round the cords to hold himself fast, for in one hand he has a little cup, and in the other a clay-pipe. He is blowing soap bubbles. The swing moves, and the bubbles float in charming changing colors : the last is still hanging to the end of the pipe, and rocks in the breeze. The swing moves. The little black dog, as light as a soap-bubble, jumps up on his hind legs to try to get into the swing. It moves, the dog falls down, barks, and is angry. They tease him; the bubble bursts!—A swing, a bursting bubble—such is my song !"

" What you relate may be very pretty, but you tell it in so melancholy a manner, and do not mention Kay."

What do the Hyacinths say ?

" There were once upon a time three sisters, quite transparent, and very beautiful. The robe of the one was red, that of the second blue, and that of the third white. They danced hand in hand beside the calm lake in the clear moonshine. They were not elfin maidens, but mortal children. A sweet fragrance was smelt, and the maidens vanished .in the wood; the fragrance grew stronger

a a

——three coffins, and in them three lovely maidens, glided out of the forest and across the lake: the shining glow-worms flew around like little floating lights.   Do the dancing maidens sleep, or are they dead? The odour of the flowers says they are corpses; the evening bell tolls for the dead!"

"You make me quite sad," said little Gerda. "I cannot help thinking of the dead maidens.   Oh! is little Kay really dead? The Roses have been in the earth, and they say no."

"Ding, dong!" sounded the Hyacinth bells. "We do not toll for little Kay; we do not know him.   That is our way of singing, the only one we have."

And Gerda went to the Ranunculuses, that looked forth from among the shining green leaves.

"You are a little bright sun!" said Gerda. "Tell me if you know where I can find my playfellow."

And the Ranunculus shone brightly, and looked again at Gerda. What song could the Rananculus sing?   It was one that said nothing about Kay either.

"In a small court the bright sun was shining in the first days of spring. The beams glided down the white walls of a neighbor's house, and close by the fresh yellow flowers were growing, shining like gold in the warm sun-rays. An old grandmother was sitting in the air ; her grand-daughter, the poor and lovely servant just come for a short visit. She knows her grandmother. There was gold, pure virgin gold in that blessed kiss. There, that is my little story," said the Ranunculus

"My poor old grandmother!" sighed Gerda. "Yes, she is longing for me, no doubt : she is sorrowing for me, as she did for little Kay. But I will soon come home, and then I will bring Kay with me. It is of no use asking the flowers; they only know their own old rhymes, and can tell me nothing." And she tucked up her frock, to enable her to run quicker; but the Narcissus gave her a knock on the leg, just as she was going to jump over it. So she stood still, looked at the long yellow flower, and asked, "You perhaps know something?" and she bent down to the Narcissus. And what did it say ?

"I can see myself—I can see myself! Oh, how odorous I am! Up in the little garret there stands, half-dressed, a little Dancer. She stands now on one leg, now on both; she despises the whole world; yet she lives only in imagination. She pours water out of the teapot over a piece of stuff which she holds in her hand; it is the bodice; cleanliness is a fine thing. The white dress is hanging on the hook; it was washed in the teapot, and dried on the roof. She puts it on, ties a saffron-colored kerchief round her neck, and then the gown looks whiter. I can see myself—I can see myself!"

"That's nothing to me," said little Gerda. "That does not concern me." And then off she ran to the further end of the garden.

The gate was locked, but she shook the rusted bolt till it was loosened, and the gate opened; and little Gerda ran off barefooted into the wide world. She looked round her thrice, but no one followed her. At last she could run no longer; she sat down on a large stone, and when she looked about her, she saw that the summer had passed; it was late in the autumn, but that one could not remark in the beautiful garden, where there was always sunshine, and where there were flowers the whole year round.

"Dear me, how long I have staid!" said Gerda. "Autumn is come. I must not rest any longer." And she got up to go further.

Oh, how tender and wearied her little feet were! All around it looked so cold and raw : the long willow-leaves were quite yellow, and the fog dripped from them like water; one leaf fell after the other : the sloes only stood full of fruit, which set one's teeth on edge. Oh, how dark and comfortless it was in the dreary world!

––––––

FOURTH STORY.

THE PRINCE AND PRINCESS.

GERDA was obliged to rest herself again, when, exactly opposite to her, a large Raven came hopping over the white snow. He had long been looking at Gerda and shaking his head; and now he said, "Caw! caw!" Good

day! good day! He could not say it better;
but he felt a sympathy for the little girl, and
asked her where she was going all alone.
The word "alone" Gerda understood quite
well, and felt how much was expressed by it;
so she told the Raven her whole history, and
asked if he had not seen Kay.

The Raven nodded very gravely, and said,
"It may be—it may be!"

"What, do you really think so?" cried the
little girl; and she nearly squeezed the Raven to death, so much did she kiss him.

"Gently, gently," said the Raven. "I
think I know; I think that it may be little
Kay. But now he has forgotten you for the
Princess."

"Does he live with a Princess?" asked
Gerda.

"Yes,—listen," said the Raven; "but it
will be difficult for me to speak your language. If you understand the Raven language I can tell you better."

"No, I have not learnt it," said Gerda;
"but my grandmother understands it, and
she can speak gibberish too. I wish I had
learnt it."

"No matter," said the Raven ; "I will tell you as well as I can ; however, it will be bad enough." And then he told all he knew.

"In the kingdom where we now are 'there lives a Princess, who is extraordinarily clever ; for she has read all the newspapers in the whole world, and has forgotten them again,—so clever is she. She was lately, it is said, sitting on her throne,—which is not very amusing after all,—when she began humming an old tune, and it was just, 'Oh, why should I not be married?' 'That song is not without its meaning,' said she, and so then she was determined to marry ; but she would have a husband who knew how to give an answer when he was spoken to,—not one who looked only as if he were a great personage, for that is so tiresome. She then had all the ladies of the court drummed together ; and when they heard her intention, all were very pleased, and said, 'We are very glad to hear it ; it is the very thing we were thinking of.' You may believe every word I say," said the Raven ; "for I have a tame sweetheart that hops about in the palace quite free, and it was she who told me all this.

" The newspapers appeared forthwith with a border of hearts and the initials of the Princess; and therein you might read that every good-looking young man was at liberty to come to the palace and speak to the Princess; and he who spoke in such wise as showed he felt himself at home there, that one the Princess would choose for her husband.

"Yes, yes," said the Raven, you may believe it; it is as true as I am sitting here. People came in crowds; there was a crush and a hurry, but no one was successful either on the first or second day. They could all talk well enough when they were out in the street; but as soon as they came inside the palace-gates, and saw the guard richly dressed in silver, and the lackeys in gold on the staircase, and the large illuminated saloons, then they were abashed; and when they stood before the throne on which the Princess was sitting, all they could do was to repeat the last word they had uttered, and to hear it again did not interest her very much. It was just as if the people within were under a charm, and had fallen into a trance till they came out again into the street; for then,—

oh, then,—they could chatter enough. There was a whole row of them standing from the town-gates to the palace. I was there myself to look," said the Raven. "They grew hungry and thirsty; but from the palace they got nothing whatever, not even a glass of water. Some of the cleverest, it is true, had taken bread and butter with them : but none shared it with his neighbor, for each thought, 'Let him look hungry, and then the Princess won't have him.' "

" But Kay—little Kay," said Gerda, "when did he come ? was he among the number?"

" Patience, patience; we are just come to him. It was on the third day, when a little personage without horse or equipage, came marching right boldly up to the palace; his eyes shone like yours, he had beautiful long hair, but his clothes were very shabby."

" That was Kay," cried Gerda, with a voice of delight. "Oh, now I've found him !" and she clapped her hands for joy.

" He had a little knapsack at his back," said the Raven.

" No, that was certainly his sledge, ' said

Gerda; "for when he went away he took his sledge with him."

"That may be," said the Raven; "I did not examine him so minutely; but I know from my tame sweetheart, that when he came into the courtyard of the palace, and saw the body-guard in silver, the lackeys on the staircase, he was not the least abashed; he nodded, and said to them, 'It must be very tiresome to stand on the stairs; for my part, I shall go in.' The saloons were gleaming with lustres,—privy councillors and excellencies were walking about barefooted, and wore gold keys; it was enough to make any one feel uncomfortable. His boots creaked, too, so loudly, but still he was not at all afraid."

"That's Kay for certain," said Gerda. "I know he had on new boots; I have heard them creaking in grandmama's room."

"Yes, they creaked," said the Raven. "And on he went boldly up to the Princess, who was sitting on a pearl as large as a spinning-wheel. All the ladies of the court, with their attendants and attendants' attendants, and all the cavaliers, with their gentlemen and gentlemen's gentlemen, stood round ; and the nearer they stood to the door, the prouder they looked.   It was hardly possible to look at the gentleman's gentleman, so very haughtily did he stand in the doorway."

"It must have been terrible," said little Gerda.   "And did Kay get the Princess?"

"Were I not a Raven, I should have taken the Princess myself, although I am promised. It is said he spoke as well as I speak when I talk Raven language ; this I learned from my tame sweetheart. He was bold and nicely behaved ; he had not come to woo the Princess, but only to hear her wisdom. She pleased him, and he pleased her."

"Yes, yes ; for certain that was Kay," said Gerda.   "He was so clever ; he could reckon fractions in his head. Oh, won't you take me to the palace?"

"That is very easily said," answered the Raven. "But how are we to manage it? I'll speak to my tame sweetheart about it : she must advise us ; for so much I must tell you, such a little girl as you are will never get permission to enter."

"Oh, yes I shall," said Gerda ; "when

Kay hears that I am here, he will come out directly to fetch me."

"Wait for me here on these steps," said the Raven. He moved his head backwards and forwards and flew away.

The evening was closing in when the Raven returned. "Caw—caw!" said he. "She sends you her compliments; and here is a roll for you. She took it out of the kitchen, where there is bread enough. You are hungry, no doubt. It is not possible for you to enter the palace, for you are barefooted: the guards in silver, and the lackeys in gold, would not allow it; but do not cry, you shall come in still. My sweetheart knows a little back stair that leads to the bedchamber, and she knows where she can get the key of it."

And they went into the garden in the large avenue, where one leaf was falling after the other; and when the lights in the palace had all gradually disappeared, the Raven led little Gerda to the back door, which stood half open.

O, how Gerda's heart beat with anxiety and longing! It was just as if she had been about to do something wrong; and yet she only wanted to know if little Kay was there. Yes, he must be there. She called to mind his intelligent eyes, and his long hair, so vividly, she could quite see him as he used to laugh when they were sitting under the roses at home. " He will, no doubt, be glad to see you, —to hear what a long way you have come for his sake ; to know how unhappy all at home were when he did not come back."

Oh, what a fright and a joy it was!

They were now on the stairs. A single lamp was burning there; and on the floor stood the tame Raven, turning her head on every side and looking at Gerda, who bowed as her grandmother had taught her to do.

" My intended has told me so much good of you, my dear young lady," said the tame Raven. " Your tale is very affecting. If you will take the lamp, I will go before. We will go straight on, for we shall meet no one."

" I think there is somebody just behind us," said Gerda ; and something rushed past : it was like shadowy figures on the wall; horses with flowing manes and thin legs, huntsmen, ladies and gentlemen on horseback.

9

"They are only dreams," said the Raven. "They come to fetch the thoughts of the high personages to the chase; 'tis well, for now you can observe them in bed all the better. But let me find, when you enjoy honor and distinction, that you possess a grateful heart."

"Tut! that's not worth talking about," said the Raven of the woods.

They now entered the first saloon, which was of rose-colored satin, with artificial flowers on the wall. Here the dreams were rushing past, but they hastened by so quickly that Gerda could not see the high personages. One hall was more magnificent than the other; one might indeed well be abashed; and at last they came into the bedchamber. The ceiling of the room resembled a large palm-tree with leaves of glass, of costly glass; and in the middle, from a thick golden stem, hung two beds, each of which resembled a lily. One was white, and in this lay the Princess; the other was red, and it was here that Gerda was to look for little Kay. She bent back one of the red leaves and saw a brown neck—Oh! that was Kay! She called him quite loud by name, held the lamp towards him—the dreams rushed back again into the chamber—he awoke, turned his head, and—it was not little Kay!

The Prince was only like him about the neck; but he was young and handsome. And out of the white lily leaves the Princess peeped, too, and asked what was the matter. Then little Gerda cried, and told her her whole history, and all that the Ravens had done for her.

"Poor little thing!" said the Prince and the Princess. They praised the Ravens very much, and told them they were not at all angry with them, but they were not to do so again. However, they should have a reward.

"Will you fly about here at liberty," asked the Princess; "or would you like to have a fixed appointment as court ravens, with all the broken bits from the kitchen?"

And both the Ravens nodded, and begged for a fixed appointment; for they thought of their old age, and said, "it was a good thing to have a provision for their old days."

And the Prince got up and let Gerda sleep in his bed, and more than this he could not

do.   She folded her little hands and thought,
" how good men and animals are!" and she
then fell asleep and slept soundly.   All the
dreams flew in again, and they now looked
like the angels; they drew a little sledge, in
which little Kay sat and nodded his head;
but the whole was only a dream, and therefore it all vanished as soon as she awoke.

The next day she was dressed from head
to foot in silk and velvet.   They offered to
let her stay at the palace, and lead a happy
life; but she begged to have a little carriage
with a horse in front, and for a small pair of
shoes; then, she said, she would again go
forth in the wide world and look for Kay.

Shoes and a muff were given her; she
was, too, dressed very nicely; and when she
was about to set off, a new carriage stopped
before the door.   It was of pure gold, and the
arms of the Prince and Princess shone like a
star upon it; the coachman, the footmen,
and the outriders, for outriders were there,
too, all wore golden crowns.   The Prince
and the Princess assisted her into the carriage
themselves, and wished her all success.   The
Raven of the woods, who was now married,

accompanied her for the first three miles. He sat beside Gerda, for he could not bear riding backwards; the other Raven stood in the doorway, and flapped her wings; she could not accompany Gerda, because she suffered from headache since she had had a fixed appointment and ate so much. The carriage was lined inside with sugar-plums, and in the seats were fruits and gingerbread.

"Farewell! farewell!" cried Prince and Princess; and Gerda wept, and the Raven wept. Thus passed the first miles; and then the Raven bade her farewell, and this was the most painful separation of all. He flew into a tree, and beat his black wings as long as he could see the carriage, that shone from afar like a sunbeam.

FIFTH STORY,

THE LITTLE ROBBER-MAIDEN.

THEY drove through the dark wood; but the carriage shone like a torch, and it dazzled

b b

the eyes of the robbers, so that they could not bear to look at it.

" 'T is gold! 't is gold!" cried they; and they rushed forward, seized the horses, knocked down the little postilion, the coachman, and the servants, and pulled little Gerda out of the carriage.

"How plump, how beautiful she is! She must have been fed on nut-kernels," said the old female Robber, who had a long, scrubby beard, and bushy eyebrows that hung down over her eyes; "she is as good as a fatted lamb! how nice she will be!" And then she drew out a knife, the blade of which shone so that it was quite dreadful to behold.

"Oh!" cried the woman at the same moment. She had been bitten in the ear by her own little daughter, who hung at her back; and who was so wild and unmanageable, that it was quite amusing to see her. "You naughty child!" said the mother: and now she had not time to kill Gerda.

"She shall play with me," said the little Robber-child; "she shall give me her muff, and her pretty frock; she shall sleep in my bed!" And then she gave her mother another bite, so that she jumped, and ran round with the pain ; and the Robbers laughed, and said, " Look, how she is dancing with the little one !"

" I will go into the carriage," said the little Robber-maiden ; and she would have her will, for she was very spoiled and very head-strong.   She and Gerda got in ; and then away they drove over the stumps of felled trees, deeper and deeper into the woods. The little Robber-maiden was as tall as Gerda, but stronger, broader-shouldered, and of dark complexion ; her eyes were quite black ; they looked almost melancholy.   She embraced little Gerda, and said, " They shall not kill you as long as I am not displeased with you. You are, doubtless, a Princess ?"

" No," said little Gerda ; who then related all that had happened to her, and how much she cared about little Kay.

The little Robber-maiden looked at her with a serious air, nodded her head slightly, and said, " They shall not kill you, even if I am angry with you : then I will do it my-self ;" and she dried Gerda's eyes, and put both her hands in the handsome muff, which was so soft and warm.

At length the carriage stopped. They were in the midst of the court-yard of a robber's castle. It was full of cracks from top to bottom; and out of the openings magpies and rooks were flying; and the great bull-dogs, each of which looked as if he could swallow a man, jumped up, but they did not bark, for that was forbidden.

In the midst of the large, old, smoking hall burnt a great fire on the stone floor. The smoke disappeared under the stones, and had to seek its own egress. In an immense caldron soup was boiling; and rabbits and hares were being roasted on a spit.

"You shall sleep with me to-night, with all my animals," said the little Robber-maiden. They had something to eat and drink; and then went into a corner, where straw and carpets were lying. Beside them, on laths and perches, sat nearly a hundred pigeons, all asleep, seemingly; but yet they moved a little when the Robber-maiden came. "They are all mine." said she; at the same time seizing one that was next to her by the legs

and shaking it so that its wings fluttered.
"Kiss it," cried the little girl, and flung the
pigeon in Gerda's face. "Up there is the
rabble of the wood," continued she, pointing
to several laths which were fastened before a
hole high up in the wall ; "that's the rabble ;
they would all fly away immediately, if they
were not well fastened in. And here is my
dear old Bac ;" and she laid hold of the
horns of a reindeer, that had a bright copper
ring round its neck, and was tethered to the
spot. "We are obliged to lock this fellow
in too, or he would make his escape. Every
evening I tickle his neck with my sharp
knife ; he is so frightened at it !" and the
little girl drew forth a long knife, from a
crack in the wall, and let it glide over the
reindeer's neck. The poor animal kicked ;
the girl laughed, and pulled Gerda into bed
with her.

"Do you intend to keep your knife while
you sleep? asked Gerda ; looking at it
rather fearfully.

"I always sleep with the knife," said the
little Robber-maiden ; "there is no knowing
what may happen. But tell me now, once

more, all about little Kay; and why you
have started off in the wide world alone."
And Gerda related all, from the very beginning: the wood-pigeons cooed above in their
cage, and the others slept. The little Robber-maiden wound her arm round Gerda's
neck, held the knife in the other hand, and
snored so loud that every body could hear
her; but Gerda could not close her eyes,
for she did not know whether she was to live
or die. The Robbers sat round the fire, sang
and drank; and the old female Robber
jumped about so, that it was quite dreadful
for Gerda to see her.

Then the Wood-pigeons said, " Coo! coo!
we have seen little Kay! A white hen
carries his sledge; he himself sat in the
carriage of the Snow-Queen, who passed
here, down just over the wood, as we lay in
our nest. She blew upon us young ones;
and all died except we two. Coo! coo!"

"What is that you say up there?" cried
little Gerda. "Where did the Snow-Queen
go to? Do you know any thing about it?"

"She is no doubt gone to Lapland; for

there is always snow and ice there. Only ask the reindeer, who is tethered there."

"Ice and snow is there! Thére it is, glorious and beautiful!" said the Reindeer. "One can spring about in the large shining valleys! The Snow-Queen has her summer tent there; but her fixed abode is high up towards the North Pole, on the Island called Spitzbergen."

"Oh, Kay! poor little Kay!" sighed Gerda.

"Do you choose to be quiet?" said the Robber-maiden. "If you don't, I shall make you."

In the morning Gerda told her all that the Wood-pigeons had said; and the little maiden looked very serious, but she nodded her head, and said, "That's no matter—that's no matter. Do you know where Lapland lies!" asked she of the Reindeer.

"Who should know better than I?" said the animal; and his eyes rolled in his head. "I was born and bred there;—there I leapt about on the fields of snow.

"Listen," said the Robber-maiden to Gerda. "You see that the men are gone; but my mother is still here, and will remain.

However, towards morning she takes a draught out of the large flask, and then she sleeps a little : then I will do something for you." She now jumped out of bed, flew to her mother; with her arms round her neck, and pulling her by the beard, said, "Good morrow, my own sweet nanny-goat of a mother." And her mother took hold of her nose, and pinched it till it was red and blue ; but this was all done out of pure love.

When the mother had taken a sup at her flask, and was having a nap, the little Robber-maiden went to the Reindeer, and said, "I should very much like to give you still many a tickling with the sharp knife, for then you are so amusing ; however, I will untether you, and help you out, so that you may go back to Lapland. But you must make good use of your legs ; and take this little girl for me to the palace of the Snow-Queen, where her play-fellow is. You have heard, I suppose, all she said ; for she spoke loud enough, and you were listening."

The Reindeer gave a bound for joy. The Robber-maiden lifted up little Gerda, and took the precaution to bind her fast on the

Reindeer's back; she even gave her a small cushion to sit on. "Here are your worsted leggins, for it will be cold; but the muff I shall keep for myself, for it is so very pretty. But I do not wish you to be cold. Here is a pair of lined gloves of my mother's; they just reach up to your elbow. On with them! Now you look about the hands just like my ugly old mother!"

And Gerda wept for joy.

"I can't bear to see you fretting," said the little Robber-maiden. "This is just the time when you ought to look pleased. Here are two loaves and a ham for you, so that you won't starve." The bread and the meat were fastened to the Reindeer's back; the little maiden opened the door, called in all the dogs, and then with her knife cut the rope that fastened the animal, and said to him, "Now, off with you; but take good care of the little girl!"

And Gerda stretched out her hands with the large wadded gloves towards the Robber-maiden, and said, "Farewell!" and the Reindeer flew on over bush and bramble

c c

through the great wood, over moor and heath, as fast as he could go.

" Ddsa! ddsa!" was heard in the sky.   It was just as if somebody was sneezing.

" These are my old northern-lights," said the Reindeer, "look how they gleam !   And on he now sped still quicker,—day and night on he went: the loaves were consumed, and the ham too; and now they were in Lapland.

SIXTH STORY.

THE LAPLAND WOMAN AND THE FINLAND WOMAN.

SUDDENLY they stopped before a little house, which looked very miserable : the roof reached to the ground; and the door was so low, that the family were obliged to creep upon their stomachs when they went in or out.   Nobody was at home except an old Lapland woman, who was dressing fish

by the light of an oil lamp. And the Reindeer told her the whole of Gerda's history,
but first of all his own; for that seemed to
him of much greater importance. Gerda
was so chilled that she could not speak.

"Poor thing," said the Lapland woman,
"you have far to run still. You have more
than a hundred miles to go before you get to
Finland; there the Snow-Queen has her
country-house, and burns blue lights every
evening. I will give you a few words from
me, which I will write on a dried haberdine,
for paper I have none; this you can take
with you to the Finland woman, and she
will be able to give you more information
than I can."

When Gerda had warmed herself, and
had eaten and drunk the Lapland woman
wrote a few words on a dried haberdine,
begged Gerda to take care of them, put her
on the Reindeer, bound her fast, and away
sprang the animal. "Ddsa! ddsa!" was
again heard in the air; the most charming
blue lights burned the whole night in the sky,
and at last they came to Finland. They

knocked at the chimney of the Finland woman; for as to a door, she had none.

There was such a heat inside that the Finland woman herself went about almost naked. She was diminutive and dirty. She immediately loosened little Gerda's clothes, pulled off her thick gloves and boots; for otherwise the heat would have been too great,—and after laying a piece of ice on the Reindeer's head, read what was written on the fish-skin. She read it three times : she then knew it by heart; so she put the fish into the cupboard,—for it might very well be eaten, and she never threw any thing away.

Then the Reindeer related his own story first, and afterwards that of little Gerda ; and the Finland woman winked her eyes, but said nothing.

"You are so clever," said the Reindeer; "you can, I know, twist all the winds of the world together in a knot. If the seaman loosens one knot, then he has a good wind ; if a second, then it blows pretty stiffly ; if he undoes the third and fourth, then it rages so that the forests are upturned. Will you give the little maiden a potion, that she may possess the strength of twelve men, and vanquish the Snow-Queen ?"

"The strength of twelve men !" said the Finland woman. "Much good that would be !" Then she went to a cupboard, and drew out a large skin rolled up. When she had unrolled it, strange characters were to be seen written thereon ; and the Finland woman read at such a rate that the perspiration trickled down her forehead.

But the Reindeer begged so hard for little Gerda, and Gerda looked so imploringly with tearful eyes at the Finland woman, that she winked, and drew the Reindeer aside into a corner, where they whispered together, while the animal got some fresh ice put on his head.

"'T is true little Kay is at the Snow-Queen's, and finds every thing there quite to his taste ; and he thinks it the very best place in the world ; but the reason of that is, he has a splinter of glass in his eye, and in his heart. These must be got out first ; otherwise he will never go back to mankind.

and the Snow-Queen will retain her power over him."

"But can you give little Gerda nothing to take which will endue her with power over the whole?"

"I can give her no more power than what she has already. "Don't you see how great it is? Don't you see how men and animals are forced to serve her; how well she gets through the world barefooted? She must not hear of her power from us; that power lies in her heart, because she is a sweet and innocent child! If she cannot get to the Snow-Queen by herself, and rid little Kay of the glass, we cannot help her. Two miles hence the garden of the Snow-Queen begins; thither you may carry the little girl. Set her down by the large bush with red berries, standing in the snow; don't stay talking, but hasten back as fast as possible." And now the Finland woman placed little Gerda on the Reindeer's back, and off he ran with all imaginable speed.

"Oh! I have not got my boots! I have not brought my gloves!" cried little Gerda. She remarked she was without them from the cutting frost; but the Reindeer dared not stand still; on he ran till he came to the great bush with the red berries, and there he set Gerda down, kissed her mouth, while large bright tears flowed from the animal's eyes, and then back he went as fast as possible. There stood poor Gerda now, without shoes or gloves, in the very middle of dreadful icy Finland.

She ran on as fast as she could. There then came a whole regiment of snow-flakes, but they did not fall from above, and they were quite bright and shining from the Aurora Borealis. The flakes ran along the ground, and the nearer they came the larger they grew. Gerda well remembered how large and strange the snow-flakes appeared when she once saw them through a magnifying-glass; but now they were large and terrific in another manner—they were all alive. They were the outposts of the Snow-Queen. They had the most wondrous shapes; some looked like large ugly porcupines; others like snakes knotted together, with their heads sticking out; and others, again, like small fat bears, with the hair

standing on end : all were of dazzling whiteness—all were living snow-flakes.

Little Gerda repeated the Lord's Prayer.
The cold was so intense that she could see
her own breath, which came like smoke out
of her mouth. It grew thicker and thicker,
and took the form of little angels, that grew
more and more when they touched the earth.
All had helms on their heads, and lances and
shields in their hands ; they increased in
numbers ; and when Gerda had finished the
Lord's Prayer, she was surrounded by a
whole legion. They thrust at the horrid
snow-flakes with their spears, so that they
flew into a thousand pieces ; and little Gerda
walked on bravely and in security. The
angels patted her hands and feet ; and then
she felt the cold less, and went on quickly
towards the palace of the Snow-Queen.

But now we shall see how Kay fared. He
never thought of Gerda, and least of all that
she was standing before the palace.

SEVENTH STORY.

WHAT TOOK PLACE IN THE PALACE OF THE SNOW-
QUEEN, AND WHAT HAPPENED AFTERWARD.

THE walls of the palace were of driving snow, and the windows and doors of cutting winds. There were more than a hundred halls there, according as the snow was driven by the winds. The largest was many miles in extent; all were lighted up by the power-ful Aurora Borealis, and all were so large, so empty, so icy cold, and so resplendent! Mirth never reigned there; there was never even a little bear-ball, with the storm for music, while the polar bears went on their hind-legs and showed off their steps. Never a little tea-party of white young lady foxes; vast, cold, and empty were the halls of the Snow-Queen. The northern-lights shone with such precision that one could tell exactly when they were at their highest or lowest degree of brightness. In the middle of the

empty, endless hall of snow, was a frozen
lake; it was cracked in a thousand pieces,
but each piece was so like the other, that it
seemed the work of a cunning artificer. In
the middle of this lake sat the Snow-Queen
when she was at home; and then she said she
was sitting in the Mirror of Understanding,
and that this was the only one and the best
thing in the world.

Little Kay was quite blue, yes nearly black
with cold; but he did not observe it, for she
had kissed away all feeling of cold from his
body, and his heart was a lump of ice. He
was dragging along some pointed flat pieces
of ice, which he laid together in all possible ways, for he wanted to make something with them; just as we have little flat
pieces of wood to make geometrical figures
with, called the Chinese Puzzle. Kay made
all sorts of figures, the most complicated, for
it was an ice-puzzle for the understanding.
In his eyes the figures were extraordinarily
beautiful, and of the utmost importance; for
the bit of glass which was in his eye caused
this. He found whole figures which represented a written word; but he never could

manage to represent just the word he wanted
—that word was " eternity ;" and the Snow-
Queen had said, " If you can discover that
figure, you shall be your own master, and I
will make you a present of the whole world
and a pair of new skates." But he could
not find it out.

"I am going now to warm lands," said
the Snow-Queen. " I must have a look
down into the black caldrons." It was the
volcanoes Vesuvius and Etna that she meant.
"I will just give them a coating of white,
for that is as it ought to be ; besides, it is
good for the oranges and the grapes." And
then away she flew, and Kay sat quite alone
in the empty halls of ice that were miles
long, and looked at the blocks of ice, and
thought and thought till his skull was almost cracked. There he sat quite benumbed
and motionless ; one would have imagined
he was frozen to death.

Suddenly little Gerda stepped through the
great portal into the palace. The gate
was formed of cutting winds ; but Gerda repeated her evening prayer, and the winds
were laid as though they slept ; and the

little maiden entered the vast, empty, cold halls. There she beheld Kay: she recognised him, flew to embrace him, and cried out, her arms firmly holding him the while, "Kay, sweet little Kay! Have I then found you at last?"

But he sat quite still, benumbed and cold. Then little Gerda shed burning tears; and they fell on his bosom, they penetrated to his heart, they thawed the lumps of ice, and consumed the splinters of the looking-glass; he looked at her, and she sang the hymn:

> " The rose in the valley is blooming so sweet,
> And angels descend there the children to greet."

Hereupon Kay burst into tears; he wept so much that the splinter rolled out of his eye, and he recognised her, and shouted, "Gerda, sweet little Gerda! where have you been so long? And where have I been?" He looked round him. "How cold it is here!" said he; "how empty and cold!" And he held fast by Gerda, who laughed and wept for joy. It was so beautiful, that even the blocks of ice danced about for joy; and when they were tired and laid themselves down, they formed exactly the letters which the Snow-Queen had told him to find out; so now he was his own master, and he would have the whole world and a pair of new skates into the bargain.

Gerda kissed his cheeks, and they grew quite blooming; she kissed his eyes, and they shone like her own; she kissed his hands and feet, and he was again well and merry. The Snow-Queen might come back as soon as she liked; there stood his discharge written in resplendent masses of ice.

They took each other by the hand, and wandered forth out of the large hall; they talked of their old grand-mother, and of the roses upon the roof; and wherever they went, the winds ceased raging, and the sun burst forth. And when they reached the bush with the red berries, they found the Reindeer waiting for them. He had brought another, a young one, with him, whose udder was filled with milk, which he gave to the little ones, and kissed their lips. They then carried Kay and Gerda,—first to the Finland woman, where they warmed themselves in the warm room, and learned what they were to do on their journey home ; and they went to the Lapland woman, who made some new clothes for them and repaired their sledges.

The Reindeer and the young hind leaped along beside them, and accompanied them to the boundary of the country. Here the first vegetation peeped forth ; here Kay and Gerda took leave of the Lapland woman. "Farewell ! farewell !" said they all. And the first green buds appeared, the first little birds began to chirrup ; and out of the wood came, riding on a magnificent horse, which Gerda knew (it was one of the leaders in the golden carriage), a young damsel with a bright-red cap on her head, and armed with pistols. It was the little Robber-maiden, who, tired of being at home, had determined to make a journey to the north ; and afterwards in another direction, if that did not please her. She recognised Gerda immediately, and Gerda knew her too. It was a joyful meeting.

"You are a fine fellow for tramping about," said she to little Kay ; "I should like to know, faith, if you deserve that one should run from one end of the world to the other for your sake ?"

But Gerda patted her cheeks, and inquired for the Prince and Princess.

"They are gone abroad," said the other.

"But the Raven?" asked little Gerda.

"Oh! the Raven is dead," answered she. "His tame sweetheart is a widow, and wears a bit of black worsted round her leg; she laments most piteously, but it's all mere talk and stuff! Now tell me what you've been doing and how you managed to catch him."

And Gerda and Kay both told their story.

And "Schnipp-schnapp-schnurre-basselurre," said the Robber-maiden; and she took the hands of each, and promised that if she should some day pass through the town where they lived, she would come and visit them; and then away she rode. Kay and Gerda took each other's hand: it was lovely spring weather, with abundance of flowers and of verdure. The church-bells rang, and the children recognised the high towers, and the large town; it was that in which they dwelt. They entered and hastened up to their grand-mother's room, where every thing was standing as formerly. The clock said "tick! tack!" and the finger moved

round; but as they entered, they remarked
that they were now grown up.   The roses on
the leads hung blooming in at the open window; there stood the little children's chairs,
and Kay and Gerda sat down on them, holding each other by the hand; they both had forgotten the cold empty splendor of the Snow-
Queen, as though it had been a dream.   The
grand-mother sat in the bright sunshine, and
read aloud from the Bible: "Unless ye become as little children, ye cannot enter the
kingdom of heaven."

And Kay and Gerda looked in each other's
eyes, and all at once they understood the old
hymn :

> " The rose in the valley is blooming so sweet,
>   And angels descend there the children to greet."

There sat the two grown-up persons;
grown-up, and yet children; children at least
in heart; and it was summer-time; summer
glorious summer!

THE LEAP-FROG.

FLEA, a Grasshopper, and a Leap-frog once wanted to see which could jump highest ; and they invited the whole world, and every body else besides who chose to come, to see the festival. Three famous jumpers were they, as every one would say, when they all met together in the room.

"I will give my daughter to him who jumps highest," exclaimed the King ; "for it is not so amusing where there is no prize to jump for."

The Flea was the first to step forward. He had exquisite manners, and bowed to the company on all sides ; for he had noble blood, and was, moreover, accustomed to the society

d d   157

of man alone; and that makes a great differ
ence.

Then came the Grasshopper. He was
considerably heavier, but he was well-man-
nered, and wore a green uniform, which he
had by right of birth; he said, moreover,
that he belonged to a very ancient Egyptian
family, and that in the house where he then
was, he was thought much of. The fact
was, he had been just brought out of the
fields, and put in a pasteboard house, three
stories high, all made of court-cards, with the
colored side inwards; and doors and windows cut out of the body of the Queen of
Hearts. "I sing so well," said he, "that sixteen native grasshoppers who have chirped
from infancy, and yet got no house built of
cards to live in, grew thinner than they were
before for sheer vexation when they heard
me."

It was thus that the Flea and the Grasshopper gave an account of themselves, and
thought they were quite good enough to
marry a Princess.

The Leap-frog said nothing; but people
gave it as their opinion, that he therefore

thought the more; and when the house-dog snuffed at him with his nose, he confessed the Leap-frog was of good family. The old councillor, who had had three orders given him to make him hold his tongue, asserted that the Leap-frog was a prophet; for that one could see on his back, if there would be a severe or mild winter, and that was what one could not see even on the back of the man who writes the almanac.

"I say nothing, it is true," exclaimed the King; "but I have my own opinion, notwithstanding."

Now the trial was to take place. The Flea jumped so high that nobody could see where he went to; so they all asserted he had not jumped at all; and that was dishonorable.

The Grasshopper jumped only half as high; but he leaped into the King's face, who said that was ill-mannered.

The Leap-frog stood still for a long time lost in thought; it was believed at last he would not jump at all.

"I only hope he is not unwell," said the house-dog; when, pop! he made a jump all on one side into the lap of the Princess, who was sitting on a little golden stool close by.

Hereupon the King said, "There is nothing above my daughter; therefore to bound up to her is the highest jump that can be made; but for this, one must possess understanding, and the Leap-frog has shown that he *has* understanding. He is brave and intellectual."

And so he won the Princess.

"It's all the same to me," said the Flea; "she may have the old Leap-frog, for all I care. I jumped the highest; but in this world merit seldom meets its reward. A fine exterior is what people look at now-a-days."

The Flea then went into foreign service, where, it is said, he was killed.

The Grasshopper sat without on a green bank, and reflected on worldly things; and he said too, "Yes, a fine exterior is every thing—a fine exterior is what people care about." And then he began chirping his peculiar melancholy song, from which we have taken this history; and which may, very possibly, be all untrue, although it does stand here printed in black and white.

Part XXX.

THIRTEEN NEW STORIES;

AND

ADDRESS TO YOUNG READERS.

THE OLD HOUSE.

————

N the street, up there, was an old, a very old house,— it was almost three hundred years old, for that might be known by reading the great beam on which the date of the year was carved : together with tulips and hop-binds there were whole verses spelled as in former times, and over every window was a distorted face cut out in the beam. The one story stood forward a great

9

way over the other; and directly under the
eaves was a leaden-spout with a dragon's
head; the rain-water should have run out of
the mouth, but it ran out of the belly, for
there was a hole in the spout.

All the other houses in the street were so
new and so neat, with large window-panes
and smooth walls, one could easily see that
they would have nothing to do with the old
house: they certainly thought, "How long
is that old decayed thing to stand here as a
spectacle in the street? And then the projecting windows stand so far out, that no
one can see from our windows what happens in that direction! The steps are as
broad as those of a palace, and as high as to
a church tower. The iron railings look
just like the door to an old family vault,
and then they have brass tops,—that's so
stupid!"

On the other side of the street were also
new and neat houses, and they thought just
as the others did; but at the window opposite the old house there sat a little boy with
fresh rosy cheeks and bright beaming eyes:
he certainly liked the old house best, and

that both in sunshine and moonshine. And when he looked across at the wall where the mortar had fallen out, he could sit and find out there the strangest figures imaginable; exactly as the street had appeared before, with steps, projecting windows, and pointed gables; he could see soldiers with halberds, and spouts where the water ran, like dragons and serpents. *That* was a house to look at; and there lived an old man, who wore plush breeches; and he had a coat with large brass buttons, and a wig that one could see was a real wig. Every morning there came an old fellow to him who put his rooms in order, and went on errands; otherwise, the old man in the plush breeches was quite alone in the old house. Now and then he came to the window and looked out, and the little boy nodded to him, and the old man nodded again, and so they became acquaintances, and then they were friends, although they had never spoken to each other,—but that made no difference. The little boy heard his parents say, "The old man opposite is very well off, but he is so very, very lonely!"

The Sunday following, the little boy took

something, and wrapped it up in a piece of paper, went down stairs, and stood in the doorway; and when the man who went on errands came past, he said to him—

"I say, master! will you give this to the old man over the way from me? I have two pewter soldiers—this is one of them, and he shall have it, for I know he is so very, very lonely."

And the old errand man looked quite pleased, nodded, and took the pewter soldier over to the old house. Afterwards there came a message; it was to ask if the little boy himself had not a wish to come over and pay a visit; and so he got permission of his parents, and then went over to the old house.

And the brass balls on the iron railings shone much brighter than ever; one would have thought they were polished on account of the visit; and it was as if the carved-out trumpeters—for there were trumpeters, who stood in tulips, carved out on the door—blew with all their might, their cheeks appeared so much rounder than before. Yes, they blew—"Traveratra! the little boy comes trateratra!"—and then the door opened.

The whole passage was hung with portraits of knights in armor, and ladies in silken gowns; and the armor rattled, and the silken gowns rustled! And then there was a flight of stairs which went a good way upwards, and a little way downwards, and then one came on a balcony which was in a very dilapidated state, sure enough, with large holes and long crevices, but grass grew there and leaves out of them altogether, for the whole balcony outside, the yard, and the walls, were overgrown with so much green stuff, that it looked like a garden; but it was only a balcony. Here stood old flower-pots with faces and asses' ears, and the flowers grew just as they liked. One of the pots was quite overrun on all sides with pinks, that is to say, with the green part; shoot stood by shoot, and it said quite distinctly, "The air has cherished me, the sun has kissed me, and promised me a little flower on Sunday!—a little flower on Sunday!"

And then they entered a chamber where the walls were covered with hog's leather, and printed with gold flowers.

> "The gilding decays,
> But hog's leather stays!"

said the walls.

And there stood easy chairs, with such high backs, and so carved out, and with arms on both sides. "Sit down! sit down!" said they. "Ugh! how I creak; now I shall certainly get the gout, like the old clothes-press, ugh!"

And then the little boy came into the room where the projecting windows were, and where the old man sat.

"I thank you for the pewter soldier, my little friend!" said the old man, "and I thank you because you come over to me."

"Thankee! thankee!" or "cranky! cranky!" sounded from all the furniture; there was so much of it, that each article stood in the other's way, to get a look at the little boy.

In the middle of the wall hung a picture representing a beautiful lady, so young, so glad, but dressed quite as in former times, with clothes that stood quite stiff, and with powder in her hair; she neither said "thankee, thankee!" nor "cranky, cranky" but looked with her mild eyes at the little boy, who directly asked the old man, "Where did you get her?"

"Yonder, at the broker's," said the old man, "where there are so many pictures hanging. No one knows or cares about them, for they are all of them buried; but I knew her in by-gone days, and now she has been dead and gone these fifty years!"

Under the picture, in a glazed frame, there hung a *bouquet* of withered flowers; they were almost fifty years old; they looked so very old !

The pendulum of the great clock went to and fro, and the hands turned, and every thing in the room became still older; but they did not observe it.

"They say at home," said the little boy, "that you are so very, very lonely!"

"Oh!" said he, "the old thoughts, with what they may bring with them, come and visit me, and now you also come! I am very well off!"

Then he took a book with pictures in it down from the shelf; there were whole long processions and pageants, with the strangest characters, which one never sees now-a-days; soldiers like the knave of clubs, and citizens with waving flags: the tailors had theirs, with a pair of shears held oy two lions,—and the shoemakers thejrs, without boots, but with an eagle that had two heads, for the shoemakers must have everything so that they can say, it is a pair!--Yes, that was a picture book!

The old man now went into the other room to fetch preserves, apples, and nuts;— yes, it was delightful over there in the old house.

"I cannot bear it any longer!" said the pewter soldier, who sat on the drawers; "it is so lonely and melancholy here! but when one has been in a family circle one cannot accustom oneself to this life! I cannot bear it any longer! the whole day is so long, and the evenings are still longer! here it is not at all as it is over the way at your home, where your father and mother spoke so pleasantly, and where you and all your sweet children made such a delightful noise. Nay, how lonely the old man is!—do you think that he gets kisses? do you think he gets mild eyes, or a Christmas tree?—He will get nothing but a grave .—I can bear it no longer !"

"You must not let it grieve you so much," said the little boy ; "I find it so very delightful here, and then all the old thoughts, with what they may bring with them, they come and visit here."

"Yes, it's all very well, but I see nothing of them, and I don't know them !" said the pewter soldier, "I cannot bear it !"

"But you must !" said the little boy.

Then in came the old man with the most pleased and happy face, the most delicious preserves, apples, and nuts, and so the little boy thought no more about the pewter soldier.

The little boy returned home happy and pleased, and weeks and days passed away, and nods were made to the old house, and from the old house, and then the little boy went over there again.

The carved trumpeters blew, "trateratra! there is the little boy! trateratra!" and the swords and armor on the knights' portraits rattled, and the silk gowns rustled ; the hog's-leather spoke, and the old chairs had the gout

2

in their legs and rheumatism in their backs:
Ugh!—it was exactly like the first time, for
over there one day and hour was just like
another.

"I cannot bear it!" said the pewter soldier,
"I have shed pewter tears! it is too melancholy! rather let me go to the wars and lose
arms and legs! it would at least be a change.
I cannot bear it longer!—Now, I know what
it is to have a visit from one's old thoughts,
with what they may bring with them! I
have had a visit from mine, and you may be
sure it is no pleasant thing in the end; I was
at last about to jump down from the drawers.

"I saw you all over there at home so distinctly, as if you really were here; it was
again that Sunday morning; all you children
stood before the table and sung your Psalms,
as you do every morning. You stood devoutly
with folded hands; and father and mother
were just as pious; and then the door was
opened, and little sister Mary, who is not two
years old yet, and who always dances when
she hears music or singing, of whatever kind
it may be, was put into the room—though she
ought not to have been there—and then she

began to dance, but could not keep time, because the tones were so long ; and then she
stood, first on the one leg, and bent her head
forwards, and then on the other leg, and bent
her head forwards—but all would not do. You
stood very seriously all together, although
it was difficult enough ; but I laughed to myself, and then I fell off the table, and got a
bump, which I have still—for it was not right
of me to laugh. But the whole now passes
before me again in thought, and everything
that I have lived to see ; and these are the old
thoughts, with what they may bring with them.

"Tell me if you still sing on Sundays?
Tell me something about little Mary! and
how my comrade, the other pewter soldier,
lives! Yes, he is happy enough, that's sure!
I cannot bear it any longer!"

"You are given away as a present!" said
the little boy; "you must remain. Can you
not understand that?"

The old man now came with a drawer, in
which there was much to be seen, both "tin
boxes" and "balsam boxes," old cards, so
large and so gilded, such as one never sees

them now. And several drawers were opened, and the piano was opened ; it had landscapes on the inside of the lid, and it was so hoarse when the old man played on it ! and then he hummed a song.

"Yes, she could sing that !" said he, and nodded to the portrait, which he had bought at the broker's, and the old man's eyes shone so bright !

"I will go to the wars! I will go to the wars !" shouted the pewter soldier as loud as he could, and threw himself off the drawers right down on the floor.

What became of him ? The old man sought, and the little boy sought ; he was away, and he stayed away.

"I shall find him !" said the old man ; but he never found him. The floor was too open —the pewter soldier had fallen through a crevice, and there he lay as in an open tomb.

That day passed, and the little boy went home, and that week passed, and several weeks too. The windows were quite frozen, the little boy was obliged to sit and breathe on them to get a peep-hole over to the old house, and there the snow had been blown

:nto all the carved work and inscriptions; it lay quite up over the steps, just as if there was no one at home;—nor was there any one at home—the old man was dead!

In the evening there was a hearse seen before the door, and he was borne into it in his coffin: he was now to go out into the country, to lie in his grave. He was driven out there, but no one followed; all his friends were dead, and the little boy kissed his hand to the coffin as it was driven away.

Some days afterwards there was an auction at the old house, and the little boy saw from his window how they carried the old knights and the old ladies away, the flower-pots with the long ears, the old chairs, and the old clothes-presses. Something came here, and something came there; the portrait of her who had been found at the broker's came to the broker's again; and there it hung, for no one knew her more—no one cared about the old picture.

In the spring they pulled the house down, for, as people said, it was a ruin. One could see from the street right into the room with the hog's-leather hanging, which was slashed

and torn ; and the green grass and leaves
about the balcony hung quite wild about the
falling beams.—And then it was put to rights.

"That was a relief," said the neighboring
houses.

*   *   *   *   *   *   *

A fine house was built there, with large
windows, and smooth white walls; but before it, where the old house had in fact stood,
was a little garden laid out, and a wild grape-
vine ran up the wall of the neighboring house.
Before the garden there was a large iron railing with an iron door, it looked quite splendid,
and people stood still and peeped in, and the
sparrows hung by scores in the vine, and
chattered away at each other as well as they
could, but it was not about the old house, for
they could not remember it, so many years
had passed,—so many that the little boy had
grown up to a whole man, yes, a clever man,
and a pleasure to his parents; and he had
just been married, and, together with his little
wife, had come to live in the house here,
where the garden was ; and he stood by her
there whilst she, planted a field-flower that
she found so pretty ; she planted it with her

little hand, and pressed the earth around it with her fingers. Oh! what was that? She had stuck herself. There sat something pointed, straight out of the soft mould.

It was —— yes, guess!—it was the pewter soldier, he that was lost up at the old man's, and had tumbled and turned about amongst the timber and the rubbish, and had at last laid for many years in the ground.

The young wife wiped the dirt off the soldier, first with a green leaf, and then with her fine handkerchief—it had such a delightful smell, that it was to the pewter soldier just as if he had awaked from a trance.

"Let me see him," said the young man. He laughed, and then skook his head. "Nay, it cannot be he; but he reminds me of a story about a pewter soldier which I had when I was a little boy!" And then he told his wife about the old house, and the old man, and about the pewter soldier that he sent over to him because he was so very, very lonely; and he told it as correctly as it had really been, so that the tears camê into the eyes of his young wife, on account of the old house and the old man.

h h

"It may possib'y be, however, that it is the same pewter soldier!" said she, "I will take care of it, and remember all that you have told me ; but you must show me the old man's grave!"

" But I do not know it," said he, " and no one knows it! all his friends were dead, no one took care of it, and I was then a little boy!"

"How very, very lonely he must have been!" said she.

" Very, very lonely!" said the pewter soldier ; "but it is delightful not to be forgotten!"

" Delightful !" shouted something close by ; but no one, except the pewter soldier, saw that it was a piece of the hog's-leather hangings ; it had lost all its gilding, it looked like a piece of wet clay, but it had an opinion, and it gave it :

> " The gilding decays,
> But hog's leather stays!"

This the pewter soldier did not believe.

THE DROP OF WATER.

HAT a magnifying glass is, you surely know—such a round sort of spectacle-glass that makes everything full a hundred times larger than it really is. When one holds it before the eye, and looks at a drop of water out of the pond, then one sees above a thousand strange creatures. It looks almost like a whole plateful of shrimps springing about among each other, and they are so ravenous, they tear one another's arms and legs, tails and sides, and yet they are glad and pleased in their way.

Now, there was once an old man, who was called by every body Creep-and-Crawl; for that was his name. He would always make the best out of everything, and when he could not make anything out of it, he resorted to witchcraft.

Now, one day he sat and held his magnifying glass before his eye, and looked at a drop of water that was taken out of a little pool in the ditch. What a creeping and crawling was there! all the thousands of small creatures hopped and jumped about, pulled one another, and pecked one another.

"But this is abominable!" said Creep-and-Crawl, "Can one not get them to live in peace and quiet, and each mind his own business?" And he thought and thought, but he could come to no conclusion, and so he was obliged to conjure. "I must give them a color, that they may be more discernible!" said he; and so he poured something like a little drop of red wine into the drop of water, but it was bewitched blood from the lobe of the ear— the very finest sort for a penny; and then all the strange creatures became rose-colored over the whole body. It looked like a whole town of naked savages.

"What have you got there?" said another old wizard, who had no name, and that was just the best of it.

"Why," said Creep-and-Crawl, "if you can guess what it is, I will make you a present of it; but it is not so easy to find out when one does not know it!"

The wizard who had no name looked through the magnifying glass. It actually appeared like a whole town, where all the inhabitants ran about without clothes! it was terrible, but still more terrible to see how the one knocked and pushed the other, bit each other, and drew one another about. What was undermost should be topmost, and what was topmost should be undermost!—See there, now! his leg is longer than mine!—whip it off, and away with it! There is one that has a little lump behind the ear, a little innocent lump, but it pains him, and so it shall pain him still more! And they pecked at it, and they dragged him about, and they ate him, and all on account of the little lump. There sat one as still as a little maid, who only wished for peace and quietness, but she must be brought out and they dragged her, and they pulled her, and they devoured her!

"It is quite amusing!" said the wizard.

"Yes; but what do you think it is?" asked Creep-and-Crawl. "Can you find it out!"

"It is very easy to see," said the other, "it is some great city, they all resemble each other. A great city it is, that's sure!"

"It is ditch-water!" said Creep-and-Crawl.

THE HAPPY FAMILY.

EALLY, the largest green leaf in this country is a dock-leaf; if one holds it before one, it is like a whole apron, and if one holds it over one's head in rainy weather, it is almost as good as an umbrella, for it is so immensely large. The burdock never grows alone, but where there grows one there always grow several: it is a great delight, and all this delightfulness is snails' food. The great white snails which persons of quality in former times made fricassees of, ate, and said, "Hem, hem! how delicious!" for they thought

29

it tasted so delicate—lived on dock leaves, and therefore burdock seeds were sown.

Now, there was an old nanor-house, where they no longer ate snails, they were quite extinct ; but the burdocks were not extinct, they grew and grew all over the walks and all the beds; they could not get the mastery over them—it was a whole forest of burdocks. Here and there stood an apple and a plumb-tree, or else one never would have thought that it was a garden ; all was burdocks, and there lived the two last venerable old snails.

They themselves knew not how old they were, but they could remember very well that there had been many more; that they were of a family from foreign lands, and that for them and theirs the whole forest was planted. They had never been outside it, but they knew that there was still something more in the world, which was called the manor-house, and that there they were boiled, and then they became black, and were then placed on a silver dish; but what happened further they knew not; or, in fact, what it was to be boiled, and to lie on a silver dish, they could not possibly imagine; but it was said to be delightful, and particularly genteel. Neither the chafers, the toads, nor the earth-worms, whom they asked about it could give them any information,—none of them had been boiled or laid on a silver dish.

The old white snails were the first persons of distinction in the world, that they knew; the forest was planted for their sake, and the manor-house was there that they might be boiled and laid on a silver dish.

Now they lived a very lonely and happy life; and as they had no children themselves, they had adopted a little common snail, which they brought up as their own; but the little one would not grow, for he was of a common family; but the old ones, especially Dame Mother Snail, thought they could observe how he increased in size, and she begged father, if he could not see it, that he would at least feel the little snail's shell; and then he felt it, and found the good dame was right.

One day there was a heavy storm of rain.

"Hear how it beats like a drum on the dock leaves!" said Father Snail.

"There are also rain-drops!" said Mother Snail; "and now the rain pours right down

i i

the stalk! You will see that it will be wet
here! I am very happy to think that we
have our good house, and the little one has
his also! There is more done for us than
for all other creatures, sure enough; but can
you not see that we are folks of quality in the
world? We are provided with a house from
our birth, and the burdock forest is planted
for our sakes! I should like to know how far
it extends, and what there is outside!"

"There is nothing at all," said Father
Snail. "No place can be better than ours,
and I have nothing to wish for!"

"Yes," said the dame. "I would willingly go to the manor-house, be boiled, and laid
on a silver dish; all our forefathers have been
treated so; there is something extraordinary
in it, you may be sure!"

"The manor-house has most likely fallen
to ruin!" said Father Snail, "or the burdocks
have grown up over it, so that they cannot
come out. There need not, however, be any
haste about that; but you are always in such
a tremendous hurry, and the little one is be
ginning to be the same. Has he not been

creeping up that stalk these three days? It gives me a headache when I look up to him!"

"You must not scold him," said Mother Snail; "he creeps so carefully; he will afford us much pleasure—and we have nothing but him to live for! But have you not thought of it?—where shall we get a wife for him? Do you not think that there are some of our species at a great distance in the interior of the burdock forest?"

"Black snails, I dare say, there are enough of," said the old one—"black snails without a house—but they are so common, and so conceited. But we might give the ants a commission to look out for us; they run to and fro as if they had something to do, and they certainly know of a wife for our little snail!"

"I know one, sure enough—the most charming one!" said one of the ants; "but I am afraid we shall hardly succeed, for she is a queen!"

"That is nothing!" said the old folks; "has she a house?"

"She has a palace!" said the ant—"the finest ant's palace, with seven hundred passages!"

3

"I thank you!" said Mother Snail; "our son shall not go into an ant-hill; if you know nothing better than that, we shall give the commission to the white gnats. They fly far and wide, in rain and sunshine; they know the whole forest here, both within and without."

"We have a wife for him," said the gnats; "at a hundred human paces from here there sits a little snail in her house, on a gooseberry bush; she is quite lonely, and old enough to be married. It is only a hundred human paces!"

"Well, then, let her come to him!" said the old ones; "he has a whole forest of burdocks, she has only a bush!"

And so they went and fetched little Miss Snail. It was a whole week before she arrived; but therein was just the very best of it, for one could thus see that she was of the same species.

And then the marriage was celebrated. Six earth-worms shone as well as they could. In other respects the whole went off very quietly, for the old folks could not bear noise and merriment; but old Dame Snail made a brilliant speech. Father Snail could not speak, he was too much affected; and so they gave them as a dowry and inheritance, the whole forest of burdocks, and said—what they had always said—that it was the best in the world; and if they lived honestly and decently, and increased and multiplied, they and their children would once in the course of time come to the manor-house, be boiled black, and laid on silver dishes. After this speech was made, the old ones crept into their shells, and never more came out. They slept; the young couple governed in the forest, and had a numerous progeny, but they were never boiled, and never came on the silver dishes; so from this they concluded that the manor-house had fallen to ruins, and that all the men in the world were extinct; and as no one contradicted them, so, of course it was so. And the rain beat on the dock-leaves to make drum-music for their sake, and the sun shone in order to give the burdock forest a color for their sakes; and they were very happy, and the whole family was happy; for they, indeed were so.

MOTHER sat there with her little child. She was so down-cast, so afraid that it should die! It was so pale, the small eyes had closed them-selves, and it drew its breath so softly, now and then, with a deep respiration, as if it sighed; and the mother looked still more sorrow-fully on the little creature.

Then a knocking was heard at the door, and in came a poor old man wrapped up as in a large horse-cloth, for it warms one, and he needed it, as it was the cold winter season! Every thing out of doors was covered with ice and snow, and the wind blew so that it cut the face.

36

As the old man trembled with cold, and the little child slept a moment, the mother went and poured some ale into a pot and set it on the stove, that it might be warm for him; the old man sat and rocked the cradle, and the mother sat down on a chair close by him, and looked at her little sick child that drew its breath so deep, and raised its little hand.

"Do you not think that I shall save him?" said she, " *Our Lord* will not take him from me!"

And the old man,—it was Death himself,—he nodded so strangely, it could just as well signify yes as no. And the mother looked down in her lap, and the tears ran down over her cheeks; her head became so heavy—she had not closed her eyes for three days and nights; and now she slept, but only for a minute, when she started up and trembled with cold: "What is that?" said she, and looked on all sides; but the old man was gone, and her little child was gone—he had taken it with him; and the old clock in the corner burred, and burred, the great leaden weight ran down to the floor, bump! and then the clock also stood still.

But the poor mother ran out of the house and cried aloud for her child.

Out there, in the midst of the snow, there sat a woman in long, black clothes; and she said, "Death has been in thy chamber, and I saw him hasten away with thy little child; he goes faster than the wind, and he never brings back what he takes!"

"Oh, only tell me which way he went!" said the mother: "Tell me the way, and I shall find him!"

"I know it!" said the woman in the black clothes, "but before I tell it, thou must first sing for me all the songs thou hast sung for thy child!—I am fond of them; I have heard them before; I am Night; I saw thy tears whilst thou sang'st them!"

"I will sing them all, all!" said the mother; "but do not stop me now;—I may overtake him—I may find my child!"

But Night stood still and mute.   Then the mother wrung her hands, sang and wept, and there were many songs, but yet many more tears; and then Night said, "Go to the right, into the dark pine forest; thither I saw Death take his way with thy little child!"

The roads crossed each other in the depths of the forest, and she no longer knew whither she should go; then there stood a thorn-bush; there was neither leaf. nor flower on it, it was also in the cold winter season. and ice-flakes hung on the branches.

"Hast thou not seen Death go past with my little child?" said the mother.

"Yes," said the thorn-bush; "but I will not tell thee which way he took, unless thou wilt first warm me up at thy heart. I am freezing to death; I shall become a lump of ice!"

And she pressed the thorn-bush to her breast, so firmly, that it might be thoroughly warmed, and the thorns went right into her flesh, and her blood flowed in large drops, but the thorn-bush shot forth fresh green leaves, and there came flowers on it in the cold winter night, the heart of the afflicted mother was so warm; and the thorn-bush told her the way she should go.

She then came to a large lake, where there was neither ship nor boat. The lake was not frozen sufficiently to bear her; neither was it open, nor low enough that she could wade through it; and across it she must go if she would find her child! Then she lay down to drink up the lake, and that was an impossibility for a human being, but the afflicted mother thought that a miracle might happen nevertheless.

"Oh, what would I not give to come to my child!" said the weeping mother; and she wept still more, and her eyes sunk down in the depths of the waters, and became two precious pearls; but the water bore her up, as if she sat in a swing, and she flew in the rocking waves to the shore on the opposite side, where there stood a mile-broad, strange house, one knew not if it were a mountain with forests and caverns, or if it were built up; but the poor mother could not see it; she had wept her eyes out.

"Where shall I find Death, who took away my little child?" said she.

"He has not come here yet!" said the old grave woman, who was appointed to look after Death's great greenhouse! "How have

you been able to find the way hither? and
who has helped you?"

"*Our Lord* has helped me," said she. "He
is merciful, and you will also be so! Where
shall I find my little child?"

"Nay, I know not," said the woman, "and
you cannot see! Many flowers and trees
have withered this night; Death will soon
come and plant them over again! You certainly know that every person has his or her
life's tree or flower, just as every one happens
to be settled; they look like other plants, but
they have pulsations of the heart. Children's
hearts can also beat; go after yours, perhaps
you may know your child's; but what will
you give me if I tell you what you shall do
more?"

"I have nothing to give," said the afflicted
mother, "but I will go to the world's end for
you!"

"Nay, I have nothing to do there!" said
the woman, "but you can give me your long
black hair; you know yourself that it is fine,
and that I like! You shall have my white
hair instead!" and that's always something!"

"Do you demand nothing else?' said she,

—"that I will gladly give you!" And she gave ner her fine black hair, and got the old woman's snow-white hair instead.

So they went into Death's great greenhouse, where flowers and trees grew strangely into one another. There stood fine hyacinths under glass bells, and there stood strong-stemmed peonies; there grew water plants, some so fresh, others half sick, the water-snakes lay down on them, and black crabs pinched their stalks. There stood beautiful palm-trees, oaks, and plantains; there stood parsley and flowering thyme: every tree and every flower had its name; each of them was a human life, the human frame still lived—one in China, and another in Greenland—round about in the world. There were large trees in small pots, so that they stood so stunted in growth, and ready to burst the pots; in other places, there was a little dull flower in rich mould, with moss round about it, and it was so petted and nursed. But the distressed mother bent down over all the smallest plants, and heard within them how the human heart beat; and amongst millions she knew her child's.

"There it is!" cried she, and stretched her hands out over a little blue crocus, that hung quite sickly on one side.

"Don't touch the flower!" said the old woman, "but place yourself here, and when Death comes,—I expect him every moment, —do not let him pluck the flower up, but threaten him that you will do the same with the others. Then he will be afraid! he is responsible for them to *Our Lord*, and no one dares to pluck them up before *He* gives leave."

All at once an icy cold rushed through the great hall, and the blind mother could feel that it was Death that came.

"How hast thou been able to find thy way hither?" he asked. "How couldst thou come quicker than I?"

"I am a mother," said she.

And Death stretched out his long hand towards the fine little flower, but she held her hands fast around his, so tight, and yet afraid that she should touch one of the leaves. Then Death blew on her hands, and she felt that it was colder than the cold wind, and her hands fell down powerless.

"Thou canst not do anything against me!" said Death.

. "But that *Our Lord* can!" said she.

"I only do His bidding!" said Death. "I am His gardener, I take all His flowers and trees, and plant them out in the great garden of Paradise, in the unknown land; but how they grow there, and how it is there I dare not tell thee."

"Give me back my child!" said the mother, and she wept and prayed. At once she seized hold of two beautiful flowers close by, with each hand, and cried out to Death, "I will tear all thy flowers off, for I am in despair."

"Touch them not!" said Death. "Thou say'st that thou art so unhappy, and now thou wilt make another mother equally unhappy."

"Another mother!" said the poor woman, and directly let go her hold of both the flowers.

"There, thou hast thine eyes," said Death; "I fished them up from the lake, they shone so bright; I knew not they were thine. Take them again, they are now brighter than be fore; now look down into the deep well close by; I shall tell thee the names of the two flowers thou wouldst have torn up, and thou wilt see their whole future life—their whole human existence: and see what thou wast about to disturb and destroy."

And she looked down into the well; and it was a happiness to see how the one became a blessing to the world, to see how much happiness and joy were felt everywhere. And she saw the other's life, and it was sorrow and distress, horror, and wretchedness.

"Both of them are God's will!" said Death.

"Which of them is Misfortune's flower? and which is that of Happiness?" asked she.

"'That I will not tell thee," said Death; "but this thou shalt know from me, that the one flower was thy own child! it was thy child's fate thou saw'st,—thy own child's future life!"

Then the mother screamed with terror, "Which of them was my child? Tell it me! save the innocent! save my child from all that misery! rather take it away! take it into God's kingdom! Forget my tears, forget my prayers, and all that I have done!"

"I do not understand thee!" said Death. "Wilt thou have thy child again, or shall I go with it there, where thou dost not know!"

Then the mother wrung her hands, fell on her knees, and prayed to our Lord: "Oh, hear me not when I pray against Thy will, which is the best! hear me not! hear me not!"

And she bowed her head down in her lap, and Death took her child and went with it into the unknown land.

.

THE FALSE COLLAR.

HERE was once a fine gentleman, all of whose moveables were a boot-jack and a hair-comb: but he had the finest false collars in the world; and it is about one of these collars that we are now to hear a story.

It was so old, that it began to think of marriage; and it happened that it came to be washed in company with a garter.

"Nay!" said the collar, "I never did see anything so slender and so fine, so soft and so neat. May I not ask your name?"

"That I shall not tell you!" said the

k k   47

"Where do you live?" asked the collar.

But the garter was so bashful, so modest, and thought it was a strange question to answer.

"You are certainly a girdle," said the collar; "that is to say an inside girdle. I see well that you are both for use and ornament, my dear young lady."

"I will thank you not to speak to me," said the garter. "I think I have not given the least occasion for it."

"Yes! when one is as handsome as you," said the collar, "that is occasion enough."

"Don't come so near me, I beg of you!" said the garter. "You look so much like those men-folks."

"I am also a fine gentleman," said the collar. "I have a boot-jack and a hair-comb."

But that was not true, for it was his master who had them: but he boasted.

"Don't come so near me," said the garter: "I am not accustomed to it."

"Prude!" exclaimed the collar; and then it was taken out of the washing-tub. It was starched, hung over the back of a chair in the sunshine, and was then laid on the ironing-blanket; then came the warm box-iron. "Dear lady!" said the collar. "Dear widow-lady! I feel quite hot. I am quite changed. I begin to unfold myself. You will burn a hole in me. Oh! I offer you my hand."

"Rag!" said the box-iron; and went proudly over the collar: for she fancied she was a steam-engine, that would go on the railroad and draw the waggons. "Rag!" said the box-iron.

The collar was a little jagged at the edge, and so came the long scissors to cut off the jagged part.

"Oh!" said the collar, "you are certainly the first opera dancer. How well you can stretch your legs out! It is the most graceful performance I have ever seen. No one can imitate you."

"I know it," said the scissors.

"You deserve to be a baroness," said the collar. "All that I have, is, a fine gentleman, a boot-jack, and a hair-comb. If I only had the barony!"

"Do you seek my hand?" said the scissors; for she was angry; and without more ado, she *cut him*, and then he was condemned.

4

"I shall now be obliged to ask the hair-comb. It is surprising how well you preserve your teeth, Miss," said the collar. "Have you never thought of being betrothed?"

"Yes, of course! you may be sure of that," said the hair comb. "I *am* betrothed—to the boot-jack!"

"Betrothed!" exclaimed the collar. Now there was no other to court, and so he despised it.

A long time passed away, then the collar came into the rag chest at the paper mill; there was a large company of rags, the fine by themselves, and the coarse by themselves, just as it should be. They all had much to say, but the collar the most; for he was a real boaster.

"I have had such an immense number of sweet-hearts!" said the collar, "I could not be in peace! It is true, I was always a fine starched-up gentleman! I had both a boot-jack and a hair-comb, which I never used! You should have seen me then, you should have seen me when I lay down!—I shall never forget *my first love*—she was a girdle, so fine, so soft, and so charming, she threw

herself into a tub of water for my sake!
There was also a widow, who became glowing hot, but I left her standing till she got
black again ; there was also the first opera
dancer, she gave me that cut which I now
go with, she was so ferocious! my own hair-
comb was in love with me, she lost all her
teeth from the heart-ache ; yes, I have lived
to see much of that sort of thing ; but I am
extremely sorry for the garter—I mean the
girdle—that went into the water-tub. I have
much on my conscience, I want to become
white paper !"

And it became so, all the rags were turned
into white paper ; but the collar came to be
just this very piece of white paper we here
see, and on which the story is printed ; and
that was because it boasted so terribly afterwards of what had never happened to it. It
would be well for us to beware, that we may
not act in a similar manner, for we can never
know if we may not, in the course of time,
also come into the rag chest, and be made
into white paper, and then have our whole
life's history printed on it, even the most secret, and be obliged to run about and tell it
ourselves, just like this collar.

THE SHADOW.

T is in the hot lands
that the sun burns,
sure enough !—there
the people become
quite a mahogany
brown, ay, and in
the *hottest* lands they
are burnt to negroes.
But now it was only to the *hot* lands that a
learned man had come from the cold; there
he thought that he could run about just as
when at home, but he soon found out his
mistake.

He, and all sensible folks, were obliged to
stay within doors,—the window-shutters and
doors were closed the whole day ; it looked
as if the whole house slept, or there was
no one at home.

52

The narrow street with the high houses, was built so that the sunshine must fall there from morning till evening—it was really not to be borne.

The learned man from the cold lands—he was a young man, and seemed to be a clever man—sat in a glowing oven; it took effect on him, he became quite meagre—even his shadow shrunk in, for the sun had also an effect on it. It was first towards evening when the sun was down, that they began to freshen up again.

In the warm lands every window has a balcony, and the people came out on all the balconies in the street—for one must have air, even if one be accustomed to be mahogany!* It was lively both up and down the street. Tailors, and shoemakers, and all the

* The word *mahogany* can be understood, in Danish, as having two meanings. In general, it means the reddish-brown wood itself; but in jest, it signifies "excessively fine," which arose from an anecdote of Nyboder, in Copenhagen, (the seamen's quarter.) A sailor's wife, who was always proud and fine, in her way, came to her neighbor, and complained that she had got a splinter in her finger. "What of?" asked the neighbor's wife. "It is a mahogany splinter," said the other. "Mahoga-

folks, moved out into the street—chairs and
tables were brought forth—and candles
burnt—yes, above a thousand lights were
burning—and the one talked and the other
sung ; and people walked and church-bells
rang, and asses went along with a dingle-
dingle-dong ! for they too had bells on. The
street boys were screaming and hooting, and
shouting and shooting, with devils and deto-
nating balls :—and there came corpse bearers
and hood wearers,—for there were funerals
with psalm and hymn,—and then the din of
carriages driving and company arriving :—
yes, it was, in truth, lively enough down in
the street. Only in that single house, which
stood opposite that in which the learned foreigner lived, it was quite still ; and yet some
one lived there, for there stood flowers in the
balcony—they grew so well in the sun's heat!
—and that they could not do unless they were
watered—and some one must water them—
there must be somebody there. The door
opposite was also opened late in the evening,

ny! it cannot be less with you !" exclaimed the woman ;—and thence the proverb, " It is so mahogany !"—
(that is, so excessively fine)—is derived.

out it was dark within, at least in the front
room ; further in there was heard the sound
of music. The learned foreigner thought it
quite marvellous, but now—it might be that
ne only imagined it—for he found everything
marvellous out there, in the warm lands, if
there had only been no sun. The stranger's
landlord said that he didn't know who had
taken the house opposite, one saw no person
about, and as to the music, it appeared to
him to be extremely tiresome. " It is as if
some one sat there, and practised a piece that
he could not master—always the same piece.
'I shall master it!' says he ; but yet he cannot master it, however long he plays."

One night the stranger awoke—he slept
with the doors of the balcony open—the curtain before it was raised by the wind, and he
thought that a strange lustre came from the
opposite neighbor's house; all the flowers
shone like flames, in the most beautiful colors, and in the midst of the flowers stood a
slender, graceful maiden,—it was as if she
also shone; the light really hurt his eyes
He now opened them quite wide—yes, he
was quite awake; with one spring he was on
 11

the floor; he crept gently behind the curtain but the maiden was gone; the flowers shone no longer, but there they stood, fresh and blooming as ever; the door was ajar, and, far within, the music sounded so soft and delightful, one could really melt away in sweet thoughts from it. Yet it was like a piece of enchantment. And who lived there? Where was the actual entrance? The whole of the ground-floor was a row of shops, and there people could not always be running through.

One evening the stranger sat out on the balcony. The light burnt in the room behind him; and thus it was quite natural that his shadow should fall on his opposite neighbor's wall. Yes! there it sat, directly opposite, between the flowers on the balcony; and when the stranger moved, the shadow also moved: for that it always does.

"I think my shadow is the only living thing one sees over there," said the learned man. "See! how nicely it sits between the flowers. The door stands half-open: now the shadow should be cunning, and go into the room, look about, and then come and tell me what it had seen. Come, now! be useful and do me a

service," said he, in jest. "Have the kind-
ness to step in. Now! art thou going?" and
then he nodded to the shadow, and the shadow nodded again. "Well then, go! but
don't stay away."

The stranger rose, and his shadow on the
opposite neighbor's balcony rose also; the
stranger turned round and the shadow also
turned round. Yes! if any one had paid
particular attention to it, they would have
seen, quite distinctly, that the shadow went
in through the half-open balcony-door of their
opposite neighbor, just as the stranger went
into his own room, and let the long curtain
fall down after him.

Next morning, the learned man went out
to drink coffee and read the newspapers.

"What is that?" said he, as he came out
into the sunshine. "I have no shadow! So
then, it has actually gone last night, and not
come again. It is really tiresome!"

This annoyed him: not so much because
the shadow was gone, but because he knew
there was a story about a man without a
shadow.* It was known to everybody at

*Peter Schlemihl, the shadowless man.

home, in the cold lands; and if the learned man now came there and told his story, they would say that he was imitating it, and that he had no need to do. He would, therefore, not talk about it at all; and that was wisely thought.

In the evening he went out again on the balcony. He had placed the light directly behind him, for he knew that the shadow would always have its master for a screen, but he could not entice it. He made himself little; he made himself great: but no shadow came again. He said, "Hem! hem!" but it was of no use.

It was vexatious; but in the warm lands every thing grows so quickly; and after the apse of eight days he observed, to his great oy, that a new shadow came in the sunshine. In the course of three weeks he had a very fair shadow, which, when he set out for his home in the northern lands, grew more and more in the journey, so that at last it was so long and so large, that it was more than sufficient.

The learned man then came home, and he wrote books about what was true in the

world, and about what was good and what
was beautiful; and there passed days and
years,—yes! many years passed away.

One evening, as he was sitting in his room,
there was a gentle knocking at the door.

"Come in!" said he; but no one came in;
so he opened the door, and there stood before
him such an extremely lean man, that he
felt quite strange. As to the rest, the man
was very finely dressed,—he must be a gentleman.

"Whom have I the honor of speaking to?"
asked the learned man.

"Yes! I thought as much," said the fine
man. "I thought you would not know me.
I have got so much body. I have even got
flesh and clothes. You certainly never
thought of seeing me so well off. Do you
not know your old shadow? You certainly
thought I should never more return. Things
have gone on well with me since I was last
with you. I have, in all respects, become
very well off. Shall I purchase my freedom
from service? If so, I can do it;" and then
he rattled a whole bunch of valuable seals
that hung to his watch, and he stuck his

hand in the thick gold chain he wore around his neck ;—nay ! how all his fingers glittered with diamond rings; and then all were pure gems.

"Nay; I cannot recover from my surprise!" said the learned man : "what is the meaning of all this?"   •

"Something common, is it not," said the shadow : "but you yourself do not belong to the common order; and I, as you know well, have from a child followed in your footsteps, As soon as you found I was capable to go out alone in the world, I went my own way. I am in the most brilliant circumstances, but there came a sort of desire over me to see you once more before you die; you will die, I suppose? I also wished to see this land again,—for you know. we always love our native land. I know you have got another shadow again; have I anything to pay to it or you? If so, you will oblige me by saying what it is."

"Nay, is it really thou?" said the learned man : "it is most remarkable: I never imagined that one's old shadow could come again as a man."

"Tell me what I have to pay," said the shadow; "for I don't like to be in any sort of debt."

"How canst thou talk so?" said the learned man; "what debt is there to talk about? Make thyself as free as any one else. I am extremely glad to hear of thy good fortune: sit down, old friend, and tell me a little how it has gone with thee, and what thou hast seen at our opposite neighbor's there—in the warm lands."

"Yes, I will tell you all about it," said the shadow, and sat down: "but then you must also promise me, that, wherever you may meet me, you will never say to any one here in the town that I have been your shadow. I intend to get betrothed, for I can provide for more than one family."

"Be quite at thy ease about that," said the learned man; "I shall not say to any one who thou actually art: here is my hand—I promise it, and a man's bond is his word."

"A word is a shadow," said the shadow, "and as such it must speak."

It was really quite astonishing how much of a man it was. It was dressed entirely in black, and of the very finest cloth; it had patent leather boots, and a hat that could be folded together, so that it was bare crown and brim; not to speak of what we already know it had—seals, gold neck-chain, and diamond rings; yes, the shadow was well-dressed, and it was just that which made it quite a man.

"Now I shall tell you my adventures," said the shadow; and then he sat, with the polished boots, as heavily as he could, on the arm of the learned man's new shadow, which lay like a poodle-dog at his feet. Now this was perhaps from arrogance; and the shadow on the ground kept itself so still and quiet, that it might hear all that passed: it wished to know how it could get free, and work its way up, so as to become its own master.

"Do you know who lived in our opposite neighbor's house?" said the shadow; "it was the most charming of all beings, it was Poesy! I was there for three weeks, and that has as much effect as if one had lived three thousand years, and read all that was composed and written; that is what I say, and it is right. I have seen everything and I know everything !"

"Poesy !" cried the learned man ; "yes, yes, she often dwells a recluse in large cities ! Poesy ! yes, I have seen her,—a single short moment, but sleep came into my eyes ! She stood on the balcony and shone as the aurora borealis shines. Go on, go on ! —thou wert on the balcony, and went through the doorway, and then ——"

"Then I was in the antechamber," said the shadow. "You always sat and looked over to the antechamber. There was no light ; there was a sort of twilight, but the one door stood open directly opposite the other through a long row of rooms and saloons, and there it was lighted up. I should have been completely killed if I had gone over to the maiden ; but I was circumspect, I took time to think, and that one must always do."

"And what didst thou then see ?" asked the learned man.

"I saw everything, and I shall tell all to you : but,—it is no pride on my part,—as a free man, and with the knowledge I have, not to speak of my position in life, my excellent circumstances,—I certainly wish that you would say *you** to me!"

"I beg your pardon," said the learned man; "it is an old habit with me. *You* are perfectly right, and I shall remember it; but now *you* must tell me all *you* saw!"

"Everything!" said the shadow, "for I saw everything, and I know everything!"

"How did it look in the furthest saloon?' asked the learned man. "Was it there as in

---

* It is the custom in Denmark for intimate acquaintances to use the second person singular, "Du," (thou) when speaking to each other. When a friendship is formed between men, they generally affirm it, when occasion offers, either in public or private, by drinking to each other and exclaiming, "*thy health,*" at the same time striking their glasses together.—This is called drinking "*Duus:*"—they are then, "*Duus Brodre,*" (thou brothers,) and ever afterwards use the pronoun "*thou,*" to each other, it being regarded as more familiar than "De," (you). Father and mother, sister and brother, say *thou* to one another—without regard to age or rank. Master and mistress say *thou* to their servants—the superior to the inferior. But servants and inferiors do not use the same term to their masters, or superiors—nor is it ever used when speaking to a stranger, or any one with whom they are but slightly acquainted—they then say as in English—*you.*

the fresh woods? Was it there as in a holy church? Were the saloons like the starlit firmament when we stand on the high mountains?"

"Everything was there!" said the shadow. "I did not go quite in, I remained in the foremost room, in the twilight, but I stood there quite well; I saw everything, and I know everything! I have been in the antechamber at the court of Poesy."

"But *what did* you see? Did all the gods of the olden times pass through the large saloons? Did the old heroes combat there? Did sweet children play there, and relate their dreams?"

"I tell you I was there, and you can conceive that I saw everything there was to be seen. Had you come over there, you would not have been a man; but I became so! And besides, I learned to know my inward nature, my innate qualities, the relationship I had with Poesy. At the time I was with you, I thought not of that, but always—you know it well—when the sun rose, and when the sun went down, I became so strangely great; in the moonlight I was very near being

5

more distinct than yourself; at that time 1
did not understand my nature; it was revealed to me in the antechamber! I became
a man!—I came out matured; but you were
no longer in the warm lands;—as a man I
was ashamed to go as I did. I was in want
of boots, of clothes, of the whole human var-
nish that makes a man perceptible. I took
my way—I tell it to you, but you will not put
it in any book—I took my way to the cake
woman—I hid myself behind her; the woman didn't think how much she concealed.
I went out first in the evening; I ran about
the streets in the moonlight; I made myself
long up the walls—it tickles the back so delightfully! I ran up, and ran down, peeped
into the highest windows, into the saloons,
and on the roofs, I peeped in where no one
could peep, and I saw what no one else saw,
what no one else should see! This is, in fact,
a base world! I would not be a man if it
were not now once accepted and regarded as
something to be so! I saw the most unim-
aginable things with the women, with the
men, with parents, and with the sweet,
matchless children; I saw," said the shadow

"what no human being must know, but what, they would all so willingly know—what is bad in their neighbor. Had I written a newspaper, it would have been read! but I wrote direct to the persons themselves, and there was consternation in all the towns where I came. They were so afraid of me, and yet they were so excessively fond of me. The professors made a professor of me; the tailors gave me new clothes—I am well furnished; the master of the mint struck new coin for me, and the women said I was so handsome! and so I became the man I am. And I now bid you farewell;—here is my card—I live on the sunny side of the street, and am always at home in rainy weather!" And so away went the shadow.

"That was most extraordinary!" said the learned man

Years and days passed away, then the shadow came again.

"How goes it?" said the shadow.

"Alas!" said the learned man, "I write about the true, and the good, and the beautiful, but no one cares to hear such things; I am quite desperate, for I take it so much to heart!"

"But I don't!" said the shadow, "I become fat, and it is that one wants to become! You do not understand the world. You will become ill by it. You must travel! I shall make a tour this summer; will you go with me?—I should like to have a travelling companion! will you go with me, as shadow? It will be a great pleasure for me to have you with me; I shall pay the travelling expenses!"

"Nay, this is too much!" said the learned man.

"It is just as one takes it!"—said the shadow. "It will do you much good to travel! —will you be my shadow?—you shall have everything free on the journey!"

"Nay, that is too bad!" said the learned man.

"But it is just so with the world!" said the shadow,—"and so it will be!"—and away it went again.

The learned man was not at all in the most enviable state; grief and torment followed him, and what he said about the true, and the good, and the beautiful, was, to most

persons, like roses for a cow!—he was quite
ill at last.

"You really look like a shadow!" said his
friends to him; and the learned man trembled, for he thought of it.

"You must go to a watering-place!" said
the shadow, who came and visited him;
"there is nothing else for it! I will take you
with me for old acquaintance' sake; I will
pay the travelling expenses, and you write
the descriptions—and if they are a little
amusing for me on the way! I will go to a
watering-place,—my beard does not grow out
as it ought—that is also a sickness—and one
must have a beard! Now you be wise and
accept the offer; we shall travel as comrades!"

And so they travelled; the shadow was
master, and the master was the shadow; they
drove with each other, they rode and walked
together, side by side, before and behind, just
as the sun was; the shadow always took
care to keep itself in the master's place. Now
the learned man didn't think much about
that; he was a very kind-hearted man, and
particularly mild and friendly, and so he said
one day to the shadow: "As we have now

become companions, and in this way have grown up together from childhood, shall we not drink '*thou*' together, it is more familiar?"

"You are right," said the shadow, who was now the proper master. "It is said in a very straight-forward and well-meant manner. You, as a learned man, certainly know how strange nature is. Some persons cannot bear to touch grey paper, or they become ill; others shiver in every limb if one rub a pane of glass with a nail: I have just such a feeling on hearing you say *thou* to me; I feel myself as if pressed to the earth in my first situation with you. You see that it is a feeling; that it is not pride: I cannot allow you to say *thou* to me, but I will willingly say *thou* to you, so it is half done!"

So the shadow said *thou* to its former master.

"This is rather too bad," thought he, that I must say *you* and he say *thou*," but he was now obliged to put up with it.

So they came to a watering-place where there were many strangers, and amongst there was a princess, who was troubled with seeing too well; and that was so alarming!

She directly observed that the stranger who had just come was quite a different sort of person to all the others;—"He has come here in order to get his beard to grow, they say, but I see the real cause, he cannot cast a shadow."

She had become inquisitive; and so she entered into conversation directly with the strange gentleman, on their promenades. As the daughter of a king, she needed not to stand upon trifles, so she said, "Your complaint is, that you cannot cast a shadow?"

"Your Royal Highness must be improving considerably," said the shadow,—"I know your complaint is, that you see too clearly, but it has decreased, you are cured. I just happen to have a very unusual shadow! Do you not see that person who always goes with me? Other persons have a common shadow, but I do not like what is common to all. We give our servants finer cloth for their livery than we ourselves use, and so I had my shadow trimmed up into a man: yes, you see I have even given him a shadow. It

m m

is somewhat expensive, but I like to have something for myself!"

"What!" thought the princess, "should I really be cured! These baths are the first in the world! In our time water has wonderful powers. But I shall not leave the place, for it now begins to be amusing here. I am extremely fond of that stranger : would that his beard should not grow! for in that case he will leave us."

In the evening, the princess and the shadow danced together in the large ball-room. She was light, but he was still lighter; she had never had such a partner in the dance. She told him from what land she came, and he knew that land; he had been there, but then she was not at home; he had peeped in at the window, above and below—he had seen both the one and the other, and so he could answer the princess, and make insinuations, so that she was quite astonished; he must be the wisest man in the whole world! she felt such respect for what he knew! So that when they again danced together she fell in love with him; and that the shadow could remark, for she almost pierced him through with her eyes. So they danced once more together; and she was about to declare herself, but she was discreet; she thought of her country and kingdom, and of the many persons she would have to reign over.

"He is a wise man," said she to herself— "It is well; and he dances delightfully—that is also good; but has he solid knowledge?— that is just as important!—he must be examined."

So she began, by degrees, to question him about the most difficult things she could think of, and which she herself could not have answered; so that the shadow made a strange face.

"You cannot answer these questions?" said the princess.

"They belong to my childhood's learning," said the shadow. "I really believe my shadow, by the door there, can answer them!"

"Your shadow!" said the princess; "that would indeed be marvellous!"

"I will not say for a certainty that he can," said the shadow, "but I think so; he has now followed me for so many years. and listened to my conversation—I should think it possible. But your royal highness will permit me to observe, that he is so proud of passing himself off for a man, that when he is to be in a proper humor—and he must be so to answer well—he must be treated quite like a man."

"Oh! I like that!" said the princess.

So she went to the learned man by the door, and she spoke to him about the sun and the moon, and about persons out of and in the world, and he answered with wisdom and prudence.

"What a man that must be who has so wise a shadow!" thought she; "It will be a real blessing to my people and kingdom if I choose him for my consort—I will do it!"

They were soon agreed, both the princess and the shadow; but no one was to know about it before she arrived in her own kingdom.

"No one—not even my shadow!" said the shadow, and he had his own thoughts about it!

Now they were in the country where the princess reigned when she was at home.

"Listen, my good friend," said the shadow to the learned man. "I have now become

as happy and mighty as any one can be; I
will, therefore, do something particular for
thee! Thou shalt always live with me in
the palace, drive with me in my royal carriage, and have ten thousand pounds a year;
but then thou must submit to be called *shadow* by all and every one; thou must not
say that thou hast ever been a man; and
once a-year, when I sit on the balcony in the
sunshine, thou must lie at my feet, as a shadow shall do! I must tell thee: I am going
to marry the king's daughter, and the nuptials are to take place this evening!"

"Nay, this is going too far!" said the learned man; "I will not have it; I will not do
it! it is to deceive the whole country and the
princess too! I will tell every thing!—that
I am a man, and that thou art a shadow—
thou art only dressed up!"

"There is no one who will believe it!" said
the shadow; "be reasonable, or I will call
the guard!"

"I will go directly to the princess!" said
the learned man.

"But I will go first!" said the shadow,
and thou wilt go to prison!" and that he

was obliged to do—for the sentinels obeyed him whom they knew the king's daughter was to marry.

"You tremble !" said the princess, as the shadow came into her chamber; "has any-thing happened? You must not be unwell this evening, now that we are to have our nuptials celebrated."

"I have lived to see the most cruel thing that any one can live to see !" said the sha-dow. "Only imagine—yes, it is true, such a poor shadow-skull cannot bear much—only think, my shadow has become mad; he thinks that he is a man, and that I—now only think—that I am his shadow !"

"It is terrible !" said the princess; "but he is confined, is he not?"

"That he is. I am afraid that he will never recover."

"Poor shadow !" said the princess, he is very unfortunate; it would be a real work of charity to deliver him from the little life he has, and, when I think properly over the matter, I am of opinion that it will be neces-sary to do away with him in all stillness !"

'It is certainly hard !" said the shadow,

"for he was a faithful servant!" and then he gave a sort of sigh.

"You are a noble character!" said the princess.

The whole city was illuminated in the evening, and the cannons went off with a bum! bum! and the soldiers presented arms. That was a marriage! The princess and the shadow went out on the balcony to show themselves, and get another hurrah!

The learned man heard nothing of all this —for they had deprived him of life.

THE OLD STREET-LAMP.

AVE you heard the story about the old street lamp? It is not so very amusing, but one may very well hear it once. It was such a decent old street-lamp, that had done its duty for many, many years, but now it was to be condemned. It was the last evening,—it sat there on the post and lighted the street; and it was in just such a humor as an old figurante in a ballet, who dances for the last evening, and knows that she is to be put on the shelf to-morrow. The lamp had such a fear of the coming day, for it knew that it should then

78

be carried to the town-hall for the first time, and examined by the authorities of the city, who should decide if it could be used or not. It would then be determined whether it should be sent out to one of the suburbs, or in to the country to a manufactory ; perhaps it would be sent direct to the ironfounder's and be re-cast ; in that case it could certainly be all sorts of things : but it pained it not to know whether it would then retain the remembrance of its having been a street-lamp.

However it might be, whether it went into the country or not, it would be separated from the watchman and his wife, whom it regarded as its family. It became a street-lamp when he became watchman. His wife was a very fine woman at that time ; it was only in the evening when she went past the lamp that she looked at it, but never in the daytime. Now, on the contrary, of late years, as they had all three grown old,—the watchman, his wife, and the lamp,—the wife had always attended to it, polished it up, and put oil in it. They were honest folks that married couple, they had not cheated the lamp of a single drop. It was its last evening

n n

in the street, and to-morrow it was to be taken
to the town-hall ; these were two dark
thoughts in the lamp, and so one can know
how it burnt.   But other thoughts also passed through it ; there was so much it had
seen, so much it had a desire for, perhaps
just as much as the whole of the city authorities ; but it didn't say so, for it was a well-
behaved old lamp—it would not insult any
one, least of all its superiors.   It remembered
so much, and now and then the flames within
it blazed up,—it was as if it had a feeling of
—yes, they will also remember me !   There
was now that handsome young man—but
that is many years since,—he came with a
letter, it was on rose-colored paper ; so fine—
so fine ! and with a gilt edge ; it was so neatly
written, it was a lady's hand ; he read it
twice, and he kissed it, and he looked up to
me with his two bright eyes—they said, "I
am the happiest of men !"   Yes, only he and
I knew what stood in that first letter from
his beloved.

    I also remember two other eyes—it is
strange how one's thoughts fly about !—there
was a grand funeral here in the street, the

beautiful young wife lay in the coffin on the
velvet-covered funeral car; there were so
many flowers and wreaths, there were so
many torches burning, that I was quite forgotten—out of sight; the whole footpath was
filled with persons; they all followed in the
procession; but when the torches were out
of sight, and I looked about, there stood one
who leaned against my post and wept. I
shall never forget those two sorrowful eyes
that looked into me. Thus there passed
many thoughts through the old street-lamp,
which this evening burnt for the last time.
The sentinel who is relieved from his post
knows his successor, and can say a few words
to him, but the lamp knew not its successor;
and yet it could have given him a hint about
rain and drizzle, and how far the moon shone
on the footpath, and from what corner the
wind blew.

Now, there stood three on the kerb-stone;
they had presented themselves before the
lamp, because they thought it was the street-
lamp who gave away the office; the one of
these three was a herring's head, for it shines
in the dark, and it thought that it could be of

6

great service, and a real saving of oil, if it came to be placed on the lamp-post. The other was a piece of touchwood, which also shines, and always more than a stock-fish; besides, it said so itself, it was the last piece of a tree that had once been the pride of the forest. The third was a glow-worm; but where it had come from the lamp could not imagine; but the glow-worm was there, and it also shone, but the touchwood and the herring's head took their oaths that it only shone at certain times, and therefore it could never be taken into consideration.

The old lamp said that none of them shone well enough to be a street-lamp; but not one of them thought so; and as they heard that it was not the lamp itself that gave away the office, they said that it was a very happy thing, for that it was too infirm and broken down to be able to choose.

At the same moment the wind came from the street corner, it whistled through the cowl of the old lamp, and said to it, "What is it that I hear, are you going away to-morrow? Is it the last evening I shall meet you here? Then you shall have a present!—now I will blow up your brain-box so that you shall not only remember, clearly and distinctly, what you have seen and heard, but when anything is told or read in your presence, you shall be so clear-headed that you will also see it."

"That is certainly much!" said the old street-lamp; "I thank you much; if I be only not re-cast."

"It will not happen yet awhile," said the wind; "and now I will blow up your memory; if you get more presents than that you may have quite a pleasant old age."

"If I be only not re-cast," said the lamp; "or can you then assure me my memory?"

"Old lamp, be reasonable!" said the wind, and then it blew. The moon came forth at the same time. "What do you give?" asked the wind.

"I give nothing!" said the moon; "I am waning, and the lamps have never shone for me, but I have shone for the lamps."* So the moon went behind the clouds

---

* It is the custom in Denmark, and one deserving the severest censure, that, on those nights in which the moon shines, or, according to almanac authority, ought to shine, the street lamps are not lighted; so that, as it too frequently happens, when the moon is over-

again, for it would not be plagued. A drop
of rain then fell straight down on the lamp's
cowl, it was like a drop of water from the
eaves, but the drop said that it came from the
grey clouds, and was also a present,—and
perhaps the best of all. "I penetrate into
you, so that you have the power, if you wish
it, in one night to pass over to rust, so that
you may fall in pieces and become dust."
But the lamp thought this was a poor present,
and the wind thought the same. "Is there
no better—is there no better?" it whistled, as
loud as it could. A shooting-star then fell,
it shone in a long stripe.

"What was that?" exclaimed the herring's
head; "did not a star fall right down? I
think it went into the lamp! Well, if persons who stand so high seek the office, we
may as well take ourselves off."

And it did so, and the others did so too;

clouded. or on rainy evenings when she is totally obscur-
ed, the streets are for the most part in perfect darkness.
This petty economy is called " the magistrates' light,"
they having the direction of the lighting, paving, and
cleansing of towns.

The same management may be met with in some
other countries besides Denmark.

but the old lamp shone all at once so singularly bright."

" 'That was a fine present !" it said ; " the
bright stars which I have always pleased
myself so much about, and which shine so
beautifully,—as I really have never been able
to shine, although it was my whole aim and
endeavor,—have noticed me, a poor old-lamp,
and sent one down with a present to me,
which consists of that quality, that everything
I myself remember and see quite distinctly,
shall also be seen by those I am fond of; and
that is, above all, a true pleasure, for what
one cannot share with others is but a half
delight."

" It is a very estimable thought," said the
wind ; " but you certainly don't know that
there must be wax-candles ; for unless a wax-
candle be lighted in you there are none of
the others that will be able to see anything
particular about you. The stars have not
thought of that ; they think that everything
which shines has, at least, a wax-candle in
it. But now I am tired," said the wind, " I
will now lie down;" and so it lay down to
rest.

The next day—yes, the next day we will
spring over: the next evening the lamp lay
in the arm chair,—and where? At the old
watchman's. He had, for his long and faithful services, begged of the authorities that he
might be allowed to keep the old lamp; they
laughed at him when he begged for it, and
then gave him it; and now the lamp lay in
the arm-chair, close by the warm stove, and
it was really just as if it had become larger
on that account,—it almost filled the whole
chair. The old folks now sat at their supper, and cast mild looks at the old lamp,
which they would willingly have given a
place at the table with them. It is true they
lived in a cellar, a yard or so below ground:
one had to go through a paved front-room to
come into the room they lived in; but it was
warm here, for there was list round the door
to keep it so. It looked clean and neat, with
curtains round the bed and over the small
windows, where two strange-looking flower-
pots stood on the sill. Christian, the sailor,
had brought them from the East or West
Indies; they were of clay in the form of two
elephants, the backs of which were wanting:

but in their place there came flourishing plants out of the earth that was in them ; in the one was the finest chive,—it was the old folks' kitchen-garden,—and in the other was a large flowering geranium—this was their flower-garden. On the wall hung a large colored print of "The Congress of Vienna ;" there they had all the kings and emperors at once. A Bornholm* clock, with heavy leaden weights went " tic-tac !" and always too fast ; but the old folks said it was better than if it went too slow. They ate their suppers, and the old lamp, as we have said, lay in the arm-chair close by the warm stove. It was, for the old lamp, as if the whole world was turned upside down. But when the old watch-man looked at it, and spoke about what they had lived to see with each other, in rain and

---

* Bornholm, a Danish island in the Baltic is famous for its manufactures of clocks, potteries, and cement ; it contains also considerable coal mines, though not worked to any extent. It is fertile in minerals, chalks, potters' clay of the finest quality, and other valuable natural productions ; but, on account of the jealous nature of the inhabitants, which deters foreigners from settling there, these productions are not made so available or profitable as they otherwise might be.

drizzle, in the clear, short summer nights, and when the snow drove about so that it was good to get into the pent-house of the cellar, —then all was again in order for the old lamp, it saw it all just as if it were now present;—yes! the wind had blown it up right well,—it had enlightened it.

The old folks were so clever and industrious, not an hour was quietly dozed away; on Sunday afternoons some book was always brought forth, particularly a book of travels, and the old man read aloud about Africa, about the great forests and the elephants that were there quite wild; and the old woman listened so attentively, and now and then took a side glance at the clay elephants—her flower-pots. "I can almost imagine it!" said she; and the lamp wished so much that there was a wax candle to light and be put in it, so that she could plainly see everything just as the lamp saw it; the tall trees, the thick branches twining into one another, the black men on horseback, and whole trains of elephants, which, with their broad feet, crushed the canes and bushes.

"Of what use are all my abilities when

there is no wax candle?" sighed the lamp;
"they have only train oil and tallow candles,
and they are not sufficient."

One day there came a whole bundle of
stumps of wax candles into the cellar, the
largest pieces were burnt, and the old woman
used the smaller pieces to wax her thread
with when she sewed ; there were wax candle ends, but they never thought of putting
a little piece in the lamp.

"Here I stand with my rare abilities," said
the lamp; "I have everything within me,
but I cannot share any part with them.
They know not that I can transform the
white walls to the prettiest paper-hangings,
to rich forests, to everything that they may
wish for. They know it not!"

For the rest, the lamp stood in a corner,
where it always met the eye, and it was neat
and well scoured ; folks certainly said it was
an old piece of rubbish ; but the old man and
his wife didn't care about that, they were
fond of the lamp.

One day it was the old watchman's birth
day; the old woman came up to the lamp,
smiled, and said, "I will illuminate for him,'

and the lamp's cowl creaked, for it thought,
"They will now be enlightened!" But she
put in train oil, and no wax candle; it burnt
the whole evening; but now it knew that
the gift which the stars had given it, the best
gift of all, was a dead treasure for this life.
It then dreamt—and when one has such
abilities, one can surely dream,—that the old
folks were dead, and that it had come to an
ironfounder's to be cast anew; it was in as
much anxiety as when it had to go to the
town-hall to be examined by the authorities;
but although it had the power to fall to pieces
in rust and dust, when it wished it, yet it
did not do it; and so it came into the furnace
and was re-cast as a pretty iron candlestick,
in which any one might set a wax candle.
It had the form of an angel, bearing a nosegay, and in the centre of the nosegay they
put a wax taper, and it was placed on a
green writing-table; and the room was so
snug and comfortable: there hung beautiful
pictures—there stood many books; it was at
a poet's, and everything that he wrote, un
veiled itself round about: the room became
a deep, dark forest,—a sun-lit meadow.

where the stork stalked about; and a ship's
deck high aloft on the swelling sea!

"What power I have!" said the old lamp,
as it awoke. "I almost long to be re-cast;—
but no, it must not be as long as the old folks
live. They are fond of me for the sake of
my person. I am to them as a child, and
they have scoured me, and they have given
me train oil. After all, I am as well off as
'The Congress,'—which is something so very
grand."

From that time it had more inward peace,
which was merited by the old street-lamp.

THE DREAM OF LITTLE TUK.

H! yes, that was little Tuk: in reality his name was not Tuk, but that was what he called himself before he could speak plain : he meant it for Charles, and it is all well enough if one do but know it. He had now to take care of his little sister Augusta, who was much less than himself, and he was, besides, to learn his lesson at the same time ; but these two things would not do together at all. There sat the poor little fellow with his sister on his lap, and he sang to her all the songs he knew ; and he glanced the while from

time to time into the geography-book that lay
open before him. By the next morning he
was to have learnt all the towns in Zealand
oy heart, and to know about them all that is
possible to be known.

His mother now came home, for she had
been out, and took little Augusta on her arm.
Tuk ran quickly to the window, and read
so eagerly that he pretty nearly read his
eyes out; for it got darker and darker, but
his mother had no money to buy a candle.

"There goes the old washerwoman over
the way," said his mother, as she looked out
of the window. "The poor woman can
hardly drag herself along, and she must now
drag the pail home from the fountain: be a
good boy, Tukey, and run across and help
the old woman, won't you?"

So Tuk ran over quickly and helped her;
but when he came back again into the room
it was quite dark, and as to a light, there was
no thought of such a thing. He was now to
go to bed; that was an old turn-up bedstead;
in it he lay and thought about his geography
lesson, and of Zealand, and of all that his
master had told him. He ought, to be sure,

to have read over his lesson again, but that, you know, he could not do. He therefore put his geography-book under his pillow, because he had heard that was a very good thing to do when one wants to learn one's lesson; but one cannot, however, rely upon it entirely. Well there he lay, and thought and thought, and all at once it was just as if some one kissed his eyes and mouth: he slept, and yet he did not sleep; it was as though the old washerwoman gazed on him with her mild eyes and said, "It were a great sin if you were not to know your lesson to-morrow morning. You have aided me; I therefore will now help you; and the loving God will do so at all times." And all of a sudden the book under Tuk's pillow began scraping and scratching.

"Kickery-ki! kluk! kluk! kluk!"—that was an old hen who came creeping along, and she was from Kjöge. I am a Kjöger hen,"* said she, and then she related how

---

* Kjöge, a town in the bay of Kjöge. "To see the Kjöge hens," is an expression similar to "showing a child London," which is said to be done by taking his head in both hands, and so lifting him off the ground. At the in-

many inhabitants there were there, and about the battle that had taken place, and which, after all, was hardly worth talking about.

"Kribledy, krabledy—plump!" down fell somebody: it was a wooden bird, the popinjay used at the shooting-matches at Prästöe. Now *he* said that there were just as many inhabitants as he had nails in his body ; and he was very proud. "Thorwaldsen lived almost next door to me.*   Plump ! here I lie capitally."

But little Tuk was no longer lying down : all at once he was on horseback. On he went at full gallop, still galloping on and on. A knight with a gleaming plume, and most magnificently dressed, held him before him on the horse, and thus they rode through the wood to the old town of Bordingborg, and

vasion of the English in 1807, an encounter of a no very glorious nature took place between the British troops and the undisciplined Danish militia.

* Prästöe, a still smaller town than Kjöge.   Some hundred paces from it lies the manor-house Ny Söe, where Thorwaldsen generally sojourned during his stay in Denmark, and where he called many of his immortal works into existence.

o o

that was a large and very lively town. High
towers rose from the castle of the king, and
the brightness of many candles streamed
from all the windows; within was dance and
song, and King Waldemar and the young,
richly-attired maids of honor danced together.
The morn now came; and as soon as the sun
appeared, the whole town and the king's palace crumbled together, and one tower after
the other; and at last only a single one remained standing where the castle had been
before,* and the town was so small and poor,
and the school boys came along with their
books under their arms, and said, "2000 inhabitants!" but that was not true, for there
were not so many.

And little Tukey lay in his bed: it seemed
to him as if he dreamed, and yet as if he
were not dreaming; however, somebody was
close beside him.

"Little Tukey! little Tukey!" cried some
one near. It was a seaman, quite a little

* Bordingborg, in the reign of King Waldemar a considerable place, now an unimportant little town. One
solitary tower only, and some remains of a wall, show
where the castle once stood.

personage, so little as if he were a midshipman ; but a midshipman it was not.

"Many remembrances from Cörsör.* That is a town that is just rising into importance ; a lively town that has steam-boats and stage-coaches : formerly people called it ugly, but that is no longer true. I lie on the sea," said Cörsör ; "I have high roads and gardens, and I have given birth to a poet who was witty and amusing, which all poets are not. I once intended to equip a ship that was to sail all round the earth ; but I did not do it, although I could have done so : and then, too, I smell so deliciously, for close before the gate bloom the most beautiful roses."

Little Tuk looked, and all was red and green before his eyes ; but as soon as the confusion of colors was somewhat over, all of a sudden there appeared a wooded slope close to the bay, and high up above stood a magnificent old church, with two high pointed

* Cörsör, on the Great Belt, called, formerly, before the introduction of steam-vessels, when travellers were often obliged to wait a long time for a favorable wind, "the most tiresome of towns." The poet Baggesen was born here.

7

towers.   From out the hill-side spouted foun
tains in thick streams of water, so that there
was a continual splashing; and close beside
them sat an old king with a golden crown
upon his white head : that was King Hroar,
near the fountains, close to the town of Roeskilde, as it is now called.   And up the slope
into the old church went all the kings and
queens of Denmark, hand in hand, all with
their golden crowns; and the organ played
and the fountains rustled.   Little Tuk saw
all, heard all.   " Do not forget the diet," said
King Hroar.*

Again all suddenly disappeared.   Yes, and
whither?   It seemed to him just as if one
turned over a leaf in a book.   And now stood
there an old peasant-woman, who came from
Soröe,† where grass grows in the market-

* Roeskilde, once the capital of Denmark. The town
takes its name from King Hroar, and the many fountains
in the neighborhood. In the beautiful cathedral the
greater number of the kings and queens of Denmark
are interred. In Roeskilde, too, the members of the
Danish Diet assemble.

† Soröe, a very quiet little town, beautifully situated,
surrounded by woods and lakes. Holberg, Denmark's
Molière, founded here an academy for the sons of the

place. She had an old grey linen apron
hanging over her head and back : it was so
wet, it certainly must have been raining
"Yes, that it has," said she ; and she now
related many pretty things out of Holberg's
comedies, and about Waldemar and Absalon;
but all at once she cowered together, and her
head began shaking backwards and forwards,
and she looked as she were going to make a
spring. "Croak ! croak !" said she : "it is
wet, it is wet ; there is such a pleasant death-
like stillness in Soröe !" She was now suddenly a frog, "Croak ;" and now she was an
old woman. "One must dress according to
the weather," said she. "It is wet, it is wet.'
My town is just like a bottle ; and one gets
in by the neck, and by the neck one must get
out again ! In former times I had the finest
fish, and now I have fresh rosy-cheeked boys
at the bottom of the bottle, who learn wisdom, Hebrew, Greek,—Croak !" When she
spoke it sounded just like the noise of frogs,
or as if one walked with great boots over a

nobles. The poets Hauch and Ingemann were appointed professors here. The latter lives there still.

moor; always the same tone, so uniform and so tiring that little Tuk fell into a good sound sleep, which, by the bye, could not do him any harm.

But even in this sleep there came a dream, or whatever else it was: his little sister Augusta, she with the blue eyes and the fair curling hair, was suddenly a tall, beautiful girl, and without having wings was yet able to fly; and she now flew over Zealand—over the green woods and the blue lakes.

"Do you hear the cock crow, Tukey? cock-a-doodle-doo! The cocks are flying up from Kjöge! You will have a farm-yard, so large, oh! so very large! You will suffer neither hunger nor thirst! You will get on in the world! You will be a rich and happy man! Your house will exalt itself like King Waldemar's tower, and will be richly decorated with marble statues, like that at Prästöe. You understand what I mean. Your name shall circulate with renown all round the earth, like unto the ship that was to have sailed from Cörsör; and in Roeskilde "——

"Do not forget the diet!" said King Hroar.

"Then you will speak well and wisely,

little Tukey ; and when at last you sink into your grave, you shall sleep as quietly "——

"As if I lay in Soröe," said Tuk, awaking. It was bright day, and he was now quite unable to call to mind his dream ; that, however, was not at all necessary, for one may not know what the future will bring.

And out of bed he jumped, and read in his book, and now all at once he knew his whole lesson.   And the old washerwoman popped her head in at the door, nodded to him friendly, and said,   "Thanks, many thanks, my good child, for your help ! May the good everloving God fulfil your loveliest dream !"

Little Tukey did not at all know what he had dreamed, but the loving God knew it.

THE NAUGHTY BOY.

LONG time ago there lived an old poet, a thoroughly kind old poet. As he was sitting one evening in his room, a dreadful storm arose without, and the rain streamed down from heaven; but the old poet sat warm and comfortable in his chimney-corner, where the fire blazed and the roasting apple hissed.

"Those who have not a roof over their heads will be wetted to the skin," said the good old poet.

"Oh let me in! let me in! I am cold, and

I'm so wet!" exclaimed suddenly a child
that stood crying at the door and knocking
for admittance, while the rain poured down,
and the wind made all the windows rattle.

"Poor thing!" said the old poet, as he
went to open the door. There stood a little
boy, quite naked, and the water ran down
from his long golden hair; he trembled with
cold, and had he not come into a warm room
he would most certainly have perished in the
frightful tempest.

"Poor child!" said the old poet, as he took
the boy by the hand. "Come in, come in,
and I will soon restore thee! Thou shalt
have wine and roasted apples, for thou art
verily a charming child!" And the boy
was so really. His eyes were like two
bright stars; and although the water trickled
down his hair, it waved in beautiful curls.
He looked exactly like a little angel, but he
was so pale, and his whole body trembled
with cold. He had a nice little bow in his
hand, but it was quite spoiled by the rain,
and the tints of his many-colored arrows ran
one into the other.

The old poet seated himself beside his
p p

hearth, and took the little fellow on his lap;
he squeezed the water out of his dripping
hair, warmed his hands between his own,
and boiled for him some sweet wine. Then
the boy recovered, his cheeks again grew
rosy, he jumped down from the lap where
he was sitting, and danced round the kind
old poet.

"You are a merry fellow," said the old
man; "what's your name?"

"My name is Cupid," answered the boy.
"Don't you know me? There lies my bow;
it shoots well, I can assure you! Look, the
weather is now clearing up, and the moon
is shining clear again through the window."

"Why, your bow is quite spoiled," said
the old poet.

"That were sad indeed," said the boy,
and he took the bow in his hand and examined it on every side. "Oh, it is dry
again, and is not hurt at all; the string is
quite tight. I will try it directly." And
he bent his bow, took aim, and shot an
arrow at the old poet, right into his heart.
"You see now that my bow was not spoiled,"
said he, laughing; and away he ran.

The naughty boy! to shoot the old poet in that way; he who had taken him into his warm room, who had treated him so kindly, and who had given him warm wine and the very best apples!

The poor poet lay on the earth and wept, for the arrow had really flown into his heart.

"Fie!" said he, "how naughty a boy Cupid is! I will tell all children about him, that they may take care and not play with him, for he will only cause them sorrow and many a heart-ache."

And all good children to whom he related this story, took great heed of this naughty Cupid; but he made fools of them still, for he is astonishingly cunning. When the university students come from the lectures, he runs beside them in a black coat, and with a book under his arm. It is quite impossible for them to know him, and they walk along with him arm in arm, as if he, too, were a student like themselves; and then, unperceived, he thrusts an arrow tc their bosom. When the young maidens come from being examined by the clergyman, or go to church to be confirmed, there he is again close behind them. Yes, he is for ever following people. At the play he sits in the great chandelier and burns in bright flames, so that people think it is really a flame, but they soon discover it is something else. He roves about in the garden of the palace and upon the ramparts: yes, once he even shot your father and mother right in the heart. Ask them only, and you will hear what they'll tell you. Oh, he is a naughty boy, that Cupid; you must never have anything to do with him. He is for ever running after everbody. Only think, he shot an arrow once at your old grandmother! But that is a long time ago, and it is all past now; however, a thing of that sort she never forgets. Fie, naughty Cupid! But now you know him, and you know, too, how ill-behaved he is!

—

E really might have thought something of importance was going on in the duck-pond, but there was nothing going on.   All the ducks that were resting tranquilly on the water, or were standing in it on their heads —for that they were able to do—swam suddenly to the shore: you could see in the wet ground the traces of their feet, and hear their quacking far and near.   The water, which but just now was smooth and bright as a mirror, was quite put into commotion.   Before, one saw every tree reflected

107

in it, every bush that was near: the old
farm-house, with the holes in the roof and
with the swallow's nest under the eaves; but
principally, however, the great rose-bush,
sown, as it were, with flowers. It covered
the wall, and hung forwards over the water,
in which one beheld the whole as in a picture, except that everything was upside
down; but when the water was agitated, all
swam away and the picture was gone. Two
duck's feathers, which the fluttering ducks
had lost, were rocking to and fro: suddenly
they flew forwards as if the wind were coming, but it did not come: they were, therefore, obliged to remain where they were, and
the water grew quiet and smooth again, and
again the roses reflected themselves—they
were so beautiful, but that they did not know,
for nobody had told them. The sun shone
in between the tender leaves—all breathed
the most beautiful fragrance; and to them
it was as with us, when right joyfully we
are filled with the thought of our happiness.

"How beautiful is existence!" said each
rose. "There is but one thing I should wish
for,—to kiss the sun, because it is so bright

and warm.* The roses yonder, too, below in
the water, the exact image of ourselves—
them also I should like to kiss, and the nice
little birds below in their nest. There are
some above, too ; they stretch out their heads
and chirrup quite loud : they have no feathers
at all, as their fathers and mothers have.
They are good neighbors, those below as well
as those above. How beautiful existence is !"

The young birds above and below—those
below of course the reflection only in the
water—were sparrows : their parents were
likewise sparrows ; and they had taken possession of the empty swallow's nest of the
preceding year, and now dwelt therein as if
it had been their own property.

"Are those little duck children that are
swimming there?" asked the young spar-

* In Danish the sun is of the feminine gender, and
not, as with us, when personified, spoken of as " he."
We beg to make this observation, lest the roses' wish
" to kiss the sun," be thought unmaidenly. We are
anxious, also, to remove a stumbling block, which might
perchance trip up exquisitely-refined modern notions,
sadly shocked, no doubt, as they would be, at such an
apparent breach of modesty and decorum.—(Note of the
Translator.)

rows, when they discovered the duck's feathers on the water.

"If you *will* ask questions, do let them be
a little rational at least," said the mother.
"Don't you see that they are feathers, living
stuff for clothing such as I wear, and such as
you will wear also? But ours is finer. I
should, however, be glad if we had it up here
in our nest, for it keeps one warm. I am curious to know at what the ducks were so
frightened; at us, surely not; 'tis true I said
'chirp,' to you rather loud. In reality, the
thick-headed roses ought to know, but they
know nothing; they only gaze on themselves
and smell: for my part, I am heartily tired of
these neighbors."

"Listen to the charming little birds above,"
said the roses, "they begin to want to sing
too, but they cannot as yet. However, they
will do so by and by: what pleasure that
must afford! It is so pleasant to have such
merry neighbors!"

Suddenly two horses came galloping along
to be watered. A peasant boy rode on one,
and he had taken off all his clothes except his
large broad black hat. The youth whistled

like a bird, and rode into the pond where it was deepest; and as he passed by the rose-bush he gathered a rose and stuck it in his hat; and now he fancied himself very fine, and rode on. The other roses looked after their sister, and asked each other, "Whither is she going?" but that no one knew.

"I should like to go out into the world," thought one; "yet here at home amid our foliage it is also beautiful. By day the sun shines so warm, and in the night the sky shines still more beautifully: we can see that through all the little holes that are in it." By this they meant the stars, but they did not know any better.

"We enliven the place," said the mamma sparrow; "and the swallow's nest brings luck, so people say, and therefore people are pleased to have us. But our neighbors! Such a rose-bush against the wall produces damp; it will doubtless be cleared away, and then, perhaps, some corn at least may grow there. The roses are good for nothing except to look at and to smell, and, at most to put into one's hat. Every year—that I know from my mother—they fall away; the peasants wife collects them together and strews salt among them; they then receive a French name which I neither can nor care to pronounce, and are put upon the fire, when they are to give a pleasant odor. Look ye, such is their life; they are only here to please the eye and nose! And so now you know the whole matter."

As the evening came on, and the gnats played in the warm air and in the red clouds, the nightingale came and sang to the roses; sang that the beautiful is as the sunshine in this world, and that the beautiful lives for ever. But the roses thought that the nightingale sang his own praise, which one might very well have fancied; for that the song related to them, of that they never thought: they rejoiced in it, however, and meditated if perhaps all the little sparrows could become nightingales too.

"I understood *the song of that bird quite well*," said the young sparrows; "one word only was not quite clear to me. What was the meaning of 'the beautiful?'"

"That is nothing," said the mamma sparrow, "that is only something external. Yonder at the mansion, where the pigeons have a house of their own, and where every day peas and corn is strewn before them—I have myself eaten there with them, and you shall, too, in time ; tell me what company you keep, and I'll tell you who you are—yes, yonder at the mansion they have got two birds with green necks and a comb on their head ; they can spread out their tail like a great wheel, and in it plays every color, that it quite hurts one's eyes to look at it. These birds are called peacocks, and that is 'THE BEAUTI-FUL.' They only want to be plucked a little, and then they would not look at all different from the rest of us. I would already have plucked them, if they had not been quite so big."

"I will pluck them," chirped the smallest sparrow, that as yet had not a single feather.

In the peasant's cottage dwelt a young married couple ; they loved each other dearly, and were industrious and active : everything in their house looked so neat and pretty. On Sunday morning early the young woman came out, gathered a handful of the most

8

beautiful roses, and put them into a glass of water, which she placed on the shelf.

"Now I see that it is Sunday," said the man, and kissed his little wife. They sat down, read in the hymn-book, and held each other by the hand: the sun beamed on the fresh roses and on the young married couple.

"This is really too tiring a sight," said the mamma sparrow, who from her nest could look into the room, and away she flew.

The next Sunday it was the same, for every Sunday fresh roses were put in the glass: yet the rose-tree bloomed on equally beautiful. The young sparrows had now feathers, and wanted much to fly with their mother; she, however, would not allow it, so they were forced to remain. Off she flew; but, however, it happened, before she was aware, she got entangled in a springe of horse-hair, which some boys had set upon a bough. The horse-hair drew itself tightly round her leg, so tightly as though it would cut it in two. That was an agony, a fright! The boys ran to the spot and caught hold of the bird, and that too in no very gentle manner.

"It's only a sparrow," said they; but they, nevertheless, did not let her fly, but took her home with them, and every time she cried they gave her a tap on the beak.

There stood in the farm-yard an old man, who knew how to make shaving-soap and soap for washing, in square cakes as well as in round balls. He was a merry, wandering old man. When he saw the sparrow that the boys had caught, and which, as they said, they did not care about at all, he asked, "Shall we make something very fine of him?" Mamma sparrow felt an icy coldness creep over her. Out of the box, in which were the most beautiful colors, the old man took a quantity of gold leaf, and the boys were obliged to go and fetch the white of an egg, with which the sparrow was painted all over; on this the gold was stuck, and mamma sparrow was now entirely gilded; but she did not think of adornment, for she trembled in every limb. And the soap-dealer tore a bit off the lining of his old jacket, cut scollops in it so that it might look like a cock's comb, and stuck it on the head of the bird.

"Now, then, you shall see master gold-coat fly," said the old man, and let the sparrow go, who, in deadly fright, flew off, illumined by the beaming sun. How she shone! All the sparrows, even a crow, although an old fellow, were much frightened at the sight; they, however flew on after him, in order to learn what foreign bird it was·

Impelled by anguish and terror, he flew homewards: he was near falling exhausted to the earth. The crowd of pursuing birds increased; yes, some indeed even tried to peck at him.

"Look! there's a fellow! Look! there's a fellow!" screamed they all.

"Look! there's a fellow! Look! there's a fellow!" cried the young sparrows, as the old one approached the nest. "That, for certain, is a young peacock; all sorts of colors are playing in his feathers: it quite hurts one's eyes to look at him, just as our mother told us. Chirp! chirp! That is the beautiful!" And now they began pecking at the bird with their little beaks, so that it was quite impossible for the sparrow to get into the nest: she was so sadly used that she could not even say "Chirrup," still less, "Why, I am your own mother!" The other birds, too, now set upon the sparrow, and plucked out feather after feather ; so that at last she fell bleeding in the rose-bush below.

"Oh! poor thing!" said all the roses, "be quieted; we will hide you. Lean your little head on us."

The sparrow spread out her wings once more, then folded them close to her body, and lay dead in the midst of the family who were her neighbors,—the beautiful fresh roses.

"Chirp! chirp!" sounded from the nest. "Where can our mother be? It is quite inconceivable! It cannot surely be a trick of hers by which she means to tell us that we are now to provide for ourselves? She has left us the house as an inheritance; but to which of us is it exclusively to belong, when we ourselves have families?"

"Yes, that will never do that you stay here with me when my household is increased by the addition of a wife and children," said the smallest.

"I shall have, I should think, more wives and children than you," said the second.

"But I am the eldest," said the third. They all now grew passionate; they beat each other with their wings, pecked with their beaks, when, plump! one after the other was tumbled out of the nest. There they lay with their rage; they turned their heads on one side, and winked their eyes as they looked upward: that was their way of playing the simpleton. They could fly a little, and by practice they learned to do so still better; and they finally were unanimous as to a sign by which, when at some future time they should meet again in the world, they might recognise each other. It was to consist in a "Chirrup!" and in a thrice-repeated scratching on the ground with the left leg.

The young sparrow that had been left behind in the nest spread himself out to his full size. He was now, you know, a householder; but his grandeur did not last long: in the night red fire broke through the windows, the flames seized on the roof, the dry thatch blazed up high, the whole house was burnt, and the young sparrow with it; but the young married couple escaped, fortunately, with life. When the sun rose again, and

every thing looked so refreshed and invigo-
rated, as after a peaceful sleep, there was
nothing left of the cottage except some charred black beams leaning against the chimney,
which now was its own master. A great
deal of smoke still rose from the ground, but
without, quite uninjured, stood the rose-bush,
fresh and blooming, and mirrored every flower,
every branch, in the clear water.

"Oh! how beautifully the roses are blooming in front of the burnt-down house!" cried
a passer-by. "It is impossible to fancy a
more lovely picture. I must have that!"

And the man took a little book with white
leaves out of his pocket: he was a painter,
and with a pencil he drew the smoking
house, the charred beams, and the toppling
chimney, which now hung over more and
more. But the large and blooming rose-tree,
quite in the foreground, afforded a magnificent sight; it was on its account alone that
the whole picture had been made.

Later in the day two of the sparrows who
had been born here passed by. "Where is
the house?" asked they. "Where the nest?

q q

Chirp! chirp! All is burnt down, and our strong brother,—that is what he has got for keeping the nest. The roses have escaped well; there they are yet standing with their red cheeks. They, forsooth, do not mourn at the misfortune of their neighbors. I have no wish whatever to address them; and, besides, it is very ugly here, that's my opinion." And off and away they flew.

On a beautiful, bright, sunny autumn day —one might almost have thought it was still the middle of summer—the pigeons were strutting about the dry and nicely-swept court-yard in front of the great steps—black and white and party-colored—and they shone in the sunshine. The old mamma pigeon said to the young ones: "Form yourselves in groups, form yourselves in groups, for that makes a much better appearance."

"What little brown creatures are those running about amongst us?" asked an old pigeon, whose eyes were green and yellow. "Poor little brownies! poor little brownies!"

"They are sparrows: we have always had the reputation of being kind and gentle; we will, therefore, allow them to pick up the grain with us.   They never mix in the conversation, and they scrape a leg so prettily."

"Yes, they scratched three times with their leg, and with the left leg too, and said also "Chirrup!" It is by this they recognised each other; for they were three sparrows out of the nest of the house that had been burnt down.

"Very good eating here," said one of the sparrows.   The pigeons strutted round each other, drew themselves up, and had inwardly their own views and opinions.

"Do you see the cropper pigeon?" said one of the others.   "Do you see how she swallows the peas?   She takes too many, and the very best into the bargain!"—"Coo! coo!"—"How she puts up her top-knot, the ugly, mischievous creature!" "Coo! coo! coo!"

And every eye sparkled with malice. "Form yourselves in groups! form yourselves in groups!   Little brown creatures!   Poor little brownies!   Coo! coo!"   So it went on unceasingly, and so will they go on chattering in a thousand years to come.

The sparrows ate right bravely.   They

listened attentively to what was said, and even placed themselves in a row side by side, with the others.   It was not at all becoming to them, however.   They were not satisfied, and they therefore quitted the pigeons, and exchanged opinions about them; nestled along under the garden palisades, and, as they found the door of the room open that led upon the lawn, one of them, who was filled to satiety, and was therefore over-bold, hopped upon the threshold.   "Chirrup!" said he, "I dare to venture!"

"Chirrup!" said another, "I dare, too, and more besides!" and he hopped into the chamber.   No one was present: the third saw this, and flew still further into the room, calling out, "Either all or nothing!   However, 'tis a curious human nest that we have here; and what have they put up there?   What is that?"

Close in front of the sparrows bloomed the roses; they mirrored themselves in the water, and the charred rafters leaned against the over-hanging chimney.   But what can that be? how comes this in the room of the mansion?   And all three sparrows were about to fly away over the roses and the chimney, but they flew against a flat wall. It was all a picture, a large, beautiful picture, which the painter had executed after the little sketch.

"Chirrup!" said the sparrows, "it is nothing! It only looks like something. Chirrup! That is beautiful! Can you comprehend it? I cannot!" And away they flew, for people came into the room.

Days and months passed, the pigeons had often cooed, the sparrows had suffered cold in winter, and in summer lived right jollily: they were all betrothed and married, or whatever you choose to call it. They had young ones, and each naturally considered his the handsomest and the cleverest: one flew here, another there; and if they met they recognised each other by the "Chirrup?" and by the thrice-repeated scratching with the left leg. The eldest sparrow had remained an old maid, who had no nest and no family; her favorite notion was to see a large town, so away she flew to Copenhagen.

There one beheld a large house, painted with many bright colors, quite close to the canal, in which lay many barges laden with earthen pots and apples. The windows were broader below than above, and when the sparrow pressed through, every room appeared like a tulip, with the most varied colors and shades, but in the middle of the tulip white men were standing: they were of marble, some, too, were of plaister; but when viewed with a sparrow's eyes, they are the same. Up above on the roof stood a metal chariot, with metal horses harnessed to it; and the goddess of victory, also of metal, held the reins. It was THORWALDSEN'S MUSEUM.

"How it shines! How it shines!" said the old maiden sparrow. That, doubtless, is 'the beautiful.' Chirrup! But here it is larger than a peacock!" She remembered still what her mother, when she was a child, had looked upon as the grandest among all beautiful things. The sparrow fled down into the court: all was so magnificent. Palms and foliage were painted on the walls. In the middle of the court stood a large, blooming rose-tree; it spread out its fresh branches, with its many roses, over a grave. Thither flew the old maiden sparrow, for she saw there many of her sort. "Chirrup!"

and three scrapes with the left leg. Thus
had she often saluted, from one year's end to
the other, and nobody had answered the
greeting—for those who are once separated
do not meet again every day—till at last
the salutation had grown into a habit.   But
to-day, however, two old sparrows and one
young one answered with a " Chirrup!" and
with a thrice-repeated scrape of the left leg.

"Ah, good day, good day!" It was two
old birds from the nest, and a little one besides, of the family.   "That we should meet
here!   It is a very grand sort of place, but
there is nothing to eat here: that is 'the
beautiful! Chirrup!"

And many persons advanced from the side
apartments, where the magnificent marble
figures stood, and approached the grave that
hid the great master who had formed the
marble figures.   All stood with glorified
countenances around Thorwaldsen's grave,
and some picked up the shed rose-leaves and
carefully guarded them.   They had come
from far—one from mighty England, others
from Germany and France: the most lovely
lady gathered one of the roses and hid it in

her bosom. Then the sparrows thought that
the roses governed here, and that the whole
house had been built on account of them.
Now, this seemed to them, at all events, too
much ; however, as it was for the roses that
the persons showed all their love, they would
remain no longer. "Chirrup!" said they,
and swept the floor with their tails, and
winked with one eye at the roses. They had
not looked at them long before they convinced
themselves that they were their old neighbors. And they really were so. The
painter who had drawn the rose-bush beside
the burned-down house, had afterwards obtained permission to dig it up, and had given
it to the architect—for more beautiful roses
had never been seen—and the architect had
planted it on Thorwaldsen's grave, where it
bloomed as a symbol of the beautiful, and
gave up its red fragrant leaves to be carried
to distant lands as a remembrance.

"Have you got an appointment here in
town?" asked the sparrows.

And the roses nodded : they recognised
their brown neighbors, and rejoiced to see
them again. "How delightful it is to live

and to bloom, to see old friends again, and every day to look on happy faces! It is as if every day were a holy-day."

"Chirrup!" said the sparrows. "Yes, it is in truth our old neighbors; their origin —from the pond—is still quite clear in our memory! Chirrup! How they have risen in the world! Yes, Fortune favors some while they sleep! Ah! there is a withered leaf that I see quite plainly." And they pecked at it so long till the leaf fell off; and the tree stood there greener and more fresh, the roses gave forth their fragrance in the sunshine over Thorwaldsen's grave, with whose immortal name they were united.

THE DARNING-NEEDLE.

HERE was once upon a time a darning needle, that imagined itself so fine, that at last it fancied it was a sewing-needle.

"Now, pay attention, and hold me firmly!" said the darning-needle to the fingers that were taking it out. "Do not let me fall! If I fall on the ground, I shall certainly never be found again, so fine am I."

"Pretty well as to that," answered the fingers; and so saying, they took hold of it by the body.

"Look, I come with a train!" said the darning-needle, drawing a long thread after it, but there was no knot to the thread.

The fingers directed the needle against

128

an old pair of shoes belonging to the cook. The upper-leather was torn, and it was now to be sewed together.

"That is vulgar work," said the needle; "I can never get through it. I shall break! I shall break!" And it really did break. "Did I not say so?" said the needle; "I am too delicate."

"Now it's good for nothing," said the fingers, but they were obliged to hold it still; the cook dropped sealing-wax upon it, and pinned her neckerchief together with it.

"Well, now I am a breast-pin," said the darning-needle. "I was sure I should be raised to honor: if one is something, one is sure to get on!" and at the same time it laughed inwardly; for one can never see when a darning-needle laughs. So there it sat now as proudly as in a state-carriage, and looked around on every side.

"May I take the liberty to inquire if you are of gold?" asked the needle of a pin that was its neighbor. You have a splendid exterior, and a head of your own, but it is small, however. You must do what you can to grow, for it is not every one that is

9

bedropped with sealing-wax!" And then the darning-needle drew itself up so high that it fell out of the kerchief, and tumbled right into the sink, which the cook was at that moment rinsing out.

"Now we are going on our travels," said the needle. "If only I do not get lost!" But it really did get lost.

"I am too delicate for this world!" said the needle, as it lay in the sink, "but I know who I am, and that is always a consolation;" and the darning-needle maintained its proud demeanor, and lost none of its good-humor.

And all sorts of things swam over it— shavings, straws, and scraps of old newspapers.

"Only look how they sail by," said the needle. "They do not know what is hidden below them! I stick fast here: here I sit. Look! there goes a shaving: it thinks of nothing in the world but of itself—but of a shaving! There drifts a straw; and how it tacks about, how it turns round! Think of something else besides yourself, or else perhaps you'll run against a stone! There swims a bit of a newspaper. What's written there is long ago forgotten, and yet out it spreads itself, as if it were mighty important! I sit here patient and still: I know who I am, and that I shall remain after all!"

One day there lay something close beside the needle. It glittered so splendidly, that the needle thought it must be a diamond: but it was only a bit of a broken bottle, and because it glittered the darning-needle addressed it, and introduced itself to the other as a breast-pin.

"You are, no doubt, a diamond?"

"Yes, something of that sort." And so each thought the other something very precious, and they talked together of the world, and of how haughty it is.

"I was with a certain miss, in a little box," said the darning-needle, "and this miss was cook; and on each hand she had five fingers. In my whole life I have never seen anything so conceited as these fingers! And yet they were only there to take me out of the box and to put me back into it again!"

"Were they, then, of noble birth?" asked the broken bottle.

"Noble!" said the darning-needle; "no,

but high-minded! There were five brothers,
all descendants of the ' Finger' family. They
always kept together, although they were of
different lengths. The outermost one, little
Thumb, was short and stout; he went at
the side, a little in front of the ranks: he
had, too, but one joint in his back, so that
he could only make one bow; but he said, if
a man were to cut him off, such an one were
no longer fit for military service. Sweet-
tooth, the second finger, pryed into what was
sweet, as well as into what was sour, pointed
to the sun and moon, and he it was that
gave stress when they wrote. Longman, the
third brother, looked at the others con-
temptuously over his shoulder. Goldrim, the
fourth, wore a golden girdle round his body!
and the little Peter Playallday did nothing
at all, of which he was very proud. 'Twas
boasting, and boasting, and nothing but boasting, and so away I went."

"And now we sit here and glitter," said
the broken glass bottle.

At the same moment more water came
along the gutter; it streamed over the sides
and carried the bit of bottle away with it.

" Well, that's an advancement," said the darning-needle. "I remain where I am : I am too fine ; but that is just my pride, and as such is to be respected." And there it sat so proudly, and had many grand thoughts.

"I should almost think that I was born of a sunbeam, so fine am I ! It seems to me, too, as if the sunbeams were always seeking me beneath the surface of the water. Ah ! I am so fine, that my mother is unable to find me ! Had I my old eye that broke, I verily think I could weep ; but I would not —weep ! no, it's not genteel to weep !"

One day two boys came rummaging about in the sink, where they found old nails, farthings, and such sort of things. It was dirty work ; however, they took pleasure in it.

"Oh !" cried one who had pricked himself with the needle, "there's a fellow for you."

"I am no fellow, I am a lady !" said the darning-needle ; but no one heard it. The sealing-wax had worn off, and it had become quite black ; but black makes one look more slender, and the needle fancied it looked more delicate than ever.

"Here comes an egg-shell sailing along !'

said the boys; and then they stuck the needle upright in the egg-shell.

"The walls white and myself black," said the needle. "That is becoming! People can see me now! If only I do not get sea-sick, for then I shall snap."

But it was not sea-sick, and did not snap.

. "It is good for sea-sickness to have a stomach of steel, and not to forget that one is something more than a human being! Now my sea-sickness is over. The finer one is, the more one can endure!"

"Crack!" said the egg-shell: a wheel went over it.

"Good heavens! how heavy that presses!" said the needle. Now I shall be sea-sick! I snap!" But it did not snap, although a wheel went over it. It lay there at full length, and there it may lie still.

OST terribly cold it was; it snowed, and was nearly quite dark, and evening—the last evening of the year. In this cold and darkness there went along the street a poor little girl, bareheaded, and with naked feet. When she left ome she had slippers on, it is true; but what was the good of that? They were very large slippers, which her mother had hitherto worn; so large were they; and the poor little thing lost them as she scuffled away across the street, because of two carriages that rolled by dreadfully fast

135

One slipper was nowhere to be found; the other had been laid hold of by an urchin, and off he ran with it; he thought it would do capitally for a cradle when he some day or other should have children himself. So the little maiden walked on with her tiny naked feet, that were quite red and blue from cold. She carried a quantity of matches in an old apron, and she held a bundle of them in her hand. Nobody had bought anything of her the whole livelong day; no one had given her a single farthing.

She crept along trembling with cold and hunger—a very picture of sorrow, the poor little thing!

The flakes of snow covered her long fair hair, which fell in beautiful curls around her neck; but of that, of course, she never once now thought. From all the windows the candles were gleaming, and it smelt so deliciously of roast goose, for you know it was new year's eve; yes, of that she thought.

In a corner formed by two houses, of which one advanced more than the other, she seated herself down and cowered together. Her little feet she had drawn close up to her, but

she grew colder and colder, and to go home
she did not venture, for she had not sold any
matches and could not bring a farthing of
money : from her father she would certainly
get blows, and at home it was cold too, for
above her she had only the roof, through
which the wind whistled, even though the
largest cracks were stopped up with straw
and rags.

Her little hands were almost numbed with
cold.   Oh ! a match might afford her a world
of comfort, if she only dared take a single
one out of the bundle, draw it against the wall,
and warm her fingers by it.   She drew one
out.   "Rischt !" how it blazed, how it burnt !
It was a warm, bright flame, like a candle,
as she held her hands over it : it was a wonderful light.   It seemed really to the little
maiden as though she were sitting before a
large iron stove, with burnished brass feet
and a brass ornament at top.   The fire burned with such blessed influence ; it warmed
so delightfully.   The little girl had already
stretched out her feet to warm them too ; but
—the small flame went out, the stove vanish-

ed : she had only the remains of the burnt-out match in her hand.

She rubbed another against the wall: it burned brightly, and where the light fell on the wall, there the wall became transparent like a veil, so that she could see into the room. On the table was spread a snow-white table-cloth ; upon it was a splendid porcelain ser-vice, and the roast goose was steaming fa-mously with its stuffing of apple and dried plums.   And what was still more capital to behold was, the goose hopped down from the dish, reeled about on the floor with knife and fork in its breast, till it came up to the poor little girl; when—the match went out and nothing but the thick, cold, damp wall was left behind. [She lighted another match. Now there she was sitting under the most magnificent Christmas trees : it was still larg-er, and more decorated than the one which she had seen through the glass door in the rich merchant's house.

Thousands of lights were burning on the green branches, and gaily-colored pictures, such as she had seen in the shop-windows, looked down upon her. The little maiden stretched out her hands towards them when —the match went out. The lights of the Christmas tree rose higher and higher, she saw them now as stars in heaven; one fell down and formed a long trail of fire.

"Some one is just dead!" said the little girl; for her old grandmother, the only person who had loved her, and who was now no more, had told her, that when a star falls, a soul ascends to God.

She drew another match against the wall: it was again light, and in the lustre there stood the old grandmother, so bright and radiant, so mild, and with such an expression of love.

"Grandmother!" cried the little one; "oh, take me with you! You go away when the match burns out; you vanish like the warm stove, like the delicious roast goose, and like the magnificent Christmas tree!" And she rubbed the whole bundle of matches quickly against the wall, for she wanted to be quite sure of keeping her grandmother near her. And the matches gave such a brilliant light that it was brighter than at noon-day: never

formerly had the grandmother been so beau-
iful and so tall. She took the little maiden,
on her arm, and both flew in brightness and
in joy so high, so very high, and then above
was neither cold, nor hunger, nor anxiety—
they were with God.

But in the corner, at the cold hour of dawn,
sat the poor girl, with rosy cheeks and with
a smiling mouth, leaning against the wall—
frozen to death on the last evening of the old
year. Stiff and stark sat the child there
with her matches, of which one bundle had
been burnt. "She wanted to warm herself,"
people said : no one had the slightest sus-
picion of what beautiful things she had seen ;
no one even dreamed of the splendor in which,
with her grandmother she had entered on the
joys of a new year.

THE RED SHOES.

HERE was once a little girl who was very pret- ty and delicate, but in summer she was forced to run about with bare feet, she was so poor, and in winter wear very large wooden shoes, which made her little insteps quite red, and that looked so danger- ous !

In the middle of the village lived old Dame Shoemaker ; she sate and sewed together, as well as she could, a little pair of shoes out of old red strips of cloth ; they were very clumsy, but it was a kind thought. They were meant for the little girl. The little girl was called Karen.

On the very day her mother was buried, Karen received the red shoes, and wore them for the first time. They were certainly not intended for mourning, but she had no others, and with stockingless feet she followed the poor straw coffin in them.

Suddenly a large old carriage drove up, and a large old lady sate in it: she looked at the little girl, felt compassion for her, and then said to the clergyman:

"Here, give me the little girl, I will adopt her!"

And Karen believed all this happened on account of the red shoes, but the old lady thought they were horrible, and they were burnt. But Karen herself was cleanly and nicely dressed; she must learn to read and sew; and people said she was a nice little thing, but the looking-glass said: "Thou art more than nice, thou art beautiful!"

Now the queen once traveled through the land, and she had her little daughter with her. And this little daughter was a princess, and people streamed to the castle, and Karen was there also, and the little princess stood in her fine white dress, in a window, and let

herself be stared at; she had neither a train
nor a golden crown, but splendid red morocco
shoes. They were certainly far handsomer
than those Dame Shoemaker had made for
little Karen. Nothing in the world can be
compared with red shoes.

Now Karen was old enough to be confirmed; she had new clothes and was to have
new shoes also. The rich shoemaker in the
city took the measure of her little foot. This
took place at his house, in his room; where
stood large glass-cases, filled with elegant
shoes and brilliant boots. All this looked
charming, but the old lady could not see well,
and so had no pleasure in them. In the midst
of the shoes stood a pair of red ones, just
like those the princess had worn. How beautiful they were! The shoemaker said also
they had been made for the child of a count,
but had not fitted.

"That must be patent leather!" said the
old lady, "they shine so!"

"Yes, they shine!" said Karen, and they
fitted, and were bought, but the old lady knew
nothing about their being red, else she would
never have allowed Karen to have gone in

s s

red shoes to be confirmed. Yet such was the case.

Everybody looked at her feet; and when she stepped through the chancel door on the church pavement, it seemed to her as if the old figures on the tombs, those portraits of old preachers and preachers' wives, with stiff ruffs, and long black dresses, fixed their eyes on her red shoes. And she thought only of them as the clergyman laid his hand upon her head, and spoke of the holy baptism, of the covenant with God, and how she should be now a matured Christian; and the organ pealed so solemnly; the sweet children's voices sang, and the old music-directors sang, but Karen only thought of her red shoes.

In the afternoon, the old lady heard from every one that the shoes had been red, and she said that it was very wrong of Karen, that it was not at all becoming, and that in future Karen should only go in black shoes to church, even when she should be older.

The next Sunday there was the sacrament, and Karen looked at the black shoes, looked at the red ones—looked at them again, and put on the red shoes.

The sun shone gloriously; Karen and the old lady walked along the path through the corn; it was rather dusty there.

At the church door stood an old soldier with a crutch, and with a wonderfully long beard, which was more red than white, and he bowed to the ground, and asked the old lady whether he might dust her shoes. And Karen stretched out her little foot.

"See! what beautiful dancing-shoes!" said the soldier, "sit firm when you dance;" and he put his hand out towards the soles.

And the old lady gave the old soldier an alms, and went into the church with Karen.

And all the people in the church looked at Karen's red shoes, and all the pictures, and as Karen knelt before the altar, and raised the cup to her lips, she only thought of the red shoes, and they seemed to swim in it; and she forgot to sing her psalm, and she forgot to pray, "Our father in Heaven!"

Now all the people went out of church, and the old lady got into her carriage. Karen raised her foot to get in after her, when the old soldier said,

"Look, what beautiful dancing shoes!"

10

And Karen could not help dancing a step or two, and when she began her feet continued to dance; it was just as though the shoes had power over them. She danced round the church corner, she could not leave off; the coachman was obliged to run after and catch hold of her, and he lifted her in the carriage, but her feet continued to dance so that she trod on the old lady dreadfully. At length she took the shoes off, and then her legs had peace.

The shoes were placed in a closet at home, but Karen could not avoid looking at them.

Now the old lady was sick, and it was said she could not recover? She must be nursed and waited upon, and there was no one whose duty it was so much as Karen's. But there was a great ball in the city, to which Karen was invited. She looked at the old lady, who could not recover, she looked at the red shoes, and she thought there could be no sin in it;—she put on the red shoes, she might do that also, she thought. But then she went to the ball and began to dance.

When she wanted to dance to the right, the shoes would dance to the left, and when she wanted to dance up the room, the shoes danced back again, down the steps, into the street, and out of the city gate. She danced, and was forced to dance straight out into the gloomy wood.

Then it was suddenly light up among the trees, and she fancied it must be the moon, for there was a face; but it was the old soldier with the red beard; he sate there, nodded his head, and said, "Look, what beautiful dancing shoes!"

Then she was terrified, and wanted to fling off the red shoes, but they clung fast; and she pulled down her stockings, but the shoes seemed to have grown to her feet. And she danced, and must dance, over fields and meadows, in rain and sunshine, by night and day; but at night it was the most fearful.

She danced over the churchyard, but the dead did not dance,—they had something better to do than to dance. She wished to seat herself on a poor man's grave, where the bitter tansy grew; but for her there was neither peace nor rest; and when she danced towards the open church door, she saw an angel standing there. He wore long, white garments; he had wings which reached from his shoulders to the earth; his countenance was severe and grave; and in his hand he held a sword, broad and glittering.

"Dance shalt thou!" said he,—"dance in thy red shoes till thou art pale and cold! till thy skin shrivels up and thou art a skeleton! Dance shalt thou from door to door, and where proud, vain children dwell, thou shalt knock, that they may hear thee and tremble! Dance shalt thou ——!"

"Mercy!" cried Karen. But she did not hear the angel's reply, for the shoes carried her through the gate into the fields, across roads and bridges, and she must keep ever dancing.

One morning she danced past a door which she well knew. Within sounded a psalm; a coffin, decked with flowers, was borne forth. Then she knew that the old lady was dead, and felt that she was abandoned by all, and condemned by the angel of God.

She danced, and she was forced to dance through the gloomy night. The shoes carried her over stack and stone; she was torn till she bled; she danced over the heath till she came to a little house. Here, she knew, dwelt the executioner; and she tapped with her fingers at the window, and said, "Come out! come out! I cannot come in, for I am forced to dance!"

And the executioner said, "Thou dost not know who I am, I fancy? I strike bad people's heads off; and I hear that my axe rings!"

"Don't strike my head off!" said Karen, "then I can't repent of my sins! But strike off my feet in the red shoes!"

And then she confessed her entire sin, and the executioner struck off her feet with the red shoes, but the shoes danced away with the little feet across the field into the deep wood.

And he carved out little wooden feet for her, and crutches, taught her the psalm criminals always sing; and she kissed the hand which had wielded the axe, and went over the heath.

"Now I have suffered enough for the red shoes!" said she; "now I will go into the church that people may see me!" And she hastened towards the church door : but when she was near it, the red shoes danced before her, and she was terrified, and turned round. The whole week she was unhappy, and wept many bitter tears ; but when Sunday return-ed, she said, " Well, now I have suffered and struggled enough ! I really believe I am as good as many a one who sits in the church, and holds her head so high !"

And away she went boldly ; but she had not got farther than the churchyard gate before she saw the red shoes dancing before her ; and she was frightened, and turned back, and repented of her sin from her heart.

And she went to the parsonage, and begged that they would take her into ser-vice ; she would be very industrious, she said, and would do everything she could ; she did not care about the wages, only she wish-ed to have a home, and be with good people. And the clergyman's wife was sorry for her and took her into service ; and she was in-dustrious and thoughtful. She sate still and listened when the clergyman read the Bible in the evenings. All the children thought a deal of her; but when they spoke of dress, and grandeur, and beauty, she shook her head.

The following Sunday, when the family was going to church, they asked her whether she would not go with them; but she glanced sorrowfully, with tears in her eyes, at her crutches. The family went to hear the word of God; but she went alone into her little chamber; there was only room for a bed and chair to stand in it; and here she sate down with her prayer-book; and whilst she read with a pious mind, the wind bore the strains of the organ towards her, and she raised her tearful countenance, and said, "O God, help me!"

And the sun shone so clearly! and straight before her stood the angel of God in white garments, the same she had seen that night at the church door; but he no longer carried the sharp sword, but in its stead a splendid green spray, full of roses. And he touched the ceiling with the spray, and the ceiling rose so high, and where he had touched it there gleamed a golden star. And he touched the walls, and they widened out, and she

t t

saw the organ which was playing; she saw
the old pictures of the preachers and the
preachers' wives. The congregation sat in
cushioned seats, and sang out of their prayer-
books. For the church itself had come to the
poor girl in her narrow chamber, or else she
had come into the church. She sate in the
pew with the clergyman's family, and when
they had ended the psalm and looked up,
they nodded and said, "It is right that thou
art come!"

"It was through mercy!" she said.

And the organ pealed, and the children's
voices in the choir sounded so sweet and
soft! The clear sunshine streamed so warmly through the window into the pew where
Karen sate! Her heart was so full of sunshine, peace, and joy, that it broke. Her soul
flew on the sunshine to God, and there no
one asked after the RED SHOES.

Stories by a Mother:

Containing—Right and Wrong; or, The Story of Rosa and Agnes; and Claudine; or, Humility the Basis of all the Virtues. By the Author of "Always Happy," "True Stories from History," etc. 75 cents; extra gilt, $1 00.

Tales of Domestic Life.

By Mrs. S. C. Hall. Cloth, 75 cents; extra gilt, $1 00.

The Turtle Dove of Carmel,

And other Stories. By Mary Howitt. 37½ cents.

How to Win Love;

Or, Rhoda's Lesson. A Story for the Young. 37½ cents.

The Merchant's Daughter,

And other Tales. By Mrs. S. C. Hall. 37½ cents.

Elements of Morality.

Being Stories for Children. Translated from the German of Salztman. With Illustrations. 50 cents.

Book of Entertainment

Of Curiosities and Wonders in Nature, Art, and Mind, drawn from the most authentic sources, and carefully revised. *Third Series.* Illustrated by more than 80 Engravings. $1 00; extra gilt, $1 25.

The Story of Stories;

Or, Fun for the Little Ones. Being Rambles in the Fairyland of Italy: containing the most popular FAIRY TALES of the 16th and 17th centuries, written in Italy; the original stories and wild conceptions on which the plots of numerous dramas, romantic legends, and best tales of many authors have been formed. With Illustrations by Cruikshank. Cloth, 88 cents.

A Picture Book without Pictures,

And other Stories. From the Danish of Hans Christian Andersen. Translated by Mary Howitt, with a Memoir of the Author. 37½ cents.

PUBLISHED BY C. S. FRANCIS & CO., NEW YORK.

A Christmas Greeting.
Thirteen new Stories. From the Danish of Hans Christian Andersen. With Engravings. 87½ cents.

A Danish Story Book.
By Hans Christian Andersen. With Engravings. 87½ cents.

The Story Teller.
Tales from the Danish. By Hans Christian Andersen. With Illustrations. 87½ cents.

Little Ellie,
And other Tales. By Hans Christian Andersen.

The Ugly Duck,
And other Tales. By Hans Christian Andersen. 87½ cents.

The Officer's Widow,
And her Young Family. By Mrs. Hofland. 87½ cents.

The Clergyman's Widow,
And her Young Family. By Mrs. Hofland. 87½ cents.

The Merchant's Widow,
And her Family. By Mrs. Hofland. 87½ cents.

Fireside Tales.
By Mary Howitt. 87½ cents.

The Christmas Tree.
A Book of Stories. By Mary Howitt. 87½ cents.

Stories of Old Daniel;
Or, Tales of Wonder and Delight; containing Narratives introductory to History and Travels 50 cents.

The Swan's Egg.
By Mrs. S. C. Hall. (In press.)

Orlandino.
A new Story. By Maria Edgeworth. (In press.)

PUBLISHED BY C. S. FRANCIS & CO., NEW YORK.

Tales of Illustrious Children.
Historical Stories. By Agnes Strickland. With Engravings. 50 cents.

Rose Marian,
And the Flower Faizies. Translated by L. Maria Child. With Illustrations. 25 cents.

Bible Cartoons.
Illustrations of Scripture History. From Designs by John Franklin. Containing 16 Engravings of Scenes from the Lives of Adam, Noah, Abraham, Joseph, and Moses, with descriptions in the words of the Bible. 1 vol., 4to. 75 cents.

Ellen the Teacher.
A Tale for Youth. By Mrs. Hofland.

The Scottish Orphans.
A Moral Tale founded on an Historical Fact. By Mrs Blackford, author of "Arthur Montaith," "Eskdale Herd Boy," etc

The Good Grandmother
And her Offspring. By Mrs. Hofland.

Keeper's Travels
In Search of his Master. Reprinted from the original edition. (In press.)

The Book of Entertainment
Of Curiosities and Wonders in Nature, Art, and Mind. Drawn from the most authentic sources, and carefully revised. *Fourth Series.* With 80 Engravings. $1 00 extra gilt, $1 25.

The Barbadoes' Girl.
A Tale for Young People. By Mrs. Hofland.

Tales from Shakspeare.
For the Use of Young Persons. By Charles and Mary Lamb. With 40 Engravings. $1 00.

Cobwebs to catch Flies;
Or, Dialogues in short sentences. A new edition, revised and illustrated. 25 cents. Colored, 37½ cents.

The Daisy;
Or, Cautionary Stories in Verse. A new edition, with additional poems. 25 cents. Colored pictures, 87½ cents

The Cowslip;
Or, More Cautionary Stories in Verse. By the author of "The Daisy." 25 cents. Colored, 87½ cents.

Grandmamma's Pockets.
A Tale for Young People. By Mrs. S. C. Hall. 87½ cents.

Hans Andersen's Story Book.
With a Memoir of the Author, by Mary Howitt. 1 thick vol. Illustrated. 75 cents; extra gilt, $1 00.

Wonderful Tales from Denmark.
By Hans Christian Andersen. A new Translation. 1 thick vol. Illustrated. 75 cents; extra gilt, $1 00.

[*These two volumes contain a complete collection of Andersen's Stories for Young People.*]

Gift Book of Stories and Poems.
For Children. By Caroline Gilman. 75 cents; extra gilt, $1 00.

Domestic Tales.
By Mrs. Hofland. Being the Histories of the Officer's, the Merchant's, and the Clergyman's Widows, and their young Families. 75 cents; extra gilt, $1 00.

Mary Howitt's Story Book.
With a Portrait of the Author, and Illustrations. 1 thick vol. 75 cents; extra gilt, $1 00.

Boys' Own Book Extended:
Containing the Boy's Own Book, Paul Preston's Book of Gymnastics, and Parlor Magic; forming a complete Encyclopedia of Sports for Youth. Cloth, $1 25.

The Evening Book

Of Pleasant and Useful Reading; with 50 illustrations
1 vol. Cloth, 75 cents; extra gilt, $1.

Home Tales.

By Mrs. Hofland. Including "The Affectionate Brothers;" "The Sisters;" and the "Blind Farmer." 1
vol. with engravings by Orr, from designs by Wallin
Cloth, 75 cents; extra gilt, $1.

The Sisters;

A Domestic Tale. By Mrs. Hofland. 1 vol. Cloth, 87½
cents.

Evenings at Home;

Or, the Juvenile Budget Opened: By Dr. Aiken and
Mrs. Barbauld. Newly revised and corrected, and illustrated with fine engravings. 1 vol. 75 cents.

Swiss Family Robinson.

Part Second. Being the continuation and completion
of this interesting work. 1 vol. 62½ cents.

Early Lessons.

By Maria Edgeworth. A new uniform edition, including Harry and Lucy; Frank; Rosamond; with the
Sequels to each work. Complete in 5 thick vols., with
illustrations. Cloth, $3 75. Each work may also be
had separately.

The Summer Day Book

Of Pleasant and Useful Reading. Containing Sketches
of Natural History; Personal Adventures; Scenes of
Foreign Travel; Information on Popular Science; and
other subjects suited to interest and improve the mind.
50 engravings. Cloth, 75 cents; extra gilt, $1.

Happy Hours;

Or, Home Story Book. By Mary Cherwell, with fine
Illustrations. 50 cents.

Instinct of Animals.

Stories about the Instinct of Animals, their Characters
and Habits. By Thomas Bingley, with designs by
Landseer. 50 cents

PUBLISHED BY C. S. FRANCIS & CO., NEW YORK

PETER THE WHALER:
HIS EARLY LIFE AND ADVENTURES
THE ARCTIC REGIONS AND OTHER PARTS OF THE WORLD

WITH ILLUSTRATIONS.

CONTENTS OF THE CHAPTERS.

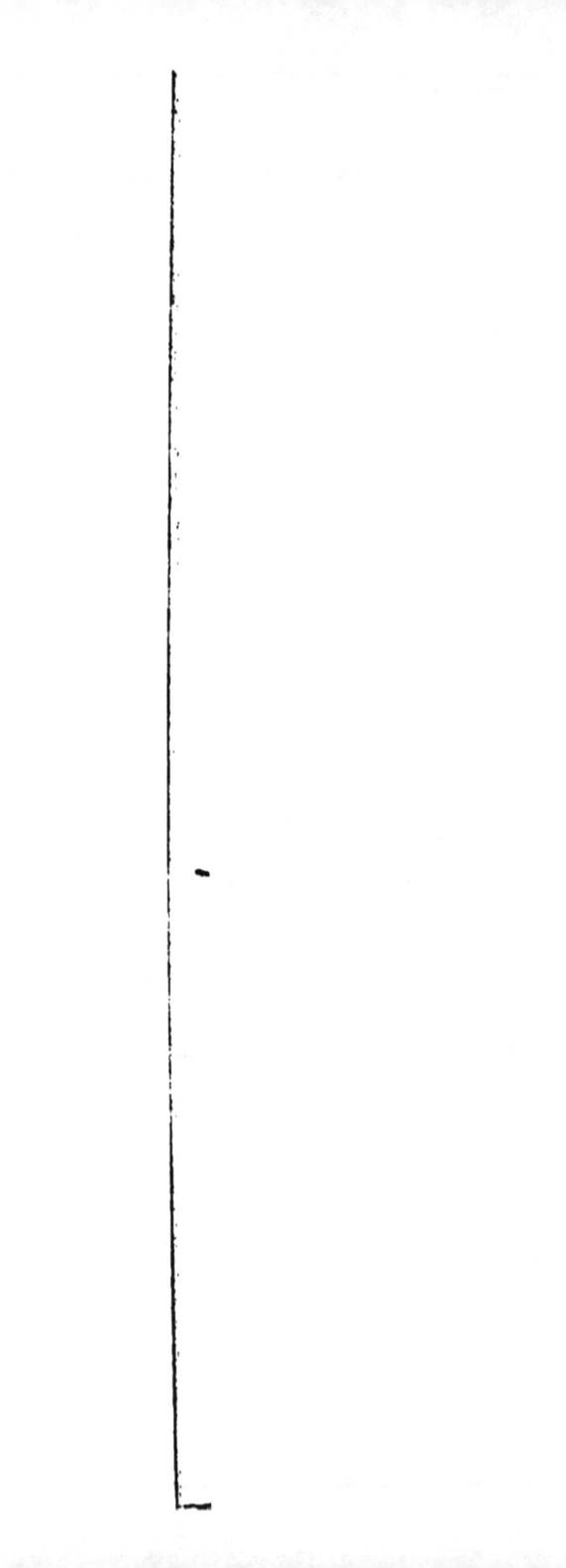

www.ingramcontent.com/pod-product-compliance
Lightning Source LLC
Chambersburg PA
CBHW022013110726
47901CB00006B/1502